Poor JUDGMENT

USA TODAY BESTSELLING AUTHOR
HEATHER M. ORGERON

Also by Heather M. Orgeron

Vivienne's Guilt
Boomerangers
Breakaway
Doppelbanger

This one's for you, Edeerie.
For thinking of me when you discovered that adult summer camps laced with booze were a thing and knowing this crazy Cajun wouldn't be able to pass up such a gold mine of drunken debauchery.

Prologue

RHETT

"OH, RHETT, YESSS..."

I squeeze harder, lapping her nipple into a firm bud through her thin top. My cock stiffens as she grinds her hips to the tempo of the music, giving me a sexy as fuck lap dance. Suddenly I have this inexplicable urge to look up, letting Monica's tit slip from my mouth. I feel smothered—like all the air has suddenly been pulled from the room.

Who is that?

"It's fine, Nick—" She digs her heels into the floor. "No, I don't want to meet—"

"Rhett." My drummer, Nick, approaches, dragging the very reluctant blonde behind him by the arm. "I'd like to introduce you to my cousin, Korie Potter. Korie, this is Rhett." He gives her a little shove, landing her on her feet, right in front of my bent knees.

My eyes peruse her sweet little body. Her long blonde hair is pulled back in a low ponytail. There's not an ounce of makeup

2 HEATHER M. ORGERON

on her face. Her eyes are a vibrant shade of emerald, and she has the most delectable little freckles dotting her cheekbones. She's wearing a black Rolling Stones tee—slightly fitted, the collar ripped so it droops a little, exposing one shoulder. One creamy, slender, tantalizing shoulder. I clear my throat, reaching around the raven-haired beauty presently situated in my lap for Korie's hand.

"I'm good," she says, not reaching back, her face scrunched like she's just gotten a whiff of something foul. "Just carry on with whatev—umm *whoever* you're doing." She whirls back on her cousin, eyes flaming. "I'm gonna go get some air."

In her haste to get away, she trips over my foot and is sent hurtling face first to the floor. Like in the movies, the music stops and every pair of eyes in the room are on her.

"Oh, shit." I slide Monica to the side. "Scuse me," I rush out, blundering to my feet, the alcohol throwing off my balance as I hop around, trying to right my pants zipper before reaching her. "My fault," I say, shoving the little douche aside who's trying to help her up. "I've got it."

He throws his hands in the air, backing away.

"Are you all right?" My fingers curl around her upper arm, and inexplicably my pulse begins to race.

Then, she turns toward me, and our eyes truly connect for the first time. Fireworks burst in my chest, and I can't seem to locate my voice. The attraction is instantaneous.

Well, it is for me at least.

She visibly stiffens. "Get your hands off of me. I'm fine."

"Just wanted to make sure you were oka—"

She shrugs out of my hold, popping to her feet and righting her clothes. "I said, I'm fine." She glances around at the slew of eyes fixed on her, sneering at all the snooty females whispering, pointing their manicured nails, and giggling in their Louboutin shoes and designer cocktail dresses. What I found hot not even five minutes ago suddenly seems pretentious and well, *boring*. "You're just making it worse," she grits.

"Right." Nodding, I withdraw my hand and bring it to my chest. "You all act like you've never seen a person trip before," I say, addressing the crowd. "Get back to it." I clap my hands loudly toward the DJ, "Music!"

With an annoyed huff, she rolls her eyes and storms off in her black Converse.

Sneakers at a Hollywood party... *Who is this girl?*

"Don't take it personally," Nick says, coming up behind me and clapping me on the shoulder. "She's Jax's daughter."

Jax Potter... Nicholas's washed-up rock star uncle, who hooked us up with our agent and helped get The Rhett Taylor Band off the ground. So, that explains why her name sounded familiar. But still doesn't account for her odd reaction toward me.

"Did I umm... Have we met before?" I stare after her until she disappears through the balcony door. "Did I offend her in some way?" I'm beginning to wonder if we've maybe hooked up and that's the reason, I feel this strange connection. But I'm positive I've never felt like this before, and she certainly doesn't seem like someone I'd easily forget.

"Nah, man. This just isn't her scene. You know Jax... wasn't easy being the one at home with her mom while he uh... did his thing." He shrugs. "I'm honestly surprised to see her here at all."

"Right," I agree as Monica's hands slink around my waist from behind. She's shimmying to the beat of the sultry music, her breasts pressed to my back, but I'm just not in it any longer. "I'll find you later," I lie, kissing the tips of her fingers and sending her off to her friends.

She pouts like a child, running a hand over my chest. "Don't forget me."

Nick laughs after she walks off. "That's probably what uh… what did it. She thinks we're all like her pops." He gives his shoulders another shrug. "Thanks for the party, man. You're the best. I'm gonna go check on Korie."

"Ahh, there you are," I say, finding Korie perched on a wicker couch with a drink in hand. It's a dark, clear night. She's staring out at the stars, all alone on the balcony off Nick's room. "So, I think maybe we got off on the wrong foot." I take a pull from my beer then clear my throat. "I wanted to find you and reintroduce myself—start over again, you know, in less… *awkward circumstances*."

Her head slowly rolls in my direction. The look in her eyes tells me she's over this conversation before it even begins. "No need. Everyone with the internet knows who you are. You're Rhett Taylor—bad boy of country music. Playboy. Womanizer."

"Ouch." I suck in a breath, bringing a hand to my chest. "Yeah…well, you see what the media wants people to see."

She rises to her feet, closing the distance between us in a few strides. The wind blows through her hair, and I get a whiff of her floral shampoo. My dick twitches. She's so close—inches away. I have to stop myself from giving in to the urge to reach out and touch her again. "What I saw when I walked in was nothing less than I expected." She plants a hand on her hip. "That wasn't the media. That was a rock star in his natural habitat." She taps a hand lightly on the front of my shirt. "I know it's probably real hard to believe, but I'm not here to go gaga and fall all over you." She smiles a lazy smile. "As disappointing as that may be for your huge...*ego*."

Did I just imagine her eyes dropping to my crotch?

"I came to see my cousin, who I haven't seen in years. The rest of this"—her hand circles the air—"is just unfortunate."

She stalks back into the house, leaving me to scrape my jaw up from the floor. Something about that sassy mouth of hers only makes me want her more.

I spend the rest of the evening lurking in the shadows of my own home, stalking a girl who wants nothing to do with me. It doesn't take her long to befriend all of the girls who were making fun of her earlier tonight, including Monica. It would seem we're all under her spell. But for some reason she's decided to give them another chance. Me? Well, I think she'd written me off before walking through the door.

I'm green with envy. I don't know what it is about this particular girl that has me feeling things I haven't felt in years... but it makes me realize just how numb I've allowed myself to become.

For the first time since I can't remember when, I'm *feeling*, and even jealousy feels a hell of a lot better than indifference.

Chapter 1

RHETT

"YOU'RE SERIOUS RIGHT NOW?" ANIKA, MY MANAGER, PACES the studio in four-inch stilettos while gnawing on the back of a pen. "You want to cancel studio time to go to...to *camp*?"

She's kinda cute when she's all riled up like this, her pale cheeks flaming red and daggers shooting from her amber eyes. I sink down further into the plush couch, crossing my arms on my chest. "It'll be fun. I'm in need of some fun. You said so yourself. A few days on the coast with other single, college-aged adults. Real people, Anika. A break from Hollywood."

"I said *after* we finish the album. Not right in the middle of recording it." Her heels clack on the wood floors as she moves to crouch before me, resting her manicured nails on the arms of my chair. Her frustration is evident in the heaviness of her breaths. She shakes her head, tossing her long chestnut braid over her left shoulder. "It's her, isn't it? She's going to be there?"

"Yes," I answer, trying to cover a smirk. "Yeah...So, there's no way I can put this off." I realize the timing isn't ideal, but it's the perfect chance to work my magic on this girl, whom I can't seem to get out of my head.

Pushing up from my knees, she's again wearing a hole into the floor. "She hates you, Rhett. This is a terrible idea. Not only for your career, but because you're going to end up *disappointed*."

What she means is depressed. My first Hollywood girlfriend did a number on me, but that was before I knew how industry relationships worked. I keep my heart guarded now—locked up tight in a suit of armor. I just want the chance to play with my sword.

"I'm curious about her," I say with a shrug, my mind wandering to my drummer Nick's birthday party, about three weeks ago. To his cousin, Korie Potter. Her long, wavy blonde ponytail, faded jeans, and Rolling Stones tee. She stood out among the sequins and glitz. Her attempt to fade into the background had the complete opposite effect. Only adding to her appeal was the easy manner with which she carried herself. She had a confidence—an honesty—about her that I don't see much in the circles I run. I can't help but smile, remembering how unimpressed she was with everything Rhett Taylor. What did she call me again? Oh, yeah. *The bad boy of country music.* Someone's been paying a little too much attention to TMZ.

At any rate, life gets rather boring when you can literally have anything you want. Any*one* you want. I hadn't realized how willing I'd become to settle until life dangled temptation, in the form of a sassy-mouthed, blonde-haired, green-eyed, fiery little vixen, right under my nose and shook things up a bit—shook *me* up a bit.

Yeah, Korie is just the challenge I need.

"The label won't like it."

Having had about enough of her negativity, I rise to my feet, towering over her five-foot frame. It's not often I ignore her advice. We've been best friends since elementary school; she's one of the few people in my life I actually trust. "I don't give a damn what they like or don't like, Anika. I'm tired. I need to rest. The boys and I *are* taking this trip."

Her pointed jaw ticks as she stares me down, arms crossed on her chest in a stance that I'm assuming she means to be intimidating. "Does she know you'll be there?"

I snort. "Of course not."

She gives one final resigned shake of her head, blowing out a laugh. "You're gonna regret this."

"Or," I say, thumping her nose because I know how much it pisses her off, "I could enjoy it very, *very* much."

"And Nick is okay with this?"

"Abso-fucking-lutely," the hulking, six-foot-three, tatted oaf himself announces, entering through the back door. "A week of tits, booze, and fun in the sun? *And* I get to watch him follow Korie around like a lovesick puppy while she hands him his balls in a sling? Sign me up for that shit."

Chapter 2

KORIE

"HELLO EVERYONE, AND WELCOME TO CAMP POUR JUDGMENT!"

My knees bounce as I glance around the cafeteria at the equally excited faces of my fellow campers. I've never done anything like this before, but with finals fast approaching, and adult life knocking at our door, my best friend, Raven, and I thought it'd be fun to burn off some pent-up energy and sexual frustration—clear our minds and libidos, if you will.

"Before we set you all free, we need to establish a few ground rules. Here at Camp Pour Judgment, we believe in the right to drink, play, and fuck responsibly."

I can't help my loud intake of breath at Camp Counselor Joe's choice of words. I mean, I knew it was a singles camp, obviously, but for him to so brazenly put it out there like that is shocking. The man is old enough to be my father.

"Don't be a buzzkill," Raven says, squeezing my upper thigh as the rest of the room erupts in cheer. The sound of the twenty-four college-aged men and women is almost deafening.

"That being said, rest assured that you will be cut off if at any point we feel you've become irresponsibly inebriated," the short balding man says, trying to keep a straight face. "Hooking up is permitted and even encouraged, so long as it is consensual. If at any point you try to force your attention on another camper, you will be evicted from the premises." His eyes naturally move to the right side of the room, where the male campers are gathered.

A few snickers and boos ring out among the group.

"We are so happy to have you all here with us for our first ever Spring Fling," his wife Essie adds to lighten the mood, narrowing her dark eyes at her husband as she snatches the mic away. She looks to be considerably younger than he is, but it could just be good genes and hair dye. Her skin is naturally tanned and flawless, her hair a mass of thick, black waves. "We'll begin each morning with a buffet-style breakfast and mimosas, served right here in this room between eight and nine a.m. For the safety of our campers, alcohol will be restricted throughout the day until our nightly themed parties, which begin at seven p.m." She holds out seven slender fingers, to be sure there's no confusion on the time. "You should have all received a detailed list of each day's activities in your welcome packets..."

"That one's mine," Raven whispers, pointing a finger at a beefy blond guy across the room. At first glance he looks kind of familiar, but the dude next to him shifts forward, hiding his face from view. "Look at the size of those feet," she hisses. "Mmm-mmm."

"Ladies," Joe interrupts, eying me and my friend pointedly, "you'll follow Essie to the left side of the property, and she'll show you to your cabins. Gentlemen, follow me." He waves a hand over his head and starts for the door before stopping abruptly and turning back around. "I almost forgot. There are lockers along the back wall there." He points to a row of rust-colored lockers that remind me of the ones we used in high school gym class. "Electronics are not permitted on the premises. You can lock your phones, laptops, and other devices up in one of those for the duration of your stay." The middle-aged man waggles a finger in our direction, indicating for us to get moving. "What happens at Camp Pour Judgment..."

"Stays at Camp Pour Judgment," his wife finishes with a sly grin.

Chapter 3

RHETT

SOMEHOW, I MANAGE TO MAKE IT THROUGH BUNK ASSIGNMENTS without being recognized. And let me tell you, when your face is constantly on the cover of gossip rags, that's no easy feat. Even with our newly grown facial hair, sunglasses, and ballcaps, I know I'll be outed sooner rather than later, and that's why I've already had Nick arrange with the counselors to have our team face Korie's in our icebreaker event, tug of war. If there's one thing I've learned since my career really took off, it's that there isn't much a little money can't buy, and I'm not above using that to my advantage.

"Up first, we have the Lush Puppies!" Essie announces, like she's introducing a boxing team into the ring. Korie, her friend, and the other two girls assigned to their cabin look less than enthused about being called up first as they join the counselors at the mic. "And on the other side of the rope, Team Tap That!"

With my ballcap low, shielding my eyes, my bandmates—Nick, Aiden, Lyle—and I make our way over to grab the opposite side of the rope.

"This isn't even fair," her dark-haired friend complains. "We don't stand a chance against a bunch of dudes."

Korie scoffs, and the sound stirs something below my belt. Why does this girl's attitude get me so fired up? "Watch and learn, Rave," she taunts, stepping around her so she's the first in line in their team of four.

She's only a few feet away and hasn't recognized me yet. Hell, she's barely spared us a single glance. My pulse races in anticipation of her reaction when she finally gets a good look at my face. She's going to go apeshit.

"The rules are quite simple," Essie announces. "At the sound of my whistle, pull. First team in the mud pit loses."

I almost feel bad about how easy this'll be, but then I have a vision of Korie with her little white tank covered in mud, and it passes.

The boys and I start out going easy on them, wanting them to believe they've got the upper hand. My shoes skid through the dirt, bringing me closer to the edge of the pit. Just when I give the signal to end the charade and yank the rope, I'm blindsided by a perky set of C-cups and go careening into four feet of sludge.

"Seriously?" Lyle, my keyboardist shouts, spitting dirt from his tongue. "They cheated."

"There was no rule against nudity," her still-laughing best friend counters, giving Korie an impressed-but-stunned look. *Interesting.* Her little distraction tactic was as much a surprise to her as it was the rest of us.

Joe and Essie confirm the girls' win, taking the opportunity to remind us that this is not a children's camp, and their ability to outwit us is completely within the rules. Essie even goes as far as to commend them for using their feminine wiles to secure their first victory.

"Nick!" Uh-oh. Looks like the jig is up. Korie's head pops through the neck of her shirt, and she's got a death stare lasered in on the guys she's just out-*titted*. "Oh my God. What're you doing here?"

He can hardly look his cousin in the face. I've never seen him so off kilter. "I did not want to see that, Kore. Jesus, haven't you ever heard of a bra?" The two-hundred-fifty-pound drummer is beet red and not making eye contact.

Slowly her eyes bounce from Nick to Lyle, and finally to my bassist, Aiden, at which point they stop moving all together. Her lips mouth the words "oh, no," and ever so hesitantly they creep in my direction.

"Oh, yes," I offer, removing my now-filthy ball cap and tossing it to her feet. My eyes slowly scan her body, pausing at the free-range nipples which are now clearly visible through her thin top. "They're even better than I've been imagining, Stick."

Chapter 4

KORIE

THIS IS NOT HAPPENING.

"Oh my God, is that—"

I roll my eyes at Raven's giddy expression. "Yes," I deadpan, crossing my arms over my chest while trying to ignore the way my heart is thundering against my ribcage. "And we are *not* happy about this."

Raven scoffs. "Girl, speak for your damn self."

Unlike me, my best friend is fascinated with all things celebrity. She's been begging for the chance to meet Nick and the rest of The Rhett Taylor Band since the day she discovered we were related, back when we were roommates during our freshman year of college.

My father, Jax Potter, was the drummer for Diesel Rose, an old rock band that was pretty popular while Nick and I were growing up. Women threw themselves at him, and he was all too happy to take advantage, leaving me to piece my heartbroken mother back together time and time again. I have nothing to do with that man anymore and want no part of a lifestyle that caused us so much heartache.

"Well, I guess the cat's out of the bag," Joe announces with a radiant smile.

Great. Even the counselors are starstruck.

"Ladies and gents, we've got some very special guests with us this week."

It takes everything in me not to visibly gag at the hero worship these clowns do not deserve.

"Everyone, say hello to Rhett Taylor and his bandmates."

Essie goes on to speak about respecting their privacy and treating them like regular people. It annoys me to no end that it even needs saying. They *are* just regular people. Disgusting, spoiled people, at that.

"Careful," Rhett breathes against my ear, causing the hairs at the nape of my neck to stand on end. His breath is minty fresh with a hint of coffee. He smells delicious. Too bad I hate him. My fists clench at my sides as a chill works its way from the top of my head to the tips of my traitorous toes. "Keep that up too long, and your face'll get stuck."

The heat of his body so close to mine sears my skin. My good sense is lost, drowning in the scent of his expensive cologne. *Stupid hormones.*

"That'd be a shame," he adds, trailing his nose up the curve of my neck. "While I quite enjoy the way you scowl at me, that's not the face I wanna see when I make you come."

My shoulders stiffen as I finally regain some semblance of control over my body and take a step away, glancing back at the insufferably handsome jackass over my shoulder. "You followed me here," I accuse, narrowing my eyes his way. I pull in a few deep breaths, trying to calm the flush I can feel rising in my cheeks.

He shrugs. "That sounds so stalkerish." Rhett runs a hand through his golden-brown mop, which, thanks to his paltry disguise, was barely touched by the mud. I cannot believe I didn't recognize them sooner. "It is entirely possible I may have seen your plans on Facebook and decided to join you. You know, to make sure you get your money's worth."

"So fucking cocky," I grit out, forgetting our audience, who are hanging on our every word.

His answering smirk simultaneously stirs butterflies in my tummy and has smoke shooting from my ears. I wish like hell I wasn't so affected by him and even more that the arrogant bastard couldn't see it. "Some things can't be helped."

"Right. Do girls actually go for—*put me down!*" I scream, when suddenly my feet are swooped out from under me as he scoops me into his arms.

"My pleasure," he croons before taking a few steps forward and tossing my ass right into the center of the pit.

"What the hell?" I sputter, swiping mud from my eyes. I didn't get the luxury of going in feet first like the guys. Oh, no. My entire body is covered. Goddamn it. I worked hard not to get mud caked in my vagina. Jesus, I even flashed my own fucking cousin.

"Just putting you in your proper place…" His eyes circle the pit. "Stick."

Stick in the mud. Fuck him.

Chapter 5

RHETT

"DUDE, IF YOU REALLY WANT IN THAT GIRL'S PANTIES, I'M NOT sure acting like a kindergartener with a crush is gonna cut it," Lyle offers, plopping down beside me on one of the logs positioned around the bonfire. "You need to be more…" He rotates his hand in the air, like he's searching for the right word. "Charming."

"What? You don't find me charming?"

"Good one," Aiden barks, clapping me on the back before laying a blanket down in the sand beside us for his lady of the night. He helps the busty redhead down between his legs, pulling her back so she's resting against his chest. Then he looks over at me and motions to his current position. He cocks a brow as if to say, "See? This is how you do it."

I roll my eyes, flipping him the bird when she isn't looking.

They've been giving me shit all afternoon over how clueless I am when it comes to wooing a woman. The truth is, I'm just not accustomed to having to work so hard to get one to want to fuck me.

After tug of war, we were given the rest of the day to mingle and to do as we pleased. I haven't seen her once. Not that I haven't been looking—I searched the kayaks and water slide while we were in the bay. Didn't see her at archery or zip lining. She must be purposely avoiding me. I can't for the life of me understand why. Okay, so maybe tossing her in the mud was taking things a bit far, but the added challenge only makes me want her that much more.

Tonight, we're all meeting around the fire to sing camp songs, tell ghost stories, and roast marshmallows. I'm trying not to be too obvious with the way my eyes are constantly searching for any glimpse of her.

"Don't say I never did anything for you," Nick says, shoving an acoustic guitar at my chest.

"What's this for?" I ask, but I'm already strumming a few chords and adjusting the knobs, tuning it by ear.

"It's your chance to impress, Korie." He gives me a look that says, *duh*. "Joe usually plays on campfire night, but I suggested since we have a real live star here that maybe you should assume the task. He was more than happy to agree."

Just then Joe and Essie walk up, carrying boxes of skewers and ingredients for s'mores. They're sporting matching smiles when they find me tinkering with the old guitar. This is the response I'm used to from people: Respect. Adoration. This I know how to work with.

"I draw the line at 'Kumbaya,'" I warn, strumming the beginning chords to "Hotel California."

Essie giggles, snuggling up beside her husband in front of the fire. "That'll do."

I channel my teenaged self, running through a few of my old favorites, and put on an impromptu concert. Informal.

Just a guy and his guitar and a bunch of strangers gathered like friends 'round a bonfire, drinking and goofing off. When I'm half through "Ain't No Sunshine" by Bill Withers, Korie and Raven finally stagger over, drinks in hand, giving me a momentary pause. They're loud, carefree, and happy. I don't even remember what that kind of freedom feels like. Every move I make is watched, recorded, and plastered on the media. Twisted to sell magazines and increase ratings.

"How 'bout 'Take Me Home, Country Roads?'" Joe asks, passing the girls a marshmallow-tipped skewer. I pretend not to notice their arrival. Try not to miss a note when my heart skips a beat. Try not to drool at the sight of those long, slender legs and the way her ass is filling those denim shorts like a second skin.

When I reach the chorus, the group joins in, singing loud and completely out of key. I honestly haven't enjoyed playing this much in years. There's no pressure. No cameras. No fear of disappointment.

At the end of the song, Essie walks over to hand me a s'more. I prop the acoustic against the log and sink my teeth in to the treat, moaning at both the decadent taste of the chocolate and the sting of the molten fluff burning my lip. When I go in for another bite, I feel the brush of the guitar against my leg and turn to find Korie slipping the strap around her neck. I damn near choke; I didn't know she played.

"I'd like to dedicate this performance to all the men out there who think they're God's gift to women," she slurs, propping a foot beside me on the log to rest the guitar on her knee. "I'm looking at you, Rhett Taylor," she says with a thick twang as she tucks her long locks behind her ears.

What follows is an absolute train wreck rendition of "What Part of No" by country legend Lorrie Morgan. She *can't* play.

Can't carry a tune. She doesn't even know half the lyrics, but the ones she does are sung with such conviction that she somehow has every one of these drunk fools entranced.

"I'll be glad to explain, if it's too hard to comprehend," she wails, abusing the strings like a toddler who's just been given her first plastic guitar. "Rhett Taylor, what part of no don't you understand?" Korie stretches the last word out in a dramatic finish before taking a bow and passing the instrument back over to me.

I'm stunned speechless. *What the hell was that?* I really want to laugh, but the triumphant look on her face tells me that might not be wise. I'm already skating on thin ice with her and need to tread carefully.

The boys and I exchange looks of sheer horror and confusion.

"Well," Nick finally says, clearing his throat, "that was... ummm, that was something, Kore."

"Thanks, cuz." She's positively beaming with pride.

His eyes grow round, and he turns his head in my direction, mouthing, *is she serious?*

"Wooooo!" Essie yells, rushing over to wrap her arms around Korie. "That was amazing and so brave!"

The girls laugh and hug, and I honestly don't know what to make of it. This must be one of those girl power things that I and the rest of the male population do not understand.

"I believe my girl just issued a challenge," Raven taunts when the theatrics wind down. "Let's hear it, country boy."

It's suddenly pin-drop quiet, but for the crackling of the fire. It only takes me about thirty seconds to think up a response...I jump right in at the chorus, "You're a crazy bitch." It's a little out of my vocal range, but I own it like a true fucking rock star.

"Buckcherry," she snorts, throwing her head back in laughter before belting out the lyrics right along with me and everyone else.

Chapter 6

KORIE

"IT'S TOO EARLY FOR THIS," I GRIPE, STILL RUBBING THE sleep from my eyes as Raven drags me, along with Kline and Lisa, our roommates and the other half of the Lush Puppies, out to join the troops.

"Listen up, bitches. The winner of today's color wars gets a liquor bar in their cabin at five p.m. That's two hours before the party starts." She eyes each one of us. "Don't come between a lush and her booze, ya got me?"

Kline and Lisa are built like athletes. Tall, muscular, fit. We certainly have an advantage with them on our side, although I'm not sure they'd feel the same about the two of us. Raven and I are lanky in comparison, but we're both fiercely competitive.

"I'm not sure how I feel about the bikini," Lisa gripes, adjusting the straps beneath her tee. "Can we keep our shirts on at least?"

Raven scoffs. "Do we want to win?" she asks. "You saw how those boys fell all over themselves at the sight of a pair of titties.

We need to work with what the good Lord gave us!"

"Look, we play basketball…we don't prance around half naked," Kline snaps.

"Well, camp is all about new experiences…breaking out of our comfort zones. And besides, if you wanted a say in the suits, you should've gotten your asses up early enough to choose them yourselves."

Well, that settles that, I think to myself as we approach the rest of the group.

"Good morning, campers!" Joe shouts into the megaphone. "I hope you've all had a good night's rest and came prepared to compete. Today we have our water wars. The relay starts with a canoe race across the bay. Once you've made it to the dock, tag your team member, who will then crab crawl across a fifty-foot Slip 'N Slide."

"Sounds easy enough, right?" Essie asks. "Wrong," she answers herself. "Because each of those Slip 'N Slides is coated in twenty bottles of baby shampoo."

"If you fall," Joe adds, "you go back to the beginning and try again."

"When you've successfully made it across, you'll tag your teammate, who will then climb up a forty-foot rope to the top of that water slide and go down on his or her stomach. Once you've reached the end, you'll tag your final teammate, who will join Joe at the zipline. He or she will zip over to the other side and capture the flag, securing the booze cart for their team!"

"Oh, we've so got this!" Raven is all business, pulling us into a huddle to assign positions.

"I think since you, Kline and Lisa, are our stronger physical competitors, that one of you should take the canoe and the other the rope climb?" I suggest, trying to figure out which task each of us is best suited for.

"I'll take the canoe," Lisa offers. "Kline, how do you feel about the rope?"

"I'm fine with it."

"Great," Raven says. "That leaves us with the Slip 'N Slide and zip line."

"I'll take the Slip 'N Slide," I offer, confident in my ability to maintain my balance across it.

Raven's face pales. "But I'm deathly afraid of heights."

Kline snorts out a laugh as she strips down to her yellow bikini. "Well, it's a good thing we're all here to break out of our comfort zones, am I right?"

I position myself at the end of the dock, and low and behold, guess who's standing there for Team Tap That?

"Lookin' real good in that teeny bikini," Rhett purrs, ogling me behind his Ray-Bans.

"Thanks," I say, trying not to stare at his perfectly sculpted chest. "Wore it just for you."

"Figured as much," he says. "I chose this suit with you in mind as well."

I've barely given him a second glance, so it isn't until this very moment I notice that he's sporting a fucking red Speedo, and one he fills out quite nicely, I might add.

"You really shouldn't have," I murmur, redirecting my attention to the starting line, where our teammates are climbing into their canoes.

Joe fires the blowhorn and they're off. Lisa is neck and neck with the four guys' teams. The other girls are still trying to figure out how to row.

"Come on, Lisa!" I shout as she starts to pull ahead.

About halfway through, the green team's canoe flips over, and the competition is down to yellow, red, and purple.

"Eat my dust," I taunt Rhett when Lisa slaps my hand and

I take off for the Slip 'N Slide. It's harder than it looks, and I fall flat on my ass just feet from the finish line and am forced back to the beginning, where my nemesis is just getting started.

"Fancy meeting you here," he says through a shit-eating grin.

"Pleasure's all yours, I'm sure."

"Oh, I'll make it good for you too, baby."

I can't even with his cockiness, so I focus on the task at hand and try to ignore the pain radiating from my tailbone from the fall I just took instead of my figurative pain in the ass competitor.

This time instead of rushing across, I glide my way slow and steady right to the finish line, tagging Kline before Rhett is even halfway through.

"Heya, cuz." *Nick.* Oh dear God, if the discomfort of seeing him spilling out of what fits his big ass like a red thong is even a fraction of what he must've felt seeing me topless…

I can't even form a response, so I'm more than thankful when Rhett finally crosses that finish line, sending him on his way.

I seriously question their choice to send Nicholas up the rope, but although Kline had a decent head start on him, they both reach the top at the same time.

The race for the flag comes down to Raven and Aiden.

And. She. Chokes.

Literally, on her vomit, at the top of the zip line, where Aiden steps around her, zipping his way to a cart of free booze.

Chapter 7

RHETT

"HOLY FUCK, RHETT. YOU'RE AN IDIOT." AIDEN CAN HARDLY breathe through guffaws when I exit the shared bathroom dressed for tonight's themed party, wearing nothing but a Domino's Pizza box around my waist like a tutu, dick and balls tucked neatly inside. The back of the box rests on the shelf of my ass, which is looking especially nice tonight, I might add, being I had it waxed for the occasion.

"The theme is 'anything but clothes.' If she can show her tits, there should be no issue with me baring my hiney."

"It is a pretty tight ass," Nick agrees, adding a final layer of duct tape to his Budweiser box kilt. "And it's not like it's anything all of America hasn't already seen," the asshole teases, making reference to a video that leaked a couple of years ago of myself and Ana Michelle, an up-and-coming actress I hooked up with, who thought it would be a great career move to *accidently* release compromising photos publicly linking the two of us.

Anika'd had a fit, spending days on the phone, tirelessly working to get them down, while I remained unphased, learning long ago not to let shit like that bug me. Rhett Taylor is nothing more than an image. An entity. A commodity. And for my own sanity, I treat my public persona as such. Few people know the real me, and their opinions are the only ones I can be bothered to care about. For some reason I couldn't begin to explain, I want to put Korie in that category—for her to see past the facade.

Lyle strolls around the corner with a navy and yellow-striped beach towel tied around his waist and a tray of shots in hand. "Nice," he says, smirking at our costumes. With his free hand, he thwacks the head of the rubber ducky protruding from the pool float that serves as Aiden's ensemble. "Pretty impressive duck ya got there."

"That's what she said." Aiden strokes the head of his duck for good measure.

Nineties dance music assaults our ears the moment we step outside. Pink and blue streaks brighten the sky as the strobe lights pulse to the beat. It's only a five-minute walk to the pavilion, but already my taint is starting to chafe due to the rubbing of the cardboard. I'm really beginning to question this costume by the time we arrive.

"It's as hot as two squirrels fucking in a sack," I groan, adjusting myself.

"I believe the saying is two rats screwing in a wool sock," a tipsy Korie offers, stumbling over her own feet. I damn near swallow my tongue as I reach out to steady her. She's wearing nothing more than strips of caution tape strategically wrapped around her breasts and hips. My eyes trail the length of her toned legs to the tips of her red-painted toes, which are usually covered in a pair of Converse sneakers. I'm pretty sure there's drool dripping from my chin when Nick barks out a laugh, pulling me from my stupor.

"I wasn't aware rodents fucking in fabric was such a common heat analogy."

"It's definitely a thing, Nicholas." I tighten my arms around her middle so she doesn't topple over when she leans forward to point her finger in his face. I'm more than a little shocked when she doesn't immediately pull away. "People at A&M say it all the time."

"You're so cultured," he teases.

She shrugs and then, as if she's only just noticed she's in my arms, her cheeks flush and she steps aside, tugging at the placement of the tape covering her tits to make sure it's still in place. The urge to untie it and garner another glimpse at her breasts is strong. "Um, there's booze over there." She points to a bar set up next to the DJ. "Raven and I are hanging by the fire…she sort of has a thing for you, Nick." Korie waggles her brows at her cousin. "Join us?"

Nick perks up like a rooster. "Yeah," he says, looking to me for confirmation. "We'll be right there."

Chapter 8

KORIE

"They're coming!" Raven tosses back another shot of whiskey, her body swaying provocatively to the sultry beat. "Don't stare. Don't make it obvious."

Alcohol swirls in my belly as I turn my head toward my best friend to avoid their gazes. Flames lick my skin. I'm hot and tingly everywhere, despite the slight nip in the night air. Trying to ignore the rapid beating in my chest, I focus on Raven, matching her moves with what I hope come off as sexy ones of my own. I want Rhett to see me as more than some frigid bitch—to want me the way I can't seem to stop myself from wanting him.

Awareness pricks my skin, and before I even hear his voice, I feel his nearness. "How much have you had to drink, Stick?" His raspy tone is pure sex. "And who knew you had moves like that?"

"There's a lot about me you don't know," I say in a flirty voice that cannot belong to me.

"Apparently." He moves to stand just inches away. I try not to ogle his chiseled abs and the V that leads down to the promised land, presently encased in a pizza box. Only Rhett Taylor could wear cardboard like it was tailor made to fit his body.

"Nice box you've got there." I giggle, and his eyes narrow just a smidge. He's not sure how to take my new attitude toward him, and quite frankly, I'm not either. But I came here for an adventure, and for some reason I'm hell bent on exploring the dick in that box.

As if reading my mind, he taunts, "You should see what's inside." Then he winks, and it's effortlessly sexy. Not at all awkward, like it'd be if I tried to do such a thing. I decide he must spend a lot of time practicing that move in the mirror to pull it off so well. Hell, if I had a face like his, I'd probably stare at myself all day too.

"I'm a little afraid of what I might find," I quip. Raising my right brow, I take a long pull from my party punch. "I hear that thing gets around." My stomach sinks at my own words, because therein lies the problem. I'm attracted to him—painfully so. But so is the rest of the female population. He could have any girl he wants, and does, regularly, if the tabloids are to be believed. I've never even had a one-night stand. Only two serious boyfriends. The thought of being just another hole for him to stick it in kinda makes me queasy. Or it did, up until about three shots ago, when I decided if I'm here to scratch an itch, why not him? I came here to be bold and daring—to find a sexy guy to have my way with. Who better than Rhett fucking Taylor? He traveled all this way to play games with me. The way I see it, I can choose to be an active player or wind up his toy, and I'd prefer to be the one pulling the strings.

"Be afraid, little one," he taunts. "I'm sure it's way more

than you could handle."

"We'll see." I bat my lashes before twirling with my arms above my head in the firelight. I feel light and woozy and free.

Rhett takes my extended hand in his, spinning me around like the Prince Charming he is anything but. "Will we?" he asks when I come back to face him, and my eyes lock with his. They're warm and hungry and command my attention. I couldn't look away if I wanted to. And it's really starting to scare me, how very much I don't want to.

"If you're lucky."

Chapter 9

RHETT

"**W**ALK WITH ME?" THE TEMPTRESS ASKS, TUGGING MY HAND toward the beach. "I need some air."

We've been dancing around the fire for nearly an hour. My dick's so hard that I'm surprised it hasn't pushed through the damn cardboard yet. I'm going to be in so much pain tomorrow, when I regain feeling in my balls. But all the discomfort's been worth it to be able to feel her tiny hands exploring my bare chest while we sway to the beat of the music. The few times I caught her appreciating my ass were definite highlights as well.

"If I didn't know better, Stick, I'd think you were trying to get me alone." I place a hand over my heart in mock surprise.

"If I didn't know better," she counters, "I'd think you were playing hard to get, Hollywood."

She gave me a nickname. *Things are getting serious quick*, I muse to myself. "Don't you go falling in love with me now," I warn in a teasing tone. I'm well aware that the danger of that happening is slim to none. The girl barely tolerates my existence…unless she's drinking, apparently, and I'm not sure what that's doing for my ego, but I'm enjoying her attention, so I don't put too much thought into it.

Her head tips back, and she laughs hysterically. "Jesus, you are full of yourself, aren't you? Don't worry, Romeo…you're safe from my affections."

"You seem awful sure." I cock my brow.

"Look, I'm just here for a good time. The last thing I'm looking to do is catch feelings."

I shrug, giving her my best lopsided grin. "Just saying…I'm rumored to be pretty irresistible."

"You're rumored to be a lot of things."

At that I bust out laughing. "How do you know every bit of it isn't true?"

"The sex change?"

"Maybe…"

"You fathered Kate Middleton and Prince William's middle child?"

Oh, that was a good one. "I mean, we were at the same resort the summer before, in the Bahamas. It could have happened."

"The penis enlargement?" Her eyes drop briefly to my crotch before bouncing back up to meet mine.

"Is complete bullshit! These killer chops aren't the only thing I was blessed with," I argue, ending the ruse to defend my manhood. "Women everywhere are just searching for a way to explain such a phenomenon."

The corners of her mouth curl into a smile. "I bet."

We leave her friend Raven and Nick dry humping on a log in front of the fire. The rest of the guys have long gone their own way. The party is in full swing, with campers linking up all over the place. It's like high school all over again, without the fear of teen pregnancy and missing curfew.

"So, what do you like to do?" Korie asks, tugging us toward the abandoned water trampoline. "You know, when you're not performing for sold-out stadiums or collecting women's panties." Her accompanying smirk is joined by a painful dose of side-eye.

"Seems you've read all there is to know about me in the papers," I counter. "I'd rather hear about you, anyway."

She takes a few long strides, putting herself ahead of me, then turns and begins walking clumsily backward. After taking a long pull from the drink still clutched in her hand, she takes her time assessing me. Emerald eyes scour every inch of my exposed body over the rim of her solo cup.

"Come on, Stick," I urge. "Who is Korie Potter?"

"Well," she says, nibbling her lower lip. "I'll be graduating in a few weeks from Texas A&M with a degree in social work."

"Oh yeah?" I ask, genuinely curious as I take her small hand in mine to help her navigate the pier. "What then?"

"Then I save the world, Hollywood." She releases my fingers to spin and damn near falls off the edge into the water.

"Whoops," she says on an exhale as I wrap my arm around her, pulling her to my chest. "I don't usually drink this much, so I'm a little off balance." Her pale cheeks flush beneath the moonlight, her shimmery eyes glowing bright. She looks fragile and dainty, a stark contrast to the hard-ass, take-no-shit Korie I'm growing used to. There's an unfamiliar tug in my chest, making me realize that maybe I like this side of her too. That this just might be more than an infatuation.

"It's okay. I don't mind saving you," I rasp, a little stunned by how much I truly mean that.

Hesitant hands comb the sides of my face, reaching into my hair and threading their way through the windblown strands. She leans in, her lips parting, breaths coming out in shallow pants. Our mouths are a fraction of an inch from touching when the Dominos box forges a barrier between us. The force causes the box to dig into my already chafed balls and I double over, seeing fucking stars.

"Oh my God! Are you okay?"

I can't tell whether she's laughing or crying as she starts to back away, looking on while I finally rip the damn thing from my body, uncaring that I'm wearing absolutely nothing underneath.

"Meat lovers," she gasps, mouth agape.

I'm already well on my way into the water when her words register. I come up sputtering, reaching beneath the surface to cup my aching sack. The freezing water feels amazing on the raw flesh. "Meat lovers?" I ask, grinning at her shocked expression. I can't blame her. The girl just got an eyeful.

"The uh—. The umm…the pizza. Definitely meat lovers," she squeaks, reaching behind her back and untying the tape from around her breasts. "Mind if I join you?" she asks as the bright yellow tape floats to the ground.

I stand there, stupefied, unable to find my voice as I watch the object of my obsession step out of the makeshift skirt that did little to cover her to begin with. With a hard swallow, I shake my head, and in what seems like an instant she's standing before me in shoulder-deep water.

Korie squeals loudly. "Jesus. Fuck! That's cold." Her jaw chatters, and she moves closer. "Let's try this again." She presses the length of her body to mine, her pebbled nipples hard against my chest and her arms laced around my neck.

"What's your favorite?" I ask when her warm breath reaches my lips.

"Huh?" I love that she's all flustered and wanting.

"Favorite pizza?" I tip her nose up with mine, so I can read her expression.

Eyes heady with desire, she all but purrs, "beef." Our eager lips crash together, her hungry tongue grappling with mine for control. She tastes delectable, like strawberries and tequila. Coupled with the scent of her coconut tanning lotion, I'm being driven to the brink.

"What else?" I ask, when her hands begin to explore below the surface, trying to keep things from going too far. She's buzzed—well on her way to drunk—and I'll be damned if she'll have that as an excuse when we finally hook up.

"Huh?" she again asks, her heart racing against my own.

I nip her lower lip. "Tell me something else?"

"About?" I try not to laugh at the frustration in her voice.

"You. I want to know all there is to know about the blonde beauty who loathes my very existence."

She backs away a little with a loud huff, looking up to see if I'm sincere. "Why? You live in L.A. You hang out with models and movie stars, for fuck's sake. My life is so boring in comparison."

"It's all fake," I say defensively, pushing long, wet strands of hair behind her shoulders.

"What is?"

"Everything." Tipping her chin up with a finger, I place a kiss on the edge of her nose. "All smoke and mirrors."

Chapter 10

KORIE

"TELL ME SOMETHING REAL. I WANT TO KNOW WHAT YOU'RE passionate about. What gets your blood going?"

I rake my eyes up and down the length of his chest, desire pooling in my center. "Really? You have to ask?"

With a shake of his head, he blows out a laugh. "Other than my notoriously impressive meat."

"Well…" I trail my hands down his back, softly cupping his ass. His hard-on digs into my stomach as his fingers trace the sensitive skin on the back of my arms, whisper soft. The sensation would tickle if I weren't so turned on at the moment. "I skate."

"Really?" His head jerks back in surprise. "Like at the roller rink?"

"No," I chuckle. "Board."

"No shit? You any good?"

I feel my own face light up. "Not bad," I answer honestly. "I've won a few local competitions. It's always been a dream to compete in the X Games, but I'm not even on their radar."

"So, get on their radar." He says it so flippantly; I'm sure the idea of having a dream and it not coming to fruition is foreign to him. He's made it, but the reality is that most of us never do. Rhett Taylor is the exception.

"It's not that easy."

"Sure it is. The question is, how bad do you really want it?" How'd we go from rubbing uglies to having an actual conversation so quickly? I'm not sober enough for this level of annoyance.

"Can we just not talk for a while?" I run my hands up his smooth chest, toying with his nipples in an attempt to redirect his attention, but it's all for naught.

"What would it take?" he persists. Taking both of my hands into his, he lifts them from the water to his mouth, pressing kisses across the knuckles, then lowers them to our sides. *Smooth.*

"Ughh," I groan. "Money…sponsorships. Attention. I'd have to get noticed by the selections committee."

"You should apply."

"I have for the last three years. They don't see me."

"Put yourself out there. Make it impossible for them not to. That's how you make it. You've got but one life, Korie Potter. Make it count."

"Seize the moment? Is that your advice, country boy?"

An almost embarrassed expression crosses his face briefly. "That's my advice."

I lock eyes with his, swallowing hard, as I reach between our bodies and wrap my fist around his length, making long strokes. "Then stop cockblocking me, cuz I'm really trying to seize this one," I whisper.

Rhett stares intently for a moment, like he's battling some

internal demons, before gripping my hips and lifting me so I can wrap my legs around his waist. His mouth molds to mine, tongue plunging urgently in and out as he backs me up to the floating trampoline, my back pressing into the rough fabric.

I reach down, guiding his thick cock to my opening, not thinking of anything but quelling the ache that's growing by the second between my thighs. The tip brushes over my clit, and I swear I've fucking died and gone to heaven.

Then he sends me crashing back to earth with a lone word. "No." It's whispered against my lips. Soft, but sure. I feel it. I hear it. But no part of me understands it. Could he be worried about pregnancy? It's the only logical excuse for his pulling away literally seconds from sealing the deal.

"I'm on the pill, Rhett. It's okay." Again, I shift to line up our centers, and once again he denies me.

"Not tonight." He's serious, and I'm irrationally angry that this world-famous manwhore doesn't want me.

"I came here to get fucked, Hollywood. Are you gonna give me my money's worth, or do I need to find it elsewhere?"

We're locked in a stare down when I feel his fingers, two—no, maybe three—slip between my folds. I'm still angry for being denied, but I haven't been touched in so long, and the way he's thrusting and grunting, lapping at my breast...Jesus, I can't think about anything but chasing this feeling.

"Oh, God. Rhett. Please don't stop."

"That's it. Give it to me, baby girl," he croons, taking my left nipple into his mouth and biting down gently.

My hands are everywhere—pulling at his hair, scoring his back. I rock and writhe and take, and he gives and gives, expecting nothing in return.

"Look at me," he orders, as his thumb presses against my clit, stroking gently, lighting every cell of my body on fire.

"I want those pretty eyes on me when you come." My pussy clenches, and I explode around his fingers. Rhett captures my scream, fucking my mouth with his tongue while I bask in the aftershocks of the greatest orgasm of my life.

"Wake up, hussy."

Raven. "Go away. I'm on vacation." I swat at the air blindly, hoping to connect with her irritating face.

"Your cousin has the most beautiful di—" she singsongs.

"Stop!" I shout, clapping a hand over her mouth. "Not another word. Ew." My other hand goes right to my forehead, trying to stop the room from spinning.

Her cynical laughter fills the cabin and sends my head pounding. Stupid hangover. "Fine. But it *was* really good."

"Happy for you."

"Did you know it was pierced?" she asks, bouncing up and down on the bed with excitement.

Okay, now I'm gagging. "He's my cousin, Raven. Why would I know any details about his penis?"

With a slight shrug and the devil in her eyes, she continues badgering me. "What about you?" she taunts. "How was Mr. Taylor? Did he live up to his reputation?"

My brain is a fog of bits and pieces of the night before. Dancing by the fire. Skinny dipping in the bay. The crush of being denied. I scoff. "That motherfucker rejected me!"

Raven's eyes narrow in disbelief. "Uh. Just how much did you have to drink? Cuz I watched him carry your naked ass into this cabin last night, and you both had hearts in your eyes."

"Is that how I got here?" I glance down at the A&M tee I

don't remember changing into. But there's a lot about last night I can't seem to see clearly.

"Oh, girl. He was gloriously naked too. You may not be able to walk today," she giggles. "They weren't lying…he must've had that thing enhanced."

I clench my thighs together. "Yeah, well, not all of the rumors are true."

"Oh, no?" she asks, eyes wide. "Tell me what mysteries you've uncovered."

Swallowing hard, I throw my head back on the pillow. "He doesn't fuck just anything with a hole between its legs." I have the sudden urge to cry, and that just pisses me off. I feel so humiliated.

"You sure?" Rave questions. "He carried you to bed and riffled through your bag for clothes…Girl, he even tucked you in and kissed your forehead before leaving."

"What a fucking psycho." I shake my head, rolling over and climbing out of my bunk to head for the bathroom, all the while fighting the urge to be sick. And it's more than just a hangover.

Chapter 11

RHETT

"**DAMN, SOMEONE'S AWAKE AND MOVING AROUND EARLY THIS** morning," Nick announces when I join him on the front porch in time to watch the sun rise. He's never been much of a sleeper, a side-effect of his ADHD. He usually takes advantage of those quiet hours to compose music, so while I'm sure it's frustrating, his insomnia is a bit of a blessing.

"Couldn't sleep." I stare out into the distance at the ocean, drowning in memories of Korie's naked form with the reflection of the moon on the bay as the perfect backdrop. The way her head was thrown back in ecstasy, the tips of her hair dipping into the water. Shit. I can still hear her sweet moans and feel the heat of her breath on my neck.

The scraping sound of Nick setting his cup of coffee on the wrought iron table between our chairs pulls me from my thoughts. He furrows his brow, eying me curiously. "You're not losing sleep over my little cousin, are you?"

I consider lying for the briefest of moments, but who am

I kidding? With all the hours Nick and I spend writing songs together, he knows me better than just about anyone else. There's an intimacy that comes with that sort of collaborative creativity, and he'd be able to see right through my bullshit, so I give it to him straight. "I think I might really like her."

"She's too good for you." *Well, damn. Tell me how you really feel.*

He's right. But that knowledge doesn't mean his lack of faith doesn't still piss me off. "I'm good enough to fuck her, but nothing more? Do you even hear yourself right now?"

"Rhett, she's a grown woman. If Korie wants to fuck around with a rock star and brag to all of her friends, that's on her," he shrugs. "But her heart is another matter entirely."

My hands clench the wooden arms of my chair so tight I'm surprised they don't splinter. With my teeth gritted, I push up to standing. "That's not your call to make." I don't know why I'm getting all worked up over a chick I barely know, but my blood is racing.

"You're right," he answers with a slow nod. "But as your *friend*, I'm asking you not to force her back into this life. There's a reason you only met her a few weeks ago. She's never wanted anything to do with it."

"I said I liked her. Chill." My laughter sounds off, even to my own ears. "I'm not proposing marriage."

I push this morning's encounter with Nick to the back of my mind as we head out to the field for today's color wars, eager to lay eyes on her again. I haven't felt butterflies like this since I first started performing on stage, and certainly never over a woman. I wonder if it happens the same with love—if the fluttering just lessens and lessens until you can't even remember when it stopped. Until you're just going through the motions. Until you reach a point where you know the love still exists deep down but can't say why.

Fuck. That shit's depressing.

"Hey, you guys!" Essie shouts into a megaphone. She and her husband are dressed in head to toe camo, face paint and all. "Today is the culmination of four days of healthy competition and what we hope will become lifelong friendships. We've decided to shake things up and pair off in boy/girl teams for the paintball competition. Joe will flip a coin. If heads wins, the gentlemen get to pick their partners. If tails is the winner, it will be ladies' choice."

Murmurs ring out among the campers, some whispering words of excitement and others sounding less than thrilled about the change up. I can't get a read on Korie, because she hasn't once looked my way since she and Raven arrived nearly ten minutes ago. For this reason, my stomach does a somersault when Joe tosses the coin into the air.

"Please, please, please," I mutter beneath my breath when Essie crouches to the ground to announce the results of the coin toss.

"Heads it is!" she calls, holding up the evidence for all to see.

"Korie's mine," I declare to the other eleven guys standing around me, just in case any of them had any thoughts of claiming her.

Nick's up to choose first. Of course he is, because he's the only one with the balls to step on me.

"Don't you fucking do it, Nick," I growl, when he looks back at me with a shit-eating grin.

His eyes of course go straight to Korie and Raven. My palms are sweating by the time he finally makes his call. "Get over here, Raven." Thank God he chose with his dick over his head.

When Stick's shoulders slump, I no longer have to wonder if she's angry with me. I know. I'm just not sure why. What the hell could have happened between the mind-blowing orgasm I gave her last night and this morning?

Three other guys are called to pick partners before me, and I watch her deflate a little more each time her name isn't called.

"Rhett, you're up. Pick your poison," Joe says, slapping me on the back as I approach him and Essie.

Poison. What an apt description. Never has a woman had me so drugged.

"I choose..." My eyes drift through each of the seven girls still standing, finally landing on the blonde whose head is rapidly shaking side to side, her lips pursed in an angry pout. "Stick."

"Dammit to hell!" she shouts, stomping over to join me.

"Lovely to see you too."

Her response is to snatch the light gray jumpsuit from Joe's hand and shove past me to the line of trees, where she removes her shoes and steps into the legs, shrugs her arms into the sleeves, and pulls the zipper up to her neck, hiding every possible inch of skin she can manage from my lust-filled eyes.

I take a moment to mourn the loss of her sexy legs in the short black Nike shorts before ambling over to join her and donning my own bee suit.

"What's your problem?" I finally ask when I can't handle the silence hanging between us.

"You didn't disappoint," she answers, coldly.

What the— "And that's a bad thing?" Why the hell are

women so damn confusing?

Her eyes roll as she accepts the goggles from Essie and proceeds to fight with fitting them to her face.

"Here," I say, taking the rubber straps from her hands. "Let me."

With a few tugs, the safety glasses are nice and snug.

She doesn't bother with thanking me but offers a curt nod instead.

"You're welcome," I say, before affixing my own goggles to my face.

"Pay attention," she whisper-hisses when Essie begins going over the game rules. "I don't like to lose."

"So, at the top of your guns there is a container called a hopper." She demonstrates with the weapon in her hand. "This is where you load the ammo. Each hopper will hold two hundred paint balls. Every team has their own color. If you run out, there will be refills located at the center of the arena on this folding table. Keep in mind there will be no cover in this area, so try to conserve your shots and make them count. The object is to be the team with the cleanest uniforms when the buzzer goes off. Play time will be one hour."

"In other words," Joe adds, "shoot, and don't get shot."

"Thanks for clarifying, hon," his wife says with an obnoxious eyeroll. "Because what I said was so confusing."

"Damn," I grumble, "are you girls all in sync today or what?"

"'Scuse me?"

"Just kidding, sunshine. I'm well aware you're not on your period."

Chapter 12

KORIE

Embarrassment colors my cheeks when I think back to last night... remembering the way I rode his fingers. So pathetic. So desperate.

"I can't stop thinking about it either," the smug asshole offers through a cocky grin.

"Well, you should...I have." I've got no doubt the bastard can see right through my lie. I can't fucking believe he turned me down and that I actually allowed him to pacify me with a finger fuck. He stole any chance I had of hooking up with someone else by monopolizing all of my time and clearly staking his claim, then failed to deliver.

"I can see that." He snickers, biting his lower lip to contain a laugh.

"Look," I growl, glancing around to be sure we don't have an audience. When I find everyone else busily loading their paint ball guns, I continue. "If you're expecting me to be impressed like your usual groupies, you're going to be disappointed. Just like I was last night."

He damn near chokes on his saliva. "*That* was disappointment?"

"If I wanted to rub one out, I could have done a better job of it myself."

Rhett stares at me in stunned silence for all of ten seconds before his attention returns to loading blue pellets of paint into his hopper.

He's annoyingly quiet while we finish loading up and head out to locate our base. Each team begins behind a huge barrel painted in their assigned color. The bases are spread out around the perimeter of the arena, which covers most of the wooded area behind the cabins.

The silence lingers between us. It's awkward, and I don't want to be the one to break it. I'm so mad—and so horny—I can hardly think straight. To make matters worse, he smells like a wet dream. Actually, much like the one I had last night after he returned me to my bed, primed and wanting.

When the blowhorn sounds signaling the start of the war, I don't even think, I just act.

"What the fu—!" Rhett's gun falls to the ground, his hands both going right for his junk. "We're on the same fucking team, psycho. What happened to not liking to lose?"

"I don't." I shrug, not feeling the least bit sorry. "And now we're even."

When his right hand begins to stroke up and down, rubbing out the sting, my mouth goes dry. I try like hell to avert my gaze but can't rip my eyes away. "Even?" he hisses.

I clear my throat, finally breaking my stare. "Matching blue balls."

Realization dawns on his face when Joe's voice sounds through the outdoor speakers. "Campers, you have thirty seconds to evacuate your bases or you'll be disqualified."

"He's talking to us, ya big tit," I say, retrieving his gun and shoving it into his hands. "Let's go. Guard my rear."

"I'd like to do something to your rear, all right," he mutters, limping behind me to a nearby cover of trees.

"What was tha—" I start, just before the sting of a bullet to the shoulder steals my breath. "Shit. That hurts."

"*I know.*"

Okay, so maybe I'm beginning to feel a little bad about popping a cap in his cock at point-blank range. "How's your dick?"

"Swollen," he teases, pulling me down on top of him to miss another hit.

"I shouldn't have done that," I rasp, trying to control my breathing, wishing I could control my manic heart. There's no way he doesn't feel it thrumming on his chest like a damn jackhammer.

"You should probably kiss it…make it feel better." His right hand lifts to cup my jaw, and he rubs his thumb over my lower lip, waggling his brows.

"Could you be more obnoxious?" I ask, shoving off of him.

"Oh, Stick. Give me a little time, I'm sure I can manage to do much worse."

"Shit!" I shout when we're bombarded with shots. In the midst of our arguing, we let our guards down and aren't even prepared to retaliate.

"This way!" Rhett yells, pushing me ahead of him through the trees. We don't stop running until we find cover behind an old tool shed, where we each take a side, defending our newfound fortress.

After we coat the enemies in blue paint, our attackers move on, and I finally have a moment to breathe.

"Come on." I look up to find Rhett pulling a loose board back and ushering me inside. "Hurry up."

"You want me to crawl in there?" I ask, already shaking my head. "There could be rats or roaches or God knows what inside."

"Already checked it out. Nothin' but a bit of dust."

"I don't want to…" I whine.

"We need a minute to settle things between us. If we stay out here, we're going to get clobbered before we can utter two words." Again, his hand waves toward the gap in the boards. "If you want to come out on top, we need a strategy. Fighting like an old married couple doesn't seem to be working for us."

I peek around my side of the building, finding we're still alone. "But isn't that against the rules?"

"Not if we don't get caught." He lifts a brow in challenge. "Scared, Stick?"

He knows just what to say to get me moving. "Not in the least."

"Good. Move it."

"Only because you asked so nicely," I snark, dropping to my knees and crawling through the narrow crack.

Rhett is right behind me, pushing his gun through the opening first and then squeezing his way inside.

"You're a mess," I observe when he rises to standing, wiping dust from his hands onto his pants but only managing to coat them in red and yellow paint.

He stares at his palms for a moment before advancing on me. "You're one to talk."

"Well," I stammer, as he backs me into a corner, smearing paint across my forehead with his knuckle, "it's all your fault."

"Is it?" His tongue darts out to wet his lower lip and for a moment, I forget my own name.

A knot becomes lodged in my throat as I stare at his mouth, silently willing him to press his lips to mine. I feel faint and can't remember why we're just standing here staring at each other. Why he's looking at me expectantly? Fuck. He probably asked me a damn question, and I was too busy drooling over him to pay attention.

Rhett clears his throat, a perceptive smile creeping across his face. "You were saying?"

Shit. I knew it was my turn. Think, Korie, think. "It's really hot in here."

"It's just me."

"Huh?" I ask, still feeling dazed and confused. It's as if English is no longer my first language, because none of the words coming out of his mouth are registering, only the seductive way his lips move around the syllables.

"You okay, Stick?"

"I…uh." I blow air up toward my eyes, trying to cool myself down. "I don't know what's wrong with me." My hand moves to my throat, pulling the zipper of my jumpsuit down a few inches, hoping it helps with the breathing issue I seem to be having.

He sucks in his lower lip, slowly gliding it through his teeth. The fucker knows I'm staring, and not even that knowledge is enough to make me look away. I've never witnessed a *lip tease.* I have the urge to shove dollars down his pants as a reward for his services.

"Did they teach you that?"

"Who?" he asks, tipping my chin up so my eyes are forced from his mouth to meet with his blue-green orbs, which are glowing with amusement and dare I hope, maybe a little desire as well. "Teach me what?"

"Lip seduction…is that a Hollywood thing?"

Chapter 13

RHETT

"WHAT?" I ASK, A LITTLE STUNNED AND ALSO VERY TURNED on by the way she's been eye-fucking me for the past few minutes.

Korie swallows hard. "Nothing...forget it."

I run my tongue to the corner of my mouth to screw with her a little. I feel like a damn fool, biting and licking and sucking my lips, but I can tell it's turning her on, so who the hell am I not to abuse this sudden lip-porn power I seem to have over her?

"Stop it."

"Stop what?" I ask, nibbling obnoxiously on my lips.

That seems to break the trance. "Why'd you bring me in here?" she asks, planting her hands on her hips. Her emerald eyes implore mine for answers? For relief?

"To explain."

Her throat clears. "What's there to explain?"

"You were drunk," I answer, thinking it'll be enough.

Heat flames in her cheeks. "It's a booze camp, Rhett... everyone was drunk."

"I don't take advantage of girls. Jesus, do you have any clue how many women would love nothing more than to cry rape and sue my ass?" But the truth is, it isn't even that. She wasn't that sloppy, and I know Korie isn't out for my money. I wanted to be sure her decision wasn't influenced even the slightest.

Her features soften to almost sympathetic, and I find myself missing the way she ogled my mouth a moment ago. "I'd never."

The honesty in those two words has my chest feeling tight. "I wanted to," I admit, lowering my mouth to a breath away from hers. "I've never wanted to fuck anyone so badly in my life."

She huffs out a laugh, reaching those long fingers up around my neck, smearing the paint into my hairline. "So, what's stopping you now?"

I gulp, placing my fingers on the metal zipper hovering just above her breasts. "Permission."

She peers up at me through hooded eyes. "Granted."

I instantly yank the zipper down to her belly button, and she steps out, letting the once-gray jumper fall to the ground. "Be quick," she warns, pulling the cropped tank over her head and shimmying out of her shorts while I strip down to my boxer briefs.

"Last night you said you were on the pill?"

"Have been for years...I'm not using you for your sperm either, Hollywood."

I nod, reaching both hands to her sides, cradling her rib cage as I roll my thumbs over her rosy nipples. "You're beautiful." I'm not usually one for pleasantries, but my God, I can't hold the words back.

She giggles, trailing her fingers over my chest, leaving a trail of red and green. "It's like finger painting."

I nod in agreement, enjoying her touch too much to form a coherent thought.

"You think it's toxic if we..." Her hand moves to my underwear, a finger trailing beneath the band.

"Nah." I swallow hard, and my dick thickens, straining for release.

"No fingers," she warns, eyeing the caked-on paint and dirt on my hands.

"Turn around for me, Stick," I order. "Put your hands on that crate."

For once the girl does as she's told, glancing back at me over her shoulder. I try not to laugh at the rainbow of color dotting her cheeks, nose, and lips.

"I'm going in dry." I hesitate, afraid I'll hurt her. All joking aside, I'm not a small guy.

She traps her lower lip between her teeth, her eyes fixed on mine. "No, you're not."

Korie stares wantonly as I drop my briefs and my cock springs free. Tugging her thong to the side, I line up with her entrance, running the tip along her slit. I spread the wetness dripping out of her pussy from her clit to her ass, teasing the tight, puckered hole.

Korie stiffens, hissing low in the back of her throat. "Rhett," she warns.

"One day," I assure her before sliding back to her slick opening and pushing slowly inside. Her warmth squeezes my cock, and I pause for a moment, enjoying the tight fit—the feel of her clenching around me.

A loud crashing sound startles us both, and for a moment I think we may be caught.

"It's just a rake," she sighs with relief. Reaching between her own legs, she begins massaging her clit in slow circles. "Don't stop, please." Korie rocks back, rolling her hips against me, practically begging me to move. And as good as it feels, there's no chance in hell this ends before we're both satiated. I'll take an ambush of paintballs to see this through.

We're like two wild animals, fucking in the wilderness, both seeming to forget that we could be busted at any moment. That there are literally two dozen other people navigating these same woods. It's pure, unadulterated need.

"Like that," she moans when I pull all the way out and ease back inside. With a tight grip on her hips, I control her frenzied movements, forcing her to slow down and savor this moment. Her legs shake with desire, and I feel her climax coming on. "J—Just like that," she whimpers, rolling her fingers faster.

Pressure builds in my groin as every cell of my body comes alive, buzzing with desire. Her body goes limp in my hold, and her knees begin to buckle.

"Not yet, Rhett," she moans. "Oh God, I'm so close."

With an arm wrapped around her waist to help keep her upright, I lick the thumb and pointer finger of my other hand and tease her nipple between them while pumping in and out in a steady rhythm.

Her pussy clenches tighter, priming me for release. Every muscle in my body tenses as I fight my own climax, trying to hold out for hers.

"I'm coming!" she shrieks, with a white-knuckled grip on the wooden crate.

Quickening my pace, I slam into her. The heat builds to unbearable just as her orgasm hits, the spasms milking my own release.

It's the first time I've ever gone bare, and I tell myself that's the reason this feels so different. Try to convince myself that somehow, it's that rubber barrier that blocks the sensations currently swirling in my chest. That it has nothing to do with the sated blonde in my arms.

That I haven't just gone and fucked up royally.

Chapter 14

KORIE

"Now, don't you go falling in love with me, Hollywood," I whisper, slinking out of his arms to retrieve my clothes.

He's strangely quiet, and I'm not quite sure what to make of it. I just want the protection of my jumper and to get the hell out of this sweatbox before we're discovered.

"That's my line," he finally says, seeming to regain his senses, and it eases a little of the insecurity I'm feeling.

"Still good," I lie, trying to ignore the butterflies swarming in my chest. "Let's get out of here," I add, not giving him the chance to say anything else that may add to the unease that's swiftly descending upon me.

Without waiting for him to finish dressing, I crawl back through the opening, standing guard at my corner. My heart is damn near beating out of my chest. It's all I hear, the echo in my head overwhelming my senses.

"You ready?" he growls into my ear, scaring me half to death.

"Jesus, Rhett…don't sneak up on me like that!"

"Hey," he whispers, spinning me around in his arms to face him. "Don't."

"Don't what?" A knot of emotion lodges in my throat. I don't understand the contradictory feelings between my head and my heart. I hate him and everything he stands for. What's with this sudden vulnerability?

"Don't make things weird, Stick. We had great sex. We both wanted it. Both enjoyed it?" He quirks a brow, and I can't help but smile that he, of all people, seems to need confirmation.

"Yeah," I sigh.

"Well, then. Let's go bust some balls!" He cocks his weapon in the air like a soldier in the movies getting ready to head out to battle.

"Let's do this."

"Well," Essie announces after all of the teams line up for inspection. "I think it's clear who our winners are—Rhett and Korie!"

Compared to everyone else, the two of us are squeaky clean. I almost feel bad about accepting victory, but there was no specific rule that you couldn't spend the hour hooking up in a tool shed, and I really hate losing, so I'm considering this a double win. I got the D *and* the V. Go team!

"What'd you two do?" Raven asks, breathing heavy and covered in every color of the rainbow from her hair to her shoes. "Hide in an underground bunker?" She laughs before throwing her arms around me and tackling me to the ground.

"Get off!" I can't catch my breath from laughing so hard as she rolls us around in the dirt.

"Much better," she says, clutching my cheeks in her hands and planting a big kiss on my forehead. "Now we match."

"Why the hell are you so happy?" I push up from the ground, dusting myself off, and can't help but smile because she's simply exuding joy.

"I think I'm in love," she sings, making goo-goo eyes at my cousin, who's presently paying her no mind, celebrating Rhett's win with the rest of their bandmates.

"Ew." I shove her playfully in the chest.

"I know you don't wanna hear this, but too bad. We're gonna be cousin-in-laws, Kore!" she squeals, and I blanch.

"Oh, fuck my life." I wave her off, heading toward Joe and Essie to collect my trophy. "Stop."

Raven skips alongside me. "It could happen."

"What's going to happen," I tell her, under my breath so no one else overhears, "is we're going to go back to Texas and graduate. We're going to get real, grown-up jobs, and they're gonna go finish recording an album. And go on tour. And fuck groupies."

Raven's mouth falls open, like it's the first time she's heard any of this. "You don't know that."

"I do," I argue. "Because I've lived it, remember?"

Her face softens, and I don't even feel bad for squashing her dreams, because I never want to see her put herself through what my mother did.

"Now, let's go get my trophy and enjoy one last night with the rock stars before *releasing them* back into the wild."

Chapter 15

RHETT

"JOE AND I WOULD LIKE TO THANK YOU ALL FOR CHOOSING TO spend your spring break with us." Essie looks around at the group, tearing up. "We hope you had a memorable time and made friendships that you'll carry with you beyond this trip."

I wonder if she cries like this at the end of every camp session, or if she's just feeling extra emotional today. Maybe she really is on her period.

"And now the moment you've all been waiting for," Joe says, taking over before his wife completely loses it. "You are free to retrieve your electronic devices, kids. Be sure to exchange numbers and remember to disconnect from time to time. True bonds aren't formed behind a screen."

Everyone rushes to the wall of lockers, collecting their belongings. I can't say I've missed mine all that much. I usually don't care to see the shit floating around on the web anyway. And to be honest, it was nice not having to worry about being secretly recorded and waking up on the cover of the Enquirer or blasted on TMZ.

"You gonna get her number?" Raven asks, brushing past me to hang all over Nick.

In all my life, I have never been so nervous to ask a girl for her phone number. But I know damn well she won't be soliciting mine. I could probably get it from Nick, but I figure I should at least try going through her first.

"Hey, Stick," I say, coming up behind her in the parking lot, where she's already exchanging numbers with a few of the other girls.

"Hollywood," she returns, a slight flush filling her cheeks. I'd bet anything she's picturing me naked.

"So, I was wondering…"

"Yeah?"

"If I could maybe call you sometime?"

"Why?" she asks, crossing her arms on her chest, scrutinizing my face like she truly can't understand it.

"What do you mean, why?" I knew she'd give me a hard time.

"It was fun," she says. "I'll never forget the shed." The blush in her cheeks spreads down her neck. "Or last night," she adds, clearing her throat, "but we both know this isn't going to go anywhere."

"Didn't ask to be your boyfriend, Stick," I tease. "Just need a way to send you dick pics."

She snorts, and I know I've got her.

"You'll be thankful for them when you've had a long day saving the world at your new job and need to unwind."

"Will you be expecting twat shots in exchange?"

I shrug, leaning in. "Maybe a tit pic when you're feeling generous?"

She blows out a long breath. "You drive a hard bargain,

Rhett Taylor."

"I'm not gonna beg for it."

She rolls her eyes, and I drop to my knees. "Okay, maybe I will."

"Jesus Christ, Rhett, get up," she hisses, looking around at everyone watching us.

"Can I pretty please get your digits, milady?" I steeple my hands in front of my face and hang my lip for effect.

"Okay. Okay. Fine…just get up!" She looks around at all the camera phones flashing away. "We're gonna be all over the internet by this afternoon," she warns, gritting her teeth.

Remaining on my knees, I unlock my phone, creating a new contact right there at her feet, *Stick*. I look up at her expectantly and begrudgingly she gives it up.

"Happy now?"

"Not yet," I say, pressing the green call button. I'm not at all surprised when the phone in her hand doesn't ring. "Cute… now give me your real number."

"Busted," Raven jeers from the sideline. Then her best friend proceeds to rattle off a set of numbers, and lo and behold, when I hit the call button, it buzzes in Korie's palm.

"All right everyone, time to load up in the vans. They'll take you to your pick-up stations and have you on your way," Essie announces.

"I gotta go," Korie says when the van beside us revs its engine. "Thanks for everything."

"Did you just thank me for sex?" I drop my jaw in mock surprise, ignoring the tight uncomfortable feeling in my chest.

"Yeah," she snarks, slapping my arm. "Nice doing business with you."

"I'd do business with you anytime." I waggle my eyebrows at her.

A huge grin spreads across her face. "Are you ever serious?" she asks, lifting her backpack to her shoulder.

I grip her chin in my hand, turning her face up to mine, and plant a long, wet kiss on her lips for all to see. She doesn't fight me on it. In fact, it's me who has to pull away when the driver honks the horn.

"I'll see you soon," I whisper against her lips.

She starts for the van, turning back just as she reaches the door to answer, "No, you won't."

"We'll see," I call out just before it slams shut and she rolls out of view.

Chapter 16

RHETT

"HOW LONG HAVE YOU BEEN SITTING THERE WATCHING ME sleep, creeper?" I don't need to open my eyes to know it's her; I've been woken by the weight of that glare so many times, I'd recognize the eerie feeling anywhere. I imagine this is the exact sensation my sister Judy complains about when being woken up with my three-year-old niece Autumn's face an inch from hers. Add in the sound of her labored breathing, and I'm mentally preparing to get my ass reamed.

I can't wait to hear what I've done this time.

"Could you at least have the decency to sit up and...I don't know?" She throws her hands in the air, exasperated. "Maybe pretend to actually give a shit, Rhett?"

Yep. She's pissed.

"To what do I owe the pleasure of your company so early in the morning, boss?" With a loud yawn, I stretch my arms above and behind my head, clutching the headboard to haul myself to sitting.

"I take it you haven't been online yet today?" she snips, drumming her fingers on the tablet clutched tightly in her lap.

Scoffing, I circle my hand around the bed, gesturing to my current state of half asleep. "I don't make a habit of browsing entertainment news sites in my dreams." My tone relays just how ludicrous that would be, although I wouldn't put it past her to do exactly that. Sweet Anika lives and breathes damage control. It's why we make a great team. I give no fucks. She gives too many. It's all about balance, right?

"Have a look," she says, rolling her eyes as she shoves an iPad, which is unsurprisingly opened to a gossip rag, at my face. The photo is one of me kneeling at Korie's feet in the parking lot of Pour Judgment. It was taken just before we parted ways yesterday, probably by one of my new so-called *friends*. I find myself sighing in disappointment even though I, of all people, should know well by now that everyone has a price.

My God, she's beautiful. Looks exactly as she did in my dream last night. Well, maybe not *exactly*. She was wearing fewer clothes.

"I was there," I say, disgust rising in my throat as I push it back without reading whatever ridiculous headline accompanies the photo. I'm not at all in the mood for this today.

"Fine!" Anika squawks, hopping to her feet. "I'll read it to you then."

"Can I stop you?" I tease, knowing there's no chance. It doesn't matter how often I tell her I don't want to hear about this stuff, she insists on freaking out over every little article. Quite frankly, it's exhausting. The girl's gonna give herself an ulcer before we're thirty. It's bad enough that she's already on high blood pressure pills at twenty-six.

"Country heart throb Rhett Taylor *proposes* to unknown," she reads, adding venom to the word, "proposes."

*Hey now...*they may be on to something. I tune out everything else she says as the most genius idea begins to formulate in my mind. Maybe this time I can use the rumor to my advantage. For once these snakes might have actually done me a favor.

"I've got to call her." I throw off the covers, stalking across the room butt naked to retrieve a pair of boxers from my dresser drawer.

Anika stutters, momentarily struck speechless, while she ogles the goods. I do enjoy screwing with her.

"Pick up your jaw," I taunt, winking her way as I step into my shorts.

The now flustered brunette mutters a string of curses beneath her breath before planting her hands on her hips, her chest red and splotchy and heaving. "This is serious. Like career-ending serious, *friend*."

"I know," I agree, retrieving my phone from the charging dock. "If you don't mind..." I motion for the door with my eyes. "I need to reach her before she gets wind of this from anyone else."

My best friend's eyes grow wide. "Are you dismissing me?"

I nod, shooing her away as if she were no more than a gnat. The truth is, I couldn't survive this crazy life without her, and she knows it. So, I make it a point to downplay that from time to time. Gotta keep her on her toes.

"We need to nip this now, Rhett...before it spreads any further."

She reaches for her phone and sudden panic wells in my chest. "Don't," I say, stopping her hand, "Don't do anything until I've had the chance to talk to Korie."

Another sigh. "Just tell me it isn't true, and I'll leave you to your call." Worry lines wrinkle her forehead as she stares at me intently, all but begging with those doe eyes of hers for me to put this gossip to sleep.

"Give me a little time to figure this out." I smooth the creases in her forehead with the pad of my thumb. "Until then...keep your big mouth shut. Got it?"

Anika's features soften to my touch. She pulls her arms tightly across her chest, looking up at me from beneath her long lashes. "Why do I feel like you're about to do something really stupid?"

I shrug, grab her by the shoulders, and spin her toward the hall, before giving her a pat on the ass to get her moving. "You always feel that way."

With her lower lip trapped between her teeth, she hesitates in the doorway. "Rhett..."

"Go."

As soon as the door clicks into place, I retrieve the forgotten device from her vacated seat to study the picture a little harder. In my outstretched hand sits a black box with the top flipped open. It's the style of box that can only mean one thing.

"Damn," I mutter, impressed by how realistic the image appears. There's no sign of the cellphone that was clutched in my palm. My eyes are latched onto hers, waiting with bated breath. Who would believe looking at this that I was simply trying to get the girl's number?

No one.

Shit. I've got to reach her before they figure out who this mystery girl is and she wakes up to press banging down her door.

The first five calls are sent to voicemail, before she finally gives in and picks up. "What do you want?"

I muffle a laugh at the irritation in her tone. "Morning, Stick...miss me yet?"

"How ever did you know?" she groans, her voice laden with sleep.

"It's okay. You don't have to be embarrassed. I miss you too."

"I thought I was pretty clear when I told you this wasn't happening, Hollywood?"

"Yeah. I know what you said, but I really do need to see you," I insist, calculating how long it would take me to reach her in Texas. "So, you're just gonna have to get over that."

"Not happening," she repeats. I hear the smile in her voice and my chest puffs up.

"This is serious, Korie." I manage to sound just like Anika, and chuckle to myself, which must confuse the hell out of Stick, not having been privy to the tantrum she just threw in my bedroom.

"Fine," she huffs. "Whatever you have to say can be said over the phone. Hurry it up so I can go back to sleep."

"We have a bit of a situation..."

I hear shuffling in the background and clearly envision her leaping from the bed. "Oh my God. Is Nick okay? Did—did something happen?"

"He's fine. This concerns the two of us. We need to talk, though. In person. And it has to be today."

"I don't know what you're trying to pull, but I've got class and you've got to record an album. We. Are. Not. Doing. This."

"Stay in your house," I order, switching her over to speaker phone so I can throw on a shirt and jeans. "Don't answer the phone for anyone but me. Don't open your door for anyone but me." I pick back up the phone and shoot off a quick text to Nick to get us on the first flight to Houston and a car from there to College Station, and that I'll explain on the way to the airport. "You're not going to class..." I trail off, retrieving my toiletries from the bathroom counter. "You can't go anywhere, actually. And go double check that your doors are locked."

"Okaaay. Rhett, you're really freaking me out. I can't even tell if you're serious right now."

"Oh," I add, shoving my shaving kit and a few changes of clothes into a bag. "No internet either."

Chapter 17

KORIE

"**W**HAT'S HE SAYING?" **M**Y PULSE IS FREAKING RACING AND **I** try peeking over at Raven's phone while she's busily texting away with my cousin. Unlike myself, she's not panicked at all. She doesn't care why…she's just thrilled for another chance to hook up with Nick. "Rhett's not talking to me at all."

"You really wanna know?" she asks, waggling her brows.

"Dude. I'm dying here. There are news vans for three different stations outside our apartment. Yes, of course I'm serious."

"He said…" She squirms in her seat, clearing her throat. "'I'm rubbing my cock ring on your cli—'"

"Stop!" I shove her in the shoulder, damn near knocking her off our couch. "He's sexting you from the air?"

"Mmhmm," she says, red-faced and giggling like a teenager. "There's a pic too," she taunts, waving her phone side to side. "Wanna see?"

I'm fairly certain she's just messing with me. I mean who

takes a picture of their dick on a plane? *Nick.* That's who. I shudder at the thought. Can't be too careful with these freaks. "No, thanks."

No longer wanting to be anywhere near their conversation, I begin pacing the living room, my bare feet leaving tracks in the shag carpet. I'm going out of my mind with worry. The shades are drawn tight, but every few minutes I split the blinds and sneak a peek. It looks like a damn press conference is being held on the front lawn, and my best friend is all but flicking her bean across the room. We had to take the house phone off the hook because it wouldn't stop ringing. Worst of all, my mom is beside herself with worry. I can't answer her calls, because I know the first thing she'll do is blurt out whatever it is she's read online, and I promised to give Rhett the opportunity to tell me. So, I had Raven text her and tell her not to believe anything she's seen on the web and that I'd call her as soon as I could to explain. What exactly I'll be explaining…well, that is the million-dollar question, isn't it?

I'm about thirty seconds from breaking down and checking the celebrity news when "Crazy Bitch" finally blares from the phone in my back pocket. *Yeah. Yeah. Stop judging me. It doesn't mean anything. I just happen to like the song.*

"Are you almost here?" I answer, sounding as out of breath as I feel.

"Well, hello to you too, Stick." His tone is too light and relaxed for someone putting me through this kind of hell. Patience is not one of the many virtues I possess. "Just landed. We have a car picking us up from a secret location. It's a black Navi with tinted windows. Nick's been chatting with Raven about the layout, and I think we've figured out a course of action."

"Wai—what?"

"We can't just walk up to the door like commoners, Korie. I'm sort of a big deal, you know."

Oh, Jesus. "And let's not forget, so modest too."

He continues barking orders like I haven't even spoken. The ass has been doing that a lot today, and he's going to hear just how much I don't appreciate it as soon as I figure out what the hell is going on.

"The driver is gonna pull up as close as he can to your unit. Nick and I will be in disguise. Don't wait for us to knock, because we'll be running through the equivalent of a herd of rabid dogs. Just unlock the door and move out of the way."

I nod, as if he can see me.

What the hell have I gotten myself into?

My heart is racing a million miles a minute when their *inconspicuous* ride pulls up. Seriously, what the hell were they thinking? If they truly didn't want to cause a scene, they should have taken a damn Volkswagen Bug or something. Disguised or not, there is no way anyone out there doesn't assume whoever's in that car is newsworthy. Considering they're all camped outside my apartment, and I know it isn't because they're dying to meet me…it's safe to assume the media already have a pretty good idea who might be showing up.

"Now! Go, go, go," Raven screeches, pushing me toward the door. "Unlock it."

I miss watching them make their big run for it. But judging by the guffaws coming from my best friend over by the window, I bet it's as good as the two of them barreling into the apartment and falling into a heap of limbs on our floor. And what the hell are they wearing? *Pajamas?* With…*tails?*

After slamming the door in the clamoring horde of reporters' faces and securing both of the locks, I turn to confront the ridiculous sight before me. "I think you fooled 'em," I snark. "Good job, boys. If music doesn't work out, I'm sure you two could make it as spies."

I take a deep breath, bracing my back against the door. A sudden warmth spreads through my veins as my body reacts to his nearness.

"Sloth onesies?" Raven barks, trying to catch her breath.

"What? Did you think a hat and glasses was gonna throw them off our scent?" Rhett laughs, peeling himself off of Nick. "Might as well give 'em something to talk about."

"Besides, our faces are covered," Nick adds, making his way over to wrap Raven up in his claws. "They'll never prove it's us. Any pictures they've taken are useless."

Now that I've had a moment to regain my senses, it's time to get to the bottom of this. "All right. Enough of the foolishness…what the hell are you two doing here?" My eyes bounce from one idiot to the next. It's so hard to take them seriously when they're dressed for trick or treat.

"Go ahead and pull up TMZ," Rhett instructs as he unzips and steps out of his costume, revealing a fitted vintage Merle Haggard tee and distressed jeans.

Raven and I waste no time reaching for our phones.

"Millions of hearts around the globe shattered this morning when they awakened to learn that one of Hollywood's most eligible bachelors has been snagged." I read the caption aloud, studying the doctored photo that makes it look like Rhett proposed in the parking lot yesterday. "I don't get it…"

"They think we're engaged," he explains, the corner of his mouth curling into an amused grin.

How stupid does he think I am? "I understand that much. What doesn't make any sense is why it's such a big deal? Surely things like this happen to you on a daily basis. Can't you just make some public statement explaining that the photo is doctored and the engagement bogus?"

"I could," he agrees, dropping down to one knee and pulling a black box, nearly identical to the one in the article, from behind his back. "But instead, I'm going to live on the edge. Stick, will you do me the absolute honor of pretending to want to marry me? What do you say? Will you wear my ring? Be my partner in crime? My plus one to all red-carpet events? Korie Potter, will you be my fake fiancée?"

My throat swells shut, thick with words I can't seem to formulate.

"Oh my God!" Raven squeals. "Holy shit, we're going to be famous!" Her hands clamp down on my shoulders, and she gives them a good squeeze. "This is like...*almost* romantic."

"Why?" I ask, tuning her out. The one syllable word is the only one I can manage. What the hell is this boy up to, and why does he want to make me a part of it?

"Quite simply," he says, removing the huge rock from the cushion and holding it out for all to see, "you need me."

That breaks whatever trance I seem to have fallen under. "I most certainly don't need anyone. Least of all you."

"What better way to be seen?" he asks, his face sobering. "The games are in five and a half months. That's plenty of time for us to get you on their radar...*use me.*"

"You came all this way to stop me from correcting this ludicrous rumor—to help me?" I'm completely dumbfounded. It's selfless and beyond generous and the last thing I'd ever expect from a man of his position.

He nods, mussing his hair nervously. *Jesus, does he have to look so hot doing that?*

"Why? Why, Rhett? Why on Earth would you do this for me?"

He takes my trembling left hand into his, sliding the gaudy ring onto the fourth finger, and I know it's pretend, but I still feel woozy, like I'm going to faint. "Why wouldn't I? You're my best friend's cousin, and I'm in a position to help. Let me prove to you we're not all like your father. That *I'm* not like him."

Of course, Nicholas told him about my dad.

"I'm not actually going to marry you," I warn, shocked that I'm even entertaining this bizarre idea. "You do realize that?"

"Not yet," he fires back. "But who knows what could happen in the coming months."

"Not ever," I insist, rotating my hand to test the weight of the ring.

"We'll see." He rises to his feet, giving me a panty-melting wink before stepping forward and wrapping me in his embrace, like this is already a done deal. I haven't agreed to anything yet.

"I mean it, Rhett Taylor," I say, breathing in the scent of his cologne. "Don't you go falling in love with me."

His smirk grows to a blinding smile. "Is that a yes?"

With a hard swallow, I shrug. "Couldn't you have gotten a simpler ring? This is really expensive for a *fake* engagement."

Rhett scoffs like he's offended. "I have a reputation to uphold."

"Speaking of reputations..." I pull out of his embrace, digging a finger into his chest. "Don't make me look like a fool. Do not turn me into my mother."

"Never," he promises, without a hint of a smile. "I will be the picture of monogamy. The best fake fiancé to ever exist."

My chest swells to almost bursting. And in this moment, I realize that I'm the one who'll have to find a way to keep control of my emotions, but this could work. I'll have to take some time away from volunteering at the hospital and graduate absentee, but he's exactly the exposure I need for a shot at the games. And apparently, I want it bad enough to risk my reckless heart.

"Okay," I whisper, swallowing a ton of lead. "Let's do it."

Chapter 18

RHETT

"I'LL BE BACK TO PICK YOU UP OUTSIDE OF CLASS AT EXACTLY ten o'clock."

Korie raises her brows in annoyance. "You do realize I've managed this college thing just fine on my own for four years, right? This isn't necessary."

"*This* is new." I grab her left hand and tap the ring that's only been on her finger since last night. "We need to be seen together," I rasp into her ear. "And I'm worried about the way people will react to you since the news dropped. Let me get you all squared away before I have to head back to L.A."

"Fine." She narrows her eyes, shoving my chest playfully. "Go away. See you in two hours."

Walking backward, I keep my eyes trained on hers until she's no longer in sight. I sign a few quick autographs as I make my way back to the waiting car, silently thanking God it's finals week and the students have to actually go to class. I've got a few very important things to take care of, and the last thing I need is to be trapped here all day.

"Where're we going?"

"To celebrate you passing that damn test."

"Oh yeah?" She slides closer on the back seat, so her leg rests against mine. "How do you know I didn't bomb it?"

"You have a 3.9 GPA with a week left of school. I think it's safe to say, you just made that exam your bitch."

Korie jerks her head back, eyes narrowed. "Are you spying on me?"

"I prefer the term, *studying*."

"That's kinda creepy."

"It's no creepier than you internet stalking me," I return. "Look, I need to know things if we're going to pull this off. People will be asking about you—about us."

"Okay...so, what's our story?" she asks. "How'd we meet? Because they'll all think you're batshit crazy if you tell them we met and got engaged in the span of four days."

"That's easy. We met at Nick's party, which is true. Fell madly in lust, also true.

"Maybe for you."

I choose to ignore that remark. "We've been secretly dating since. Lust quickly evolved into love, and we got engaged...a little foretelling. Not exactly a lie."

She glares at me, then purses her lips and nods. "It could work."

"It will," I assure her as the driver pulls around a strip mall, parking in the back near the dumpster. And honestly, I don't know whether I'm referring to the lie...or hoping it'll become our truth.

"Boy this place is a dump," she observes, climbing out of the door behind me with her nose pinched. "You sure know how to treat a girl in style."

"Come on, brat." I wrap an arm around her shoulders, pulling her close and plant a kiss on the top of her head. With her body firmly plastered to my side, I guide her over to the third door from the left and knock, just like Anika instructed.

Speaking of the pint-sized dictator, she's quite pissed with me right now over this whole *engagement fiasco*, as she called it, and having to push back recording again. I do sign her paychecks, so however begrudgingly, she's still managing my life from afar. But you better believe she's making her feelings on the matter known every chance she gets.

"Mr. Taylor." A balding older man with round spectacles and a cheery disposition pulls the door open with a nod. "Miss Potter. We've been expecting you. My name's Todd. I'm the day manager, and I'll be seeing to your needs personally."

I reach for Korie's hand, linking my fingers with hers and give it a reassuring squeeze. I can tell by the slight furrow of her brow that she still has no clue where we are.

"Right this way."

We're led to a private table in the manager's office at Sundae Fun Days. It's nothing fancy: a four-seater with a red and white checkered table cloth set up in front of an executive style desk. In the center is a huge array of toppings so we can dress our own dessert.

Korie is all smiles when I pull out her chair. "A little bird told me you had a thing for ice cream."

Her grin widens. "You research well. It's my favorite meal."

Before my butt is in my seat, a heaping bowl of vanilla ice cream is placed in front of us.

"Syrup?" Todd asks, balancing a tray of bottles that seems to have appeared out of thin air in one hand. "We have fudge, caramel, strawberry, cherry, pineapple, or raspberry."

"She's the boss." I nod to my left at Stick.

"We have to share?" She looks absolutely appalled.

"What? Not big enough?" I rest my forearms on the table and gawk at her. There's no way the two of us will finish this thing off before it melts, much less each our own.

"No. I just—I have this thing about eating after people."

"Seriously? You had my dick all up in your mouth last night, and you can't eat from the same bowl as me today?"

Todd's face turns beet red, but he doesn't waiver, his expression a blank slate as he calmly awaits instruction.

"Oh my God. I can't believe you just said that in front of this poor guy. I'm sorry about my boyfriend, Todd." She stammers on the word *boyfriend,* like it tastes sour on her tongue, and it bothers me a hell of a lot more than it should. Because I want this to be real, and I want her to be proud.

"Fiancé," I quickly correct, to which I'm rewarded with a glare.

"Can I at least have my own spoon?"

"Duh. I'm not putting my mouth on something that's been inside yours. How disgusting." I cringe, grab at my throat and gag theatrically as Todd reaches onto the tray, retrieving two shiny spoons, fanning one in each of our directions.

"There you are," he offers with a smile. "Would you like me to get you another bowl? It's really not a problem."

"No, thank you." Korie's flushed from her cheeks to her chest. "We'll have fudge, please."

"I'll let you know if we need anything else." I say, dismissing him as he's finishing up with the chocolate sauce.

Korie's lips twist to the side as she assesses the collection of candy, nuts, and fruits. She's putting a whole lot of thought into how to top this mountain of sugar. "Do you like gummy bears?"

"I'm a man." I shrug, thinking that's all the answer she needs, but she looks at me cock-eyed, so I elaborate. "I'll eat anything. Go ahead and dress it however you want."

She grabs a handful, sprinkling them generously over the top. Then she adds a few cherries and strawberries before double checking to be sure I don't want to add anything else. Finally, she finishes it off with a blob of whipped cream and rainbow sprinkles, and we dig in. I make sure to keep to my side, as to not disgust her any further. Just as I suspected, we don't make it through even half of the concoction.

"You ready to get out of here?" I ask when she returns from a trip to the restroom.

Korie shakes her head, slinking back into her chair. "Let's play a game," she proposes with a gleam in her eyes. "No sense in wasting all of this."

"What kind of game?" Immediately I'm skeptical, but more curious to see where this is going. She looks like the fucking cat who ate the canary.

"Mystery toppings." She retrieves a strip of black fabric from her back pocket and waves it around in the air. "Just borrowed this blindfold from our friend, Todd."

"Ladies first," I insist, holding out my hand for the blindfold, which turns out to be a cloth napkin. It's just barely long enough, but it'll do the trick.

"No peeking," she orders as I secure it around my eyes.

Naturally, I try to listen to figure out what's going on, because I don't completely trust her. But other than a slight clinking, the only sound is the air conditioner.

"Open up."

Here goes nothing. I close my mouth around the spoon,

moaning as if it's the best thing I've ever tasted. It's more candy than ice cream. I suck the cream off the toppings, rolling them around my tongue to decipher what I'm eating. "M&M's," I mumble when I crunch down on the tiny disk of chocolate. That one was easy. "Cherry."

"Mmmhmm," she says. "What else?"

"Something really hard and sour…" I'm not big on sweets. This date is purely for Stick's benefit, so this isn't as easy for me as it would be for most people. "I give up. I have no clue."

"It was Nerds," she says, snatching the blindfold from around my head and tightening it to fit hers. "You go."

"Give me a minute…" I study the options for a moment before placing a pecan, blueberry, and raspberry on the spoon. She obviously has a sweet tooth. So, I figure I'm better off with fruits and nuts if I'm to have any shot at tripping her up.

"Ugh," she groans, chewing with her nose all scrunched. "Blueberry, gross."

"Yeah…" *Damnit.*

"Pecan and raspberry." She beams, uncovering her eyes. "I'm right, aren't I? Point for me!"

"Yep. Go again."

She walks around the table and ties the napkin over my eyes herself this time. I'm not sure where the distrust is coming from. I didn't even get them all right last round, so I obviously wasn't cheating, but it's her game, and I play along.

"Can't see anything," I say when I feel her hand waving around in front of my face.

"Just making sure…"

I don't know what the hell is going on, but I swear I hear her smothering a laugh. "What's taking so long?"

"Almost done," she promises.

Finally, I feel the spoon tap against my lower lip and open.

"Bigger," she says, with a giggle. Against my better judgment, because I just know this girl is up to something, I open my mouth wider. She shoves a heaping pile of ice cream into my mouth, so much I almost can't close my lips around it.

Cautiously I bite down and feel a crunch. My very first thought is that she's gone and fed me a fucking bug, but then my tongue starts to burn and my entire mouth catches fire.

"Ugh!" I yell, spitting it out right onto the table, before wrenching the cloth from my face. "Jalapenos!"

She nearly falls out of her seat she's laughing so damn hard, while I shovel spoonful after spoonful of vanilla ice cream into my mouth to douse the flames.

"I'm a man. I'll eat anything," she mocks, throwing my earlier words in my face. "Some man."

"You fight dirty." Despite the sweat pouring from my eyes, because these are *not* tears y'all, and the coughing fit that won't seem to end, I can't help but laugh at my own expense. Call me impressed.

"Oh, Mr. Taylor, you have no idea…"

Chapter 19

KORIE

HE WON'T TELL ME WHERE WE'RE HEADED NEXT, AND I BELIEVE we've already established that I'm not the most patient of people. I can't believe I'm actually ditching drinks with my classmates at the pub tonight to go along with whatever Rhett has planned. My life has become a whirlwind of surprises since the moment I woke up yesterday morning. I feel upside down and turned inside out. I'm a person who likes order. Reliability. All of the things I never had growing up.

"What are we doing here?" I ask when the truck starts down a familiar back road.

Rhett pulls up Instagram on his cell, doing that thing he's been doing where he pretends he didn't just hear me speak. "Here. Type in your handle so I can follow you."

"Handle?" I snort laugh. "You sound like an old truck driver." With an eyeroll, I take the phone from his hand, typing in my username, *Korie_Sk8tes,* and try not to shiver as he breathes over my shoulder.

"Cute. A hundred and fifty-eight fans." He sounds anything but impressed. "Now follow me back."

Sighing, I retrieve my own phone from my pocket. "Pushy. Pushy." With a tsk, I do as he instructs. "Look at you all official with your blue checkmark," I tease before taking notice of his fifty-five million fans and darkening the screen. I'm so out of my element. But this is why we're doing this. I need him—him and fifty million of his devoted fans. "There, happy now?"

"Not yet, but we're getting there." He reaches for the door handle, throwing it open. "Let's go."

"Go where?" I slide across the leather seat, scrambling to keep up as he exits the car and continues around to the hatch.

"I want you to teach me to ride."

Something about this moment…that gleam in his turquoise eyes…the sincerity in his raspy tone has my stomach doing summersaults. "You're serious?" Red flags start waving around in my head.

This isn't supposed to happen. Do not start falling for him, Korie. Keep your head in the game and your eyes on the prize—the games…not Rhett. He is not the prize. Nope.

"'Course I am. Told you I wanted to know what you were passionate about…and not just in the bedroom," he adds, tucking a finger beneath my chin and tilting my face up to his. "You've seen me do my thing. Now, I wanna see you do yours."

"I don't, umm," I cough. "I don't have my board." I don't know why I'm suddenly feeling shy. I know I'm good enough. Somehow it feels intimate, sharing this with him, alone in the park. This is where I come to unwind, *by myself.* I don't want to get close to him, but despite my better judgment, I feel it happening with every moment spent in his company.

The back of the SUV pops open and there it is, along with Raven's, which I'm assuming he brought along for himself.

"You really planned this thing out," I ponder aloud, impressed by how simple yet personal our first *official* fake date is turning out to be.

"Raven helped a little," he admits, retrieving our equipment.

"What's in the bag?"

Shame colors his cheeks. "Anika bitched a fit until I agreed to use protection."

Sucking in my lips, I bite down hard trying not to howl with laughter when he opens the duffle to reveal a black helmet with a mohawk across the top, along with knee and elbow pads. "Cute," I spit out, unable to contain my hysterics.

"Laugh it up, Stick. Can't go breakin' the cash cow." Although he's smiling when he says it, I sense his underlying resentment and find myself apologizing. I'm not even sure why, because I'm not the one using him for his money...*or am I?* I'm totally taking advantage by allowing him to use his position for my own personal gain. Guilt swarms in my chest and I'm beginning to feel sick and ready to call this whole thing off.

"Don't," he says, pulling one more item from the bag. It's a pair of black Converse. *My staple.* The proud grin on his face has me melting into a puddle of swoon. *Why does he have to be so freaking adorable?* "Don't apologize just yet, cuz yours is in here." He grabs a purple Under Armour bag from the back and unzips it.

"No freaking way," I scoff when he tries to hand me a Trolls helmet, complete with pink, fluffy hair.

"You don't like Poppy?" he asks, in mock horror. "'Cuz that could be a deal breaker."

"What's a Poppy?"

"Don't you know anything?" he asks, jamming the helmet onto my head and adjusting the plastic straps beneath my chin. His fingers are rough, calloused from years of strumming the guitar. When they brush over my smooth skin, I break out in goosebumps, reminded of all the places they explored when we were fooling around last night. "She's the pink haired one...the princess, and only the most important troll." His eyes roll up dramatically. "No big deal."

I bite back another laugh. "You're awful passionate about a kid's show."

"It's my niece Autumn's favorite, and you'll score major points with her by wearing it."

He has a niece. One he seems pretty smitten with at that. How sad is it that I've never even considered the fact that he has a family? That he's more than this crazy hot, famous, well endow—

"Hey," Rhett says, resting a hand on my shoulder. "Still with me?"

"Oh!" I startle, snapping my head up from where it's wandered to his crotch. "Yeah, sorry."

After fastening his own helmet into place, he opens up to the camera on his phone. "Let's send her a picture. She's gonna love it."

"Who could say no to this face?" I pinch his scruffy cheeks between my fingers and squeeze, feeling my heartrate escalate.

"Just about no one."

And I one hundred percent believe it.

Rhett's long, toned arm stretches out, holding the phone so we're both in the frame. "Smile pretty for Princess Autumn!" He pulls me tighter with his free arm, so close I can smell the jalapeno pepper lingering on his breath.

Now, make no mistake, Rhett Taylor is a beautiful man in any situation. But Rhett Taylor beaming at the camera for his baby niece is something altogether sinful. I shouldn't be this turned on. Not by him. And certainly not while taking a picture for a toddler, but I am. Warmth radiates from my every pore as I stare back at our reflections in the glass.

"There," he says, taking a moment to fire off a message to his sister. "Let's get down to business."

Rhett follows me over to the flat section, where I drop my board and motion for him to do the same. "Let's see whatcha got."

He lowers his to his feet awkwardly and within thirty seconds of taking off, is flat on his ass. "I think I may need help."

"You have to start with your front foot on the board. You led off with your back one. It's harder to get on that way…. Front foot on the board. Push with your back foot and turn them perpendicular once you have them both on. Try it again."

"This is harder than it looks," Rhett complains when he loses his balance once more.

"It's like anything else…just takes practice."

I walk over to where he's splayed on the ground with his arms raised in the air, helping him back up. "Get back on and hold on to my shoulders till you get the hang of it."

Rhett slides his fingers beneath my hair, cupping my shoulders, and suddenly I'm short of breath. "Like this?" he asks, kneading the stiffness away with expert skill.

"Mmhmm," I murmur, rolling my neck. I swear those hands of his are pure magic.

"Shouldn't your eyes be open?"

"Probably," I say, while trying my damnedest not to purr.

Before I realize what's happening, his hands are at my waist, and he's spinning me around and lifting me onto the board to stand in front of him, my feet in the center between his—the front of his body pressed intimately to my back. "How 'bout a lesson in balance?"

The warmth of his breath on my ear causes my entire being to tremble. "Oh—okay," I agree, as he slides one of his hands along my torso, stopping just beneath my breasts. Pretty sure I'd agree to just about anything at this moment. His back foot drops to the ground, and he pushes off. Our knees bend together in sync like we were made to fit, and we lean into the motion, gliding across the cement.

"You played me," I accuse, catching his cocky smirk when I glance back at him over my shoulder.

He flashes his pearly whites, pumping his foot faster to gain speed. "Can't do any tricks," he admits. "But I was a teenaged boy once upon a time."

"You mean you weren't always a Hollywood heartbreaker?"

"I'll have you know, you're lookin' at the former stud of Oak Bend Trailer Park," he huffs just as we lose our footing and topple to the ground. I forgot he grew up there with Nick. We're cousins on my father's side but never once visited their home, mostly cuz Dad was rarely around. And when he was, he certainly wouldn't have been caught at Oak Bend Trailer Park. Who'd have thought that a rowdy bunch of boys from the wrong side of the tracks would end up where they are today?

"I can't picture you as anything but famous," I admit, rolling over onto my back to lie beside him and stare up at the clouds. "What were you like as a kid?"

He's quiet for a spell. Pensive. Then, he clears his throat. "I was loud and obnoxious, if you can believe it."

"Oh, I easily believe it."

"You're a sassy little thing. Anyone ever tell you that?"

"Once or twice. How many siblings?"

His head lulls to the side, his bright eyes holding mine captive. "Just the one sister...What is this? Twenty questions?"

"You said we needed to get to know each other, right?"

"I did say that."

"How 'bout we put our own spin on the game? We each get ten questions to use at our leisure, and no matter what, we have to promise to answer honestly. No passing. No half-truths."

"This feels like a trap."

"Got something to hide, Hollywood?"

Rhett lifts his head, resting his weight on his forearm as he towers over me. "So many things."

"Great! Then this should be fun."

Chapter 20

RHETT

"HOW MANY GIRLS HAVE YOU HAD SEX WITH?" HOW'D I KNOW
that'd be her first question?

"I'm not sure." I trail my finger along her collarbone as I
answer, enjoying the way her breathing becomes erratic. How
her nipples begin to pebble beneath the thin fabric of her gray
T-shirt. It's taking every ounce of restraint not to take things
further. It's out of pure respect for her that I don't, because I
seriously doubt she'd want to be plastered all over the web half
naked, and there's a good chance we're being watched. My cock
thickens, straining for release.

Fuck. I just can't get enough of this girl.

Korie stares at me with a look that screams *bullshit*, and it
takes me a moment to remember what we're talking about. *My
number.*

"You wanted honesty. I could easily spout off some bogus
answer, but you asked for the truth, and the truth is that I don't
know. But I had only slept with three women before our first

tour, if that counts for anything."

"Groupies." Her voice is heavy with disgust, and she looks so disappointed that my cheeks heat with shame, even though I have no reason to be embarrassed.

"Some," I admit. "They were mostly models and actresses—a few dancers."

Korie scrunches her nose, diverting her eyes from mine. "Aren't you going to ask me the same question?"

"No."

"Why not? It's only fair. Surely you're curious…"

"Because what, or who, you did before me doesn't matter. It's not like I could change any of it, even if I wanted to, and I'm not wasting my questions on trivial shit that has no bearing on our relationship."

"Fake," she interjects, while doing a piss-poor job of hiding the jealousy flaming in her bright green eyes. For someone who claims not to like me much, she's really good at sending mixed signals.

"I stand corrected…*fake* relationship."

Her head bobs in approval.

"Have you ever been in love?" I ask, deciding I'd rather know what I'm up against. Sex is just sex, unless there are feelings involved. That's when shit gets tricky. I don't fancy myself in love with Korie yet, but I do feel more strongly for her than I have for anyone else, and that's something I plan to hold on to—to see through.

"I thought so, but now I'm not so sure. I mean, I don't think you ever really get over true love, you know?"

"I've got no personal experience to draw from."

"Well," she sighs. "At any rate, I'm definitely over the guys from my past, so I don't think it was the real deal. Mom says I'll definitely know."

"How?"

"Because when you're in love, you'll be willing to do just about anything to keep them. Move heaven and earth just to be with them, no matter how badly it hurts, because no amount of pain is greater than the fear of losing your one true love."

I blanch. "That's the most depressing description of love I think I've ever heard."

"Well, she can only speak from her own experience, you know?" Her face takes on a faraway look before she fires back with the same question. "What do you think love is?"

"Question number two already?"

Korie shrugs. "Sure."

I take a moment to really consider my answer before speaking. "I believe true love is all consuming. You think of them every minute of every day, and your world suddenly revolves around this other person. Keeping them safe…making them happy. She's your best friend. Your compass. She's home." I brush a lock of stray hair from her cheek, leaning in close. "That's what I think."

Her tongue darts out to lick her lips, and she starts breathing heavy. "Where'd you get such a fanciful idea of love?"

"My parents…They were really something to watch. The way they moved around each other. How their eyes lit up when the other walked into a room. That's what I'm holding out for. What I hope to find someday."

"Were?" she whispers softly against my lips. "You said were?"

"Yeah." I hesitate for a moment, composing myself. "My mother died in a car accident when I was fifteen. Dad's never been the same. He's still as in love with her as ever, eleven years later."

Korie lifts up to sitting, cupping the sides of my face in her trembling hands, her eyes welling with tears. "I'm so sorry,

Rhett. I truly had no idea."

"Guess you need to step up your stalking game." I swallow the lump of emotion talking about Mom always brings on and close the breath of space still separating us, brushing my lips lightly against hers. Then, I grip her around the waist, pulling her to straddle me.

Korie leans over, her hair concealing us in a blonde curtain as she takes control, kissing me slowly—reverently. It's a kiss that's filled with compassion and meant to comfort. I know it won't lead to anything more, but it's enough. Hell, it's more than enough. It's perfect.

"Come on," she chirps, finally pulling herself away. Korie brushes the grass from her dark gray skinny jeans and hops back onto her board, doing a fancy jump, one she makes look effortless as she flies into the air, landing perfectly in the exact spot she began. "We're gonna work on your Ollie."

Now we're talkin'. "Call him whatever you want, just please come back and get to work on him," I beg, cupping my raging erection.

"You're something else..."

"Your driver is going the wrong way." She's a little flustered. I'm learning quickly, the girl really isn't a fan of surprises. That could be an issue.

Glancing out the window, I take in the rolling hills and gated houses, while trying to cover a smirk. "Reginald knows where he's going."

"Reginald," she croons as she leans forward, tapping my driver–slash–body guard on the shoulder. "I'm not sure what address you were given, but my apartment is back near the university."

"Miss," he answers, eying me in the rearview with a frown. Reginald doesn't like being touched. Not even by pretty girls. "I'm sorry, but you'll just have to sit back..." He reaches for her hand, shrugging it off. "And trust me."

"I don't even know you," she huffs, pulling her arm to her chest, clearly offended by his brush off.

"But you do know me." I grab the hem of her shirt and pull her to the seat. "Take a chill pill and relax."

"I'm not sure what you're up to, Hollywood, but I hardly know you either, so forgive me if I don't trust the man who's turned my well-organized life into complete freaking chaos, all in the span of twenty-four hours."

"You referring to the man who's turning his own life upside down all for the sake of making your dream come true? The one whose manager is riding his ass and whose bandmates are all pissed because he ran to your aid? Is he the man you don't trust?"

She sulks, slamming her back against the leather seat with a thoughtful pout. "No offense, but not really..." Her hand grips my thigh and squeezes to lessen the blow. "But I am appreciative, truly. Even when I don't act like it."

"Great to hear. Then I hope you can find some appreciation for this too," I say as we turn down the drive of the townhouse Raven and I picked out this morning while Korie was in class.

"Where are we?"

"Home."

She glares at me, furrowing her brow. "Whose home?"

"Yours. Well, yours and Raven's. Mine when I'm in town." I pop the door open, taking her hand and pulling her across the leather seat and out behind me. "Come on. I can't wait to show you around."

Her feet grow roots, and she plants herself on the cement drive. "You can't do this."

"Don't be ridiculous, Stick. I already did."

Her face turns fire engine red. "It's too much. I don't want to be indebted to you when this is all over."

I get really close. So close we're sharing breaths. "You asked me not to embarrass you…"

She gulps. Nods.

"Well, I'm asking the same of you. What the hell will people think if I have my fiancée living in a rinky-dink apartment, practically in the ghetto?"

Her shoulders stiffen. "It's on campus, and safe." Her argument is weak, and she knows it.

"That place looks like something straight out of a horror movie."

Korie purses her lips, her face radiating. "It's what we could afford, on our own without having to take out any loans. It's perfect."

Pinching the bridge of my nose, I try not to allow my frustration to show. "The world thinks we're together—thinks you're mine. I won't have them believe that I don't take care of what belongs to me."

"Did you forget the part where this is all pretend?" she asks, balling her angry fists at her sides. "And let me remind you, I belong to no one." Her bony finger darts out, and she stabs it into my chest. "It's one thing to take a few photos and be seen together in public. But I can't afford a place like this, Rhett. Even when I'm working, I won't be able to. What am I going to do? Move again when the jig is up? It's ridiculous!"

"There's nothing to afford. It's yours."

She stares at me for a moment while that sinks in. "What

did you do?"

"The place is in your name. Consider it an engagement present. I'll wait to give you the papers until you've come to your senses, seeing as in your current state, I don't trust you not to tear them up."

"This wasn't part of the deal. I didn't agree to any of this."

"Listen, if it's the money you're worried about, don't. I make enough to pay for this place outright in a month, easily. Financially, this is nothing to me, so stop making it a bigger deal than it needs to be."

She starts to speak, and I press a finger to her lips to silence her. "For the first time since this whole music thing started, I feel like I'm doing something important...something that matters. I know you hate him, but your father gave us a huge break in helping us land an agent and allowing us to use his studio. He changed our lives."

"Don't..." she warns. "Don't paint him a saint, because I'll call this shit off now."

"I'm not. Fuck, Kore..." My hand instinctively runs through my hair. "I know he hurt you. He let you down in a huge way, and I can't help but feel like part of that is our fault. We benefited from his lifestyle, while you suffered."

"My father is a grown-ass man. There is no one to blame for his actions but him," she adds, too easily letting me off the hook.

"Consider this my way of paying it forward. Of giving someone their break." I trace the side of her face with my thumb tenderly. "Stick, I can't think of anyone more deserving than you."

"So, I'm a charity case..."

"You're a prize, Korie Potter, and I'm playing to win."

Chapter 21

KORIE

WELL, DAMN. MY HEART'S STILL REELING AS I RELUCTANTLY
follow Rhett into the new home he's managed to wrangle me
into. *A prize.* I don't know what I want to do more... swoon like
a besotted fool or throttle his overbearing ass.

"Oh, wipe that grimace off your face, roomie... just look at
this place!" Raven's arms extend above her head and she does an
elaborate twirl in the center of the foyer. "It's fucking brilliant.
Stop scowling at our knight in tight jeans and cowboy boots
and say thank you...you know, like a normal person would." She
apparently has no problem with such an extravagant gift.

Although I feel like I've been completely railroaded into
this, with all the money he's just dropped on me, I guess a
thank you is in order. "Thanks, Hollywood. You *really* shouldn't
have."

"You're welcome." Judging by the deep dimples he's
sporting, he either doesn't sense my underlying resentment or
is choosing to ignore it. Probably the latter. Lord knows the

man is really good at only hearing what he wants.

My eyes dance around the fully furnished living area. The first thing I notice is that none of our old ratty furniture is here. There's a plush, light beige sectional with teal, yellow, and red floral throw pillows scattered about. It's nothing I'd ever have chosen, but I must admit it looks really comfortable. I can already see myself curled up next to the lamp with a glass of wine and a romance novel. A whitewashed wood coffee table in the shape of an octagon rests on a shag rug at the center of the living room. Elaborate ornamental frames house the pictures of Mom and me, and Raven and her family that formerly sat atop our old rickety entertainment center. Can't say I'm upset that disaster is nowhere to be seen. There are actual window treatments surrounding the bay windows to the right, as opposed to the cheap plastic blinds we owned just this morning.

"You do this?" I ask him, referring to the farm house chic decor that I know my punk rock bestie did not pick out.

"Pffft," he huffs. "Hired an interior decorator to do the dirty work. I wanted it to be a surprise. Raven oversaw the move, since I trusted she'd know what was important enough to keep and what was replaceable. I only had to entertain you for the day. Seriously, if it's not your style, we can get Josette back out here to make it more you."

Not accustomed to being doted on this way, I shake my head. "This is perfect. Really."

Rhett releases a loud breath. It's cute how badly he obviously wanted to impress me. "Good." Grinning ear to ear, he places a hand at the small of my back. "Just wait till you see the master suite!"

My breath catches when he ushers me through the barn doors at the end of the hall. The bed is massive. The frame is a simple distressed off-white wood, with an elegant chandelier hanging above thick, plush, blue-gray bedding. I don't even have to touch it to know I'll sink into it like a cloud. The walls are pale gray, almost white. The floor's a stonewashed wood. To my left is another set of barn doors, slid aside to reveal a master bath fit for a queen. A pedestal tub sits at the center the room with yet another chandelier dangling above. Until this moment, I always imagined myself more of a candelabra girl, but even I can't deny that it's beautiful. Oh, who am I kidding? It's nothing short of breathtaking.

"Well," he mutters, chewing the inside of his cheek. "If you hate it, like I said, it can all be ch— "

I allow myself to get swept up in the moment and jump into his arms, capturing those sinfully plump lips between my own. There's a war waging inside me, my heart and head battling it out with my rampant hormones, which seem to be taking the lead as I guide my new boy toy over to the king-sized bed.

"Woah," he breathes, capturing my hair near the nape of my neck in a fist and locking eyes with mine. He stills as the backs of his legs knock the bedframe. "I take it you're getting over—"

"Shhhh." I touch my index finger to his lips. "Don't—"

"Don't what?"

Rising up to my toes, I wrap my arms around his broad shoulders and bury my nose into the bend of his neck, inhaling deeply as I breathe in his now-familiar scent. "Less talking."

His thumb and forefinger make a zipping motion across his mouth then both of his hands land on my ass. He grips my cheeks, lifting me to wrap my legs around his waist, then climbs onto the mattress, lowering me slowly while peppering kisses from my right ear, along my jawline, my neck, and across my collar bone.

Chill bumps break out over my skin, contradictory to the way his lips strike fire to the blood running beneath the surface. I'm so hot. So damn horny. My hips buck off the bed when he lowers my shirt and takes my nipple between his teeth, the lace barrier of my bra somehow only adding to the intensity.

"Rhett." His name is a strangled moan as I fist his golden mane in my hands, my body writhing beneath his skilled touch.

"I love these tits," he says, staring down at my chest while sliding a hand behind my back and unclasping my bra. He pays equal attention to each one before continuing lower. I can hardly breathe as he traces a path down my stomach and around my belly button with his tongue while making quick work of releasing the button on my jeans.

My hips lift of their own accord, and in one quick motion, my pants are gone.

"And I love your sweet pussy," he growls. The warmth of his breath, as he slides the tip of his nose along the silky fabric barely concealing my swollen bud, has me twisting my fingers in the sheets to keep from crying out.

"Ohh," I moan at the sensation of him slipping my panties aside and inserting a finger, slowly pumping in and out, trailing his tongue along the length of my body, working his way back to my mouth.

"I love these perfect little lips, and the sounds you make when I touch you here." His finger glides from my entrance to circle my clit. "And here," he whispers before nibbling on the lobe of my ear and pushing back inside.

Rhett's words fuel my desire, while he strums at all of my sweet spots, working me into a frenzy. A true artist, the man plays my body by sound—so attuned to every whimper. Every hiss. Every moan.

But it's the sinking feeling I get each time he says the

L-word that sends me crashing back to reality. I know they're only words and he's not actually *in love* with me, but I also know the warmth swirling in my chest to be a dangerous thing. It brings me to my senses, reminding me of what's at stake. *The games.* There's no way my heart will make it out of this arrangement unscathed. A little bruising, I can handle, but he can't break what I don't give him.

"Stop!" I say, squirming out from beneath his body and righting my underwear. The confusion in his face makes me feel like such a tease.

"Did I do something wrong?" he asks, swiping his thumb across his kiss-swollen lips.

"W—we agreed this wasn't going anywhere." I stare up at the ceiling as to not be deterred by the frown that meets my comment. "I get it," I huff, still trying to catch my breath. "You want to look like the perfect fiancé. You've got your reputation, and heaven knows it's bigger than mine. So, I'll let you do this," I say, referring to the house. "But lines are being blurred. We're not in public right now."

"Okay..."

"So, we don't have to keep pretending behind closed doors, all right? There's no sense in making this harder on either of us."

He nods, solemnly. "Before I go, can I ask a question?"

"Go 'head." I hold up two fingers to let him know I'm still keeping track.

The corner of his mouth quirks into a playful smile. "Have you gone and fallen in love with me already, Miss Potter?"

"Not yet," I rasp, getting lost in the depth of his turquoise eyes. *But I'm not sure how much longer I can give that answer and still remain truthful.*

Chapter 22

KORIE

It's nearing three in the morning, and I can still hear Rhett, Raven, and Nicholas cutting up in the living room when the pain of my screaming bladder forces me awake. The pillow stuffed over my face only serves to slightly muffle the noise down the hall but does nothing to alleviate the urge for the bathroom. With a loud groan, I throw off the covers and head for the barn doors.

I'm annoyed with myself for the way I behaved earlier. When the hell did I become such a buzz kill? And who do I think I am, asking the man to be faithful for the duration of this fake engagement and then not putting out? Do I actually believe he's suddenly going to become celibate for my benefit?

Sure, princess. He's probably got pussy thrown at him daily. Hell, maybe even hourly. You ain't that special.

After climbing back into the enormous bed and settling myself beneath the plush linens, I retrieve my cell from under the pillow. Now wide awake, I open up the Instagram app, hoping to kill some time. *Rhett Taylor tagged you in a post.* Oh shit. I wouldn't blame him if it was an announcement calling this entire charade off after what happened between us earlier.

Of course, that's not what it is, because if I've learned anything about Mr. Taylor thus far, it's that he's completely unlike any of my assumptions. I can't help the goofy grin that overtakes my entire face, nor the fluttering sensation in my tummy, when the selfie we took at the skatepark earlier appears on the screen. Jesus, he has to be the sexiest fucking thing to ever grace two legs, even sporting something as ridiculous as a black mohawk helmet. His smile is downright panty wetting. Those lips, so full and kissable. Eyes so bright in the glow of the afternoon sun that they look otherworldly. The scruff dusting his chin and cheeks has me clenching my thighs, and dear Lord, those dimples. Yeah, everything about Rhett Taylor screams sex. And cautions me to run far and fast before the damage left in his wake is beyond repair.

After staring an obscene amount of time, my eyes finally make it to the caption. "Poppy's got nothin' on my princess. Enjoying watching my girl do her thing on this beautiful day."

Over three thousand hearts. My mouth falls open when I click over to my profile to see that the number of followers has already grown to over five thousand, all from one shared photo.

When the chatter finally dies down, I fire off a text apologizing to Rhett for shutting down on him earlier. He doesn't have to do this for me, and I'm acting like a total brat.

Almost immediately, my phone lights up with a response.

Rhett: Don't ever apologize for telling a guy no, Stick. You should always have that option.

"Why are you so nice to me?" I type back. And I truly want to know. I've been awful to Rhett, and he continues to respond with kindness. I guess I have no clue what he sees in me, and that makes this all so hard to believe–like he and the universe are in cahoots and I'm just waiting on the bomb to drop.

Rhett: Wasn't aware being an asshole was a prerequisite for being male :P

Me: You're different than I imagined...and it kinda scares me.

Rhett: Because you didn't expect to like me back?

"Throwing out question number three already?" I send back. There's no way I'm revealing so much of myself without charging him for it.

Rhett: Sure.

Honesty. Me and my bright ideas.

Me: Yeah...

Rhett: As much as I know it killed you to do so, you've just admitted to liking me, and if you can't tell by now how much I like you, I'm gonna have to start sending up smoke signals or something. Look, Stick, this engagement might be a ruse, but our relationship doesn't have to be.

Me: Are you asking me out, Hollywood?

Rhett: Only if you're saying yes. If it's a no then I'm totally just fucking with ya.

"Can I sleep on it?" I text while my heart tries to escape through my esophagus.

Rhett: Take all the time you need. I'm not going anywhere.

Oh, but he is. Back to L.A. in a few days, and then once his tour starts up, to God knows where. Am I prepared to martyr what's left of my heart on the slim chance he doesn't rip it to shreds?

Goddamn it. I'm such an idiot for agreeing to this.

Just as I start to doze, my phone vibrates in my hand. Another text from Rhett.

Rhett: My sister invited us over for dinner tomorrow. She and Autumn would love to meet you. Will you come?

Me: Does she know?

Rhett: Know what?

Me: That we're not really together?

Rhett: Nope.

Me: You don't think you should tell her?

The little bubbles bounce on my screen for what seems like forever before the boy renders me speechless with his response.

Rhett: I'm pretty confident that by the time tomorrow arrives, we will be. But on the off chance we're not, the less people who know the details of our situation, the better. If we want the media to believe this is the real deal, we need to be as convincing as possible.

"Good morning, sleeping beau—whoa. Well, it's nothing a quick shower won't fix..." Rhett stands in the bathroom doorway, a cloud of steam trailing behind. The scent of his man-soap fills my nostrils as he takes in my bedraggled state.

On instinct, my hand goes right to the rat's nest on the

back of my head. "I was thinking of wearing it like this to meet the family. You don't approve?" Flashing him a teasing smile, I sit up, pulling the comforter to my neck.

"So..." He makes his way over to stand beside the bed. Once again, skipping right to his own agenda. I swear the man thinks I speak just to exercise my mouth. "Looks like you slept *real* good after our little talk."

"Is that your not-so-polite way of telling me I look like shit?"

I'm met with a grin. The bed sinks beneath the weight of his fists pressing into the mattress on either side of my body. My head is forced back as he blocks me in and brings his face level with mine. Dear God, he smells delectable, and I'm having trouble focusing on anything but the heat of his still damp skin so close to mine. "Even with a crow's nest on your head, you're beautiful. That was a very impatient man's way of saying, okay, you slept on it, and asking if you're finally his."

"What do you think?" With a hard swallow, I scoot up my pillow, trying to put a little distance between us, so I can recover some of my wits.

"I think..." he says, taking the hint and backing away. The intensity of his stare burns like molten lava, and there's an uncomfortable silence before he reaches out, trying to run a hand through my tangles. Like a true jackass, he makes a very dramatic scene when it gets stuck. "I think it looks like you and this bed had a wild time fantasizing about your new man all night."

"That you write lyrics for a living is mind blowing."

"Know what else is mind blowing?" He snaps the towel, letting it fall to his feet. His palm wraps around his very impressive shaft, and he gives it a few strokes till it's full mast and jutting straight at my face.

My mouth fills with saliva, and I hope like hell I don't look the way I feel—like a kid drooling at the world's largest ice cream cone. My traitorous tongue rolls over my lips, revealing my position—wanton…desperate…and undeniably his.

"What'dya say, Stick? Wanna give this a go?"

"I mean, can I at least brush my teeth first?"

The sound of his laughter booms in the quiet room. "I meant us." His finger motions back and forth in the space between us. "You know…the relationship thing."

Heat floods my cheeks. "Well, how the hell was I supposed to know when you're standing here like a porn star? Jesus, you're about to poke my damn eye out!"

Flustered, I slink out of the bed. Naked as the day he was born, he follows me into the bathroom, still chuckling as he watches me line the toothbrush with paste and furiously scrub at my teeth. I brush longer than usual, using the time to stall.

"You ready?" he asks, coming up behind me to grab the brush from my hand. His eyes find mine in the glass and hold them as he rinses the bristles beneath the running water.

"To fuck?" I hate how giddy the thought makes me, the way every cell of my being is jumping up and down with excitement and I'm suddenly finding it hard to breathe.

"To fall in love," he croons.

Chapter 23

RHETT

"Uncle Rhett!" Autumn darts off the front porch, running clumsily across the vast lawn of white and yellow wildflowers, somehow managing to remain on her pudgy little feet as only a three-year-old can. Judy and her husband Ryan moved to the country shortly after she was born. Their ranch-style home sits on seven acres, more than half of it wooded. It's one of the few places I don't feel the constant need to look over my shoulder for the paparazzi, who seem to turn up everywhere I go.

Although it's only about an hour drive outside of campus, knowing that Korie's holding out on giving me her answer until we leave here made it feel more like five. I've never wanted a visit with my family to end before it's even started.

"Your highness." I greet my niece with a princely bow before swinging her up into my arms. Her little blonde curls rest on her shoulders, framing an angelic face. Her eyes, the same shade of blue as mine, are wide, and her dimples press divots in her cheeks as she beams up at me. One look from this little girl has me feeling like a million bucks. "I think you've grown a whole foot since the last time I saw you!"

Giggling, she rubs her dirt-covered hands over my cheeks. She's always loved the texture of the stubble. She freezes when she notices Korie standing behind me.

"Who's dat?" she asks with a sneer, while jerking her head back. Her reaction serves to further convince me that jealousy is engrained in the female DNA. The mean mug she has aimed at my date is nothing short of impressive.

"Autumn! This is Uncle Rhett's new girlfriend, Miss Korie. I told you he was bringing her over to meet you today, *remember?*" Judy admonishes before apologizing. "I'm so sorry, hon. The kid has no filter." My sister's hand darts out. "I'm told it's just the age and she'll grow out of it." She shrugs. "I'm Judy, by the way. Rhett's older sister. But, of course, you already know that."

"Nice to meet you." Korie takes her hand, her smile wide and blinding.

She's an absolute vision in a spaghetti-strapped black sundress that hits at the knee and matching black and white chucks. It's the first time I've seen her in a dress, and dear God does she wear it well. Her normally wavy blonde hair is blown straight and parted down the middle. Her porcelain skin is free of any makeup, save for a little black liner around her eyes. She's not one to make a fuss over her appearance, and truth be told, she doesn't need to. Korie is the definition of raw, natural beauty, a rarity in Tinseltown. Still, however minimal, I can tell she put effort into today's meeting, and it stokes the tiny ember of hope still burning inside me, that she might actually say yes. She's definitely wanting to impress someone; I can only hope it's me.

"You're even prettier in person."

Autumn harrumphs at her mother's assessment while wiggling around for me to put her down. "Her was prettier when her was wearin' dat pink Poppy hat."

My sister and I gape at each other, but the awkwardness of the moment quickly passes when Korie bursts into a fit of laughter. Leave it to the blunt honesty of a toddler to break the ice.

"Oh my God," she heaves, hand flying to her chest. "You're my pint-sized hero, sassafras."

Autumn looks at my *fiancée* like she's grown two heads. "I not a sassy ass."

Now it's her mother's turn to harrumph. "Keep tellin' yourself that, kiddo."

"Dat's so rude!" Pudgy arms cross on the tiny tyrant's chest and her lip curls into a pout.

"Sass-uh-fras," Korie corrects, smoothing the tot's windblown hair in an attempt to soothe her. "It means feisty... it's a good thing," she assures her.

My niece stares Korie down for a long moment, trying to decide whether or not to give her another shot. "Do you wanna come pway princess tea party wif me?"

Guess that's a yes.

Korie looks to both Judy and me for permission.

"It's fine with me." My sister curls an arm around Stick's shoulders, leaning close to whisper into her ear. "But I have to warn you, she can be a bit much."

"No worries." With a smile that could stretch clean across Texas, she takes Autumn's little hand and allows her to lead the way.

"We won't be far behind," I call out, wanting to reassure Korie in case she's feeling abandoned, but she simply waves her hand without looking back, as if to say *I've got this.*

"She's cute," Judy drawls once Korie is out of earshot.

"But?" Because with my sister there is *always* a but.

"This is all really sudden, Rhett." Her shoulders slump. "Are you sure about this girl? I mean...I hate to be Debbie Downer, but how do you know she isn't just after your money?"

Judy may be only three years older, but when we lost Mom, she took it upon herself to fill the role of mother. I think it gave her something else to focus on—a way to cope. It can be annoying at times, right now being a prime example. But for all her intrusiveness, I appreciate the concern enough to tolerate it.

"She's not. Believe me."

"You can't know that for sure." She draws a long breath when I shrug. "Just...be careful, little brother. I'd hate to see you get trapped by some gold-digger with stars and dollar signs in her eyes—you deserve to be with someone who can appreciate you for the amazing man you are. Because *you*. Are. Amazing!" She punctuates each word with a finger stab to the chest.

If she only knew how wrong she was about Stick and that I'm having to practically bribe her into dating me. "I'm being careful." I wrap my sister into a hug, planting a placating kiss at the top of her head. "Promise."

"You better not be taking pictures over there." Korie glares up at me over the rim of her porcelain teacup, which I know from experience is filled with apple juice.

"Even better! We're live on my Insta story." Her face pales. "My two favorite girls in one place. Dreams really do come true, y'all." I flip the camera on myself to give our audience my signature wink— and her a moment to recover—before turning it back on Korie and Autumn. "Tell everyone bye, ladies."

If looks could kill, the glare Korie just shot me while twiddling her fingers at the camera would have me reduced to nothing more than a pile of ash.

Thankfully Autumn wastes no time in stealing the show, batting her lashes and blowing kisses to her adoring fans. This isn't her first rodeo. "See y'all soon! Bye. Wuv you!"

On that note, I end the video. As I'm slipping my phone into my back pocket, a wooden slice of birthday cake nails me right in the shoulder. "Ow! What the hell was that for?"

Stick leaps to her feet. She's fighting mad, but the ten-sizes-too-small fluffy pink and purple dress she's sporting over her sundress, along with the matching floppy hat tied beneath her chin, makes it impossible not to laugh.

"This isn't funny, Hollywood. How dare you put me on the spot like that?"

I can't even look at her and maintain a straight face. "Do you trust me?"

"We've already covered this." She huffs. "Not even a little."

"Babe," I drawl, biting my lower lip to keep from laughing while reconstructing the bow on the brim of her fancy hat. "I've been doing this a long time. Believe me, they're going to eat this up…everyone is going to fall head over heels in love with you."

"Yeah, cuz dem already wuvs me." Our little eavesdropper won't be left out.

"Of course they do," her mother says, entering from the kitchen with her husband trailing behind. Their hands are both filled with serving bowls, which they swiftly unload on the dining table amidst the girls' tea party mess. That's life with a kid. Teacups on the table. Legos on the living room floor.

Barbies floating in the bathtub. I can't wait till that's my life.

"Hey bro," I greet Ryan, who must've gotten home from work while I was playing paparazzi. "Good to see ya."

"You too." His curious eyes volley between Korie and me. "You brought a girl home…this is a first. She must be someone special."

"Ryan, this is my *fiancée*, Korie Potter." His eyes grow wide as he reaches for her hand. I can't believe my sister didn't tell him before tonight. Way to put the girl on the spot. I was really hoping this evening would endear her to me, not scare her off. "Korie, your soon-to-be brother-in-law, Ryan."

"Nice to meet you." Her face softens, and a slight blush colors her cheeks as she returns his handshake, before plastering her body to the side of mine. It's an unconscious move, one that makes me puff up like a peacock as I stroke my fingers along the Velcro fasteners at her back. I'll be her security blanket any day.

After introductions are made, we take our seats around the table, Judy and Ryan on one side, Korie and me on the other, and Princess Autumn at the end.

"I feel a little underdressed," I announce, eying my T-shirt and jeans before following that up with a perusal of our two Southern belles. Korie and Autumn look fresh off the set of Gone with the Wind.

"Keep it up, peasant," Korie teases, "and you'll find yourself eating out in the stables with the animals."

Autumn, of course, laughs like it's the funniest thing she's ever heard and threatens to send me out to eat with her sheep dog, Jerry. And I ain't even mad that Stick seems to have replaced me as her favorite for the evening.

Okay, so maybe a *little* jealous…

Throughout dinner, I soak up all I can about Stick while

Ryan gives her the third degree. Like her favorite color is yellow. She's got an addiction to romance novels, which I find sort of ironic for a girl so afraid of falling in love. She hates red meat of any kind, mustard, and peanut butter. Her plans after graduation are to work for the children's hospital she's been volunteering at through college. I never thought to ask if she had a job, but apparently, she's been living off a small trust fund her grandfather left her for school. The fact that she doesn't have any real schedule to adhere to for the time being is really good for our mission. If we're going to get her into the games, we'll have to work hard and fast.

I keep catching myself starting to ask questions, and having to reign it in, because I should know all of this already about the woman I plan to marry. I definitely don't want to make my sister any more uneasy about our sudden *engagement* than she already is.

"I didn't know you worked at the hospital." I'm the first to speak as we start down the winding drive.

"You never asked."

She's right. I don't really have anything to say to that, so I focus on the drive, drumming my thumbs on the steering wheel and hoping she'll be the one to bring up the conversation I've been dying to have all day.

"I like them—your family. They're protective of you..." she muses. "Even the baby."

I catch a glimpse of her dreamy smile in my peripheral vision, and my heartbeat quickens. As happy as it makes me that she enjoyed her time with my family, I don't have the patience for another minute of small talk. "It's after," I finally blurt out.

She laughs. "You're not wasting any time are you? We haven't even made it to the highway."

"Are you kidding me?" I throw my head back onto the headrest while keeping my eyes on the road. "That was excruciating."

"Really? I thought it was so much fun."

"Stick..." With a growl, I tighten my grip on the wheel.

"Even if I agree to this, it doesn't mean I'm marrying you."

"Noted."

"This is freaking crazy...I mean, I don't even like you all that much." She fiddles with the hem of her dress. I can see that she's nervous, so I try to give her time to sort through her thoughts. For a long stretch there's nothing but silence. When I look over to make sure she hasn't fallen asleep on me, she finally breaks it.

"Rhett?"

"Yeah?"

"I meant what I said."

"What was that?"

"Don't fall in love with me."

"Stick?"

"Yeah?"

"Maybe you should heed your own advice."

Chapter 24

KORIE

HE'S GONE.

Rhett and Nick left for Los Angeles to finish recording their new album before the sun was even up over the horizon. It'll be at least three weeks until I see him again. Anika and the guys have cut us off from any more visits until they've completed their studio time. I thought I'd feel relieved once he left and things went back to some kind of normal. But I'm actually missing having him around, and it's only been a couple of hours. Although, I'm not ready to admit that to Rhett. Truth be told, I hope I never am because I'm still trying, albeit failing, not to fall in love with the hopelessly charming fucker.

"Well, look who finally decided to show her pretty face."

"Hey, Momma." I figure since I'm already having a rotten day, I might as well get this meeting over with. Take it all up the ass at once, if you will.

"I've been worried sick about you." She pulls the double doors open wider, ushering me inside. The familiar smell of home wraps around me like a warm blanket, and when her arms envelop me in a tight hug, I have the sudden urge to burst into tears.

Ugh, I'm just all sorts of hormonal today. *Gross.*

"Sorry, Ma. You know I've been busy with finals and stuff."

"Mmmhmm…and stuff…" Cocking her right brow, she takes a step back, cradling my face in her hands. Her warm caramel eyes lock with mine. Then her lower lip begins to quiver, and something inside me splinters. "What did you do, baby?"

Dammit. I was expecting to be yelled at. That I was prepared for. That I could handle.

With a resigned sigh, I turn to push the doors shut before filling her in. Rhett and I discussed at length the importance of keeping our families in the dark. So, I tell her how we met at Nick's party and embellish the weeks between then and Camp Pour Judgment. By the time I've made it through his visit to College Station and my impending trip to Los Angeles, I feel like I've run a marathon. Lying to the one person I've always been able to count on is one of the hardest things I've ever had to do. It just adds to the awesome mood I find myself in today.

My mother remains quiet while I talk. She grabs my hand, examining the ring with something akin to disgust on her face. "It's too much." She shakes her head. "This is all happening entirely too fast. What's the rush?"

I swallow down the lump that's growing larger with every lie I feed her. "You know what they say…When you know, you know, right?"

"But how? Why?" She shakes her head, gnawing on her thumb nail as she paces the marble foyer. "I taught you better than this. I wanted so much more for you. For your children. This life…" She looks around the empty mansion she once shared with my father. "It's lonely." My beautiful mother's eyes well with tears, the worry lines on her face growing deeper. "Why couldn't you just find some nice college boy?"

"It just sort of...*happened*."

"Natural disasters just happen, Korie. This is a train wreck in the making. You tie yourself to the tracks, and eventually you're going to get struck. I don't want to see you end up spending the rest of your life regretting a rash decision."

My blood heats to boiling, and the need to come to Rhett's defense is both shocking and undeniable. "He's not Dad!"

He's not Dad. Those three words run on loop in my mind while I work out my frustration at Buck Nutty's, Little Hope's indoor skate park, over the massive argument I just had with my mother. It's in this room where I fell in love with the sport. Although it's ancient and smells of teenage boys and dirty gym socks, it'll always be my favorite place to hone my craft. I know this terrain like the back of my hand.

Effortlessly I run trick after trick, landing the 360 that's been giving me hell this week like I could do it in my sleep. I'm shredding up the course, having one of the best runs of my life, when suddenly I get the feeling of being watched. The unease trips me up, and just as I go careening down the ramp, a slow clap sounds behind me.

What the—?

"That was great. Where should I send it?"

I turn to find a middle-aged man in a red and black flannel and worn jeans crouched behind a camera on a tripod. His too-long hair curls around the edges of his Etnies ball cap.

Where'd he come from?

"I'm sorry...and you are?" With some hesitation, I pop my board into my hand and walk over to meet the intruder. He looks harmless enough. Probably a damn paparazzi.

"Name's Wally. I work for Mac's Media Marketing Solutions."

"Okay...Let's try this instead. *Why* are you here filming *me?*"

"I was hired by Mr. Taylor to get some video footage for your Instagram. That was one hell of a run." His hand lifts into the air for a high five, but I'm still too much in shock over his being here to do more than stare at it, and he lowers it back to his side with an embarrassed shrug. "Yeah, so...it should get tons of engagement, and I got some great still shots as well. I'll fire 'em over to your email, and you can start posting today."

"Dammit, Rhett," I hiss. He knew I'd be visiting Mom today, and I mentioned hitting up the park before heading home. He could have given me some warning before sending the dude to scare my ass half to death.

Me: What the hell, Hollywood???

Rhett: Gonna need you to be a little more specific...

Me: Your stalking is getting out of hand. What's with the video guy?

Rhett: Ahhh, that. You're welcome.

Me: You could have given me a heads up.

Rhett: If you'd known he was filming, your nerves would have ruined it. We don't have a lot of time to pull this off. I wanted you completely in the dark and skating at your best. And it worked.

"Excuse me?" Wally interrupts my texting tirade. "If you could just let me know where to send all these files, I'll get out of your hair."

I spout off my email address and thank him for his services. After all, he was only doing his job. It's not his fault Rhett doesn't possess an ounce of common courtesy.

With my legs dangling over the edge of the half-pipe, I plop down to sift through the footage.

Me: Okay, so these are really good.

Rhett: Yeah, they are. You look hot!

Of course, Wally sent them to Rhett already. He's the one who hired him after all.

Me: Great! Because that is totally the goal...

Rhett: Well, talented, too, but looking good never hurt anyone.

He would know...

"How'd it go with DeeDee today?" Raven saunters over with a pen clutched between her teeth and order pad in hand when she finds me curling into my usual booth at Little Sicily's, the pizza place she waitresses at five nights a week.

"As bad as you're thinking." Slouching in my seat, I stare up at the dust-covered teardrop lights, remembering the way I leaped to Rhett's defense. *What was that?* "Worse, probably."

"Wanna talk about it?"

"Nope."

"Good," she snarks. "Cuz I didn't really wanna hear about

it."

I glance around to be sure none of her customers are watching then give her the finger. "Bitch."

She shrugs, poking out her tongue. "The usual?"

"You know it."

Dessert nachos for the win! There's nothing quite like a heaping plate of cinnamon chips piled high with vanilla ice cream, then drizzled in caramel and hot fudge, to end a shit-tastic day.

Raven giggles when I shovel a loaded crisp into my mouth and moan at its decadence. "I don't know how you don't have diabetes or weigh five hundred pounds by now. The shit you eat'd go straight to my ass."

I wave her away, stuffing my face while she finishes up with her shift. On the ride home, I fill her in on all the gory details of my day. Despite her earlier insistence that she didn't care to hear it, her ears perk up at the mention of the Insta photo guy. She's all about this making me famous thing.

"Did you see this?" she asks, showing me the video I uploaded before leaving the skate park.

I cast a brief glance to the side before turning my attention back to the road.

"Your page is at twelve thousand followers now…and there are hundreds of comments on this video, including one from *Melanie Binx*."

"Holy shit!" My excitement causes me to momentarily veer onto the shoulder. She's one of the pioneers of the women's skate scene and my freaking idol. "What'd she say?" I ask after righting the ship.

"Don't run us into a ditch, hooker!" She gives my shoulder a shove, like that'll improve my driving, before turning back to the phone. "Gnarly run, chicka. Hope I'll be seeing you around the circuit!"

Someone check my pulse. Pretty sure I just died.

Chapter 25

RHETT

"WHAT THE FUCK, MAN? YOU LEAVE YOUR BALLS IN TEXAS?" The track cuts just as Lyle's voice filters through the speakers into the sound booth. "Try it again. This time without sounding like a fucking girl."

I flip him off and chug a bottle of water. We've been working on the vocal for the same damn song all morning. Or rather, I've been working while they pick every fucking note apart. I can't seem to get this chorus right, and it's pissing me off.

"Needs more tractors and truck beds, Taylor," our producer, Mitch, adds, speaking into the mic. "Twang it up a bit." He points at me with a cigarette dangling between his fingers. "You've got it in you. I know you do."

The door opens and in struts Nick, flask in hand. "I've got just what he needs." Unscrewing the top, he passes it my way. "Desperate times," he says "Forget Anika. She doesn't get paid if we don't."

"Touché." I press the cool steel rim to my lips and tip my

head back, relishing the feel of the bitter heat washing over my tongue and burning its way down my throat. Warmth blooms in my stomach, spreading like a current of molten lava to my face and extremities. "Whoo!" I shout, pounding a fist on my chest. "Damn, that's good."

"Puts hair on the nuts, boy!" Nick says in his best Jax Potter impression. We recorded our first album at his Nashville studio, where he provided an endless supply of drugs and liquor. He wasn't the greatest role model for sure, but I'll give the man this much, he knows his music.

Let's just say that while under his influence, the guys and I fell into some bad habits. When it reached the point where Anika had to start making excuses and rescheduling shows, shit got old quick. Our little spitfire of a manager threatened to walk, and we cleaned up our act, leaving the partying until after our work was done. But she's not here, and no shows will be canceled if we catch a little buzz.

"Thattaboy!" Nick thumps me between the shoulder blades and heads back to join the others while I take another long pull of liquid fire to coat the vocal cords.

Mitch gives me the thumbs up and waits for me to return it before restarting the track.

Channeling my best Luke Bryan, I give it another go.

"They say every man has a weakness
Well, as it turns out mine is you
So, think long and hard before this goes too far
Cuz once you dip your toes in these waters
Babe, you best be ready to swim."

"We got it!" Mitch slaps his hands down on the soundboard before throwing a fist into the air. "That's a wrap!"

"Whiskey brings the twang!" I thrust my shot glass into the air and try not to fall off my bar stool when the motion causes me to lose my balance.

"And the tang!" Aiden adds, grabbing the girl that's been fluttering around him all night and plunging his tongue down her throat.

"Mitch said you guys nailed it."

I turn toward the familiar sound of Anika's voice as she saddles up on the stool beside me, grab a fresh shot, and raise my glass in her direction. "To whiskey!"

"Cheers," she says, smiling before combing a hand through her loose hair and throwing back the shot Nick placed on the bar in front of her. She blows out a long breath. "Shit, that's strong."

"Yeah, Annie!" Lyle cheers her on using the nickname we reserve for the days we actually still like her.

"I'm really proud of y'all."

"Uh-oh, I feel one comin' on…" Nick gets up out of his chair and Anika squeals, trying to shrink away. "Group hug!"

"Is this really necessary?" she asks through high-pitched laughter while the four of us squish her between us.

She's still fighting us off when the beginning notes to "Back that Ass Up" float through the speakers. Our group, along with most of the bar, gravitate toward the dance floor. A huge crowd begins to circle around us. The lights are pulsating and the bass is pumping, and our girl is shaking what her momma gave her. Damn, I can't help but notice how good she looks tonight, with her hair down and eyes all smoky. She's traded her signature business attire for distressed jeans and a tight, fitted tee. Her cleavage is on point.

Aiden, for one, takes notice, dropping the chick from the bar and molding the front of his body to hers. His hands land on her hips, guiding her movement to match his. The coy smile she sends over her shoulder when she turns to uncover her mystery partner is scorching hot.

"It's a damn good thing we have a strict no fraternizing with the manager rule in place," I shout at the two of them over the music. "Pretty sure that look alone just got me pregnant."

"Always said you were a pussy," Aiden quips, making a V with his first two fingers and lapping his tongue in the air between them.

Anika's cheeks heat. "Ohhh…is someone jealous?" She leaves his arms for mine. "Ready for your turn?" she asks, fluttering her lashes as she links her hands behind my neck.

"Careful, Annie," I tease. "You're starting to sound like the ho all those jealous bitches in high school thought you were."

"Burn!" That outburst comes courtesy of Lyle, followed by raucous laughter all around.

The DJ keeps with the upbeat tone, and the four of us take turns spinning our girl around the dance floor. Shots are flying and bodies are bouncing in every direction. The rest of the night is one big haze of flashing lights and thumping bass. Of sweat-soaked skin and racing hearts. Just a bunch of childhood friends reveling in realized dreams.

Times like this with Anika are few and far between. For a girl who grew up with barely a pot to piss in, she's living a good life. But it sure is nice to see a little of the hood rat we grew up with come out to play.

"This better be good, boss," I groan as I stumble across the house to her office at five in the morning. "Pretty sure I'm still a little drunk."

"Have a look for yourself," she says, turning her computer monitor around to face me. "I knew this was a terrible idea." *And Annie has left the building.*

"This isn't even close to the biggest scandal we've dealt with, Anika. You need to calm down."

Wound so tight she's visibly about to explode, she scowls at my blasé attitude from her chair behind the desk. "The issue here is that she has no publicist, or manager, or experience dealing with paparazzi. This kind of thing is going to happen over and over again."

"Then you'll handle it when trouble arises, because that's what I pay you to do. Swear to God, if you make her feel bad over this, it will not end well."

My lifelong friend's face falls, making me feel like a complete asshole. Weren't we just celebrating mere hours ago? "Like I'd ever do such a thing, Rhett. Glad to see you think so highly of me."

"Look, I'm sorry." I plant my palms on the desktop, leaning in close. "I know you wouldn't intentionally hurt anyone. It's just been a long day and night. I'm drunk, grumpy, and half asleep. We'll deal with this shit in the morning together, okay? Actual morning."

With some reluctance she nods, swallowing hard. "Sure... in the morning then."

Chapter 26

KORIE

"**W**AKE UP!"

"Ugh," I groan, pulling the comforter over my head to shield my eyes from the sudden influx of light. "I'm sleeping. Get the hell out of my room."

My full bladder threatens to burst when Raven jumps on top of me in the bed. "You're Britney two-thousand-seven famous, bitch. *Wake up!*"

"I'm serious, Raven. Get out!"

Dammit.

Now I have to pee. Annoyed as hell, I glare at her as I shove the blankets off and trudge to the bathroom, where she follows...

"Ever heard of privacy?" I grump while doing my business. If she wants to watch, that's on her.

Rave shrugs before shoving her phone screen in front of my face, not the least deterred by me being on the toilet. "Sure. But this David Wills sure hasn't."

"Oh, God, no." My gut churns as I read the caption beneath a photo of myself flipping Raven off at the restaurant last night. Guess I forgot to check for paparazzi outside of the glaring window my table is positioned against. *Fuck!*

Korie Potter caught going diva on unsuspecting waitress. Looks like someone's already getting a little too big for her britches. Rhett Taylor better rein this one in before she becomes a publicity nightmare.

"Oh, this is bad."

"Nicholas thinks it's hilarious, actually," Raven supplies, following me over to the sink where I wash my hands and brush my teeth, all the while trying not to regurgitate last night's dinner. "Anika is going a little crazy, though. You probably should call her back."

I spit and rinse and rush back to the bed to retrieve my phone from its usual spot beneath my pillow. Seventeen missed calls and texts from just about every person I know and even a few I don't.

Bile rises in my throat as I scroll through the list, reading the ones that matter.

Mom: Did you see TMZ? They have a photo of you giving Raven the finger with a nasty caption. I hate to say I told you so...but this is only the beginning if you go ahead with this insanity.

Gee. Thanks, ma.

Rhett: Don't freak out but check E-News. It's not as bad as it looks. I promise. Call me when you wake up.

And one from my cousin, Abby Jane…

AJ: OMG! Korie!!!! Did you see TMZ? HAH! They think Raven is some poor unsuspecting waitress. What a fucking riot.

Unknown: Korie, this is Anika. I've been trying to reach you for hours. Give me a call as soon as you can, please. It's important.

Ignoring all of the messages, including Rhett's, I call Anika first. I know how much the guys respect her and want more than anything to win her approval.

"Korie?" she answers, barely halfway through the first ring. "Good morning," she adds, almost as an afterthought.

"Is it?" I snort, trying for a little humor in this disastrous situation, but all I get in return is radio silence. "I'm so sorry, Anika. I didn't think..."

"Don't worry about it," she says, cutting me off. "Rhett and I have already discussed how best to proceed. We'll run a post on both of your social media accounts explaining who Raven is and that the picture was taken out of context. No big deal."

"Really?" My entire body sags with relief. "That's all there is to it?"

"Yeah," she says. "It's what we *usually* do when this sort of thing happens."

Oh, hell no.

"You mean it's what you *should* have done when the picture of me and Rhett leaked?" I ask, not missing the meaning behind the well-placed inflection in her tone. I had a feeling she might not like me before, but now I'm convinced of it. I just have no idea why.

"That Stick?" The familiar timbre of his voice soothes my ire considerably. "Lemme talk to her."

I can't make out their muffled words as the exchange is made, but I don't even care what was said once he's the one on the other side of the line. "How's my little troublemaker this morning?"

"Ugh," I groan. "So not funny."

"Welcome to the lifestyles of the rich and famous, babe. This shit comes with the territory."

"I guess. Really makes you question everything you read in the tabloids, that's for sure."

"You gonna be okay?" There he goes worrying about me again, when I've just dumped another shit storm into his lap.

"Yeah…I just don't want to cause any issues for you and the guys. The comments are pretty bad." I scroll through the list at the end of the article, wincing at all of the hate being spewed about me.

"Never read the comments, Stick. First rule of the trade. But if it really bugs you, you could let it slip who you are. If they know you're the daughter of a washed-up, somewhat famous, former musician…, it'll at least squash the idea that you're just out for fame."

"Nope. I'm sure they'll eventually figure it out on their own, but I have no desire to publicly lay claim to that man."

"I get it. Just send over a fun shot of you and Raven together. I'll have Anika whip up a statement. We'll post on our social media accounts, and in a day or two it'll be like this never happened. You'll see."

"I'm sorry," I say, hating the vulnerability in my tone. I can deal with people talking shit on me, that's not what this is about. It's knowing that my reputation could affect his career—his livelihood—that has me feeling sick to my stomach.

"No need to be," he insists. "I'm sure Raven deserved it, anyway."

It's been a week since the middle finger incident, and I'm happy to report I've managed to keep myself out of the headlines. *Go me!* I've been trying to keep a low profile, practicing my tricks and focusing on developing a real presence on social media. That shit's a full-time job in itself.

Rhett actually had me take an online class on how to Instagram. This shit is that hard core. There are all these rules I never knew about, like the best times to post and choosing appropriate hashtags. I'm supposed to respond to every comment with at least four words to keep myself in the algorithms. I've also got to go comment on some of the commenters' photos to keep my engagement up—which is what I'm currently in the middle of when his text finally comes through at almost midnight. Not that I've been waiting or anything. I'm not that desperate, y'all.

Rhett: We're finally, home. Miss me?

Me: Don't flatter yourself.

Yes. Dammit. I miss him, okay. And Ollie. Well, mostly just Ollie. *What?* Great sex is easy to get attached to. Surely it isn't his stellar personality that has me counting down the days till I see him again.

Seven. More. Days.

Rhett: If I don't, who will? I definitely can't count on my fiancée to do it :p

Me: Oh, you poor baby. Go for a stroll down the magazine aisle at Target and you'll find more flattery than you can stand.

"Hello," I answer when Rhett responds with a Facetime call. It takes a minute for the video to connect, but once his face fills the screen, there's no denying the sense of longing that falls over me.

"Just wanted to see your gorgeous face." He's lying in bed with one arm folded behind his head, looking sexier than any man has a right to. "I miss you like fucking crazy, Stick."

"Have you been drinking?" I ask, behind a grin. I love the way his voice takes on a lazy Southern drawl when he's had a few too many.

His head tips side to side and he squints his bloodshot eyes. "Maybe a little."

"So, you probably won't remember this conversation in the morning?"

"Definitely won't remember a word."

"In that case, I might miss you just a little." I pinch my fingers together in front of the screen to demonstrate just how minute.

"*Annnd* you think I'm cute?" he asks, widening his eyes like a little boy looking for reassurance.

I sigh at his neediness. "Stupidly handsome, and you know it."

His languid smile tugs on my heart. "I know. But I just wanted to make sure you knew. You seemed confused, so I had to call you to check."

"I will deny every word of this in the morning."

"What are you talkin' 'bout?" he asks, looking around the dark room. "I came home and passed right out."

Even drunk off his ass, the boy knows how to handle me. "How was your day?" I ask, trying to move the conversation from the mushy shit. "Y'all get a lot done?"

"Oh yeah." He yawns really big. "Cleaned up a few tracks. What'd you do? Besides miss me?"

"Spent a few hours with the kids at the hospital this morning, then went to the skate park."

He nods. "That's so nice…"

"It was," I agree in a whisper, sure he's about to nod off.

"Stick," he slurs, his eyes growing heavier by the second.

"Yeah?"

"Love me, yet?"

Jesus, he's persistent. "No way, José."

"You can tell me. This conversation isn't even happening, remember."

I shake my head. "Do you love me, Rhett Taylor?"

He lifts one brow. His blue eyes now nothing but slits. "I think it was love at first *slight*."

Chapter 27

RHETT

"**WHAT ARE YOU DOING THE WEEKEND OF APRIL 27?**" **I**DLY, **I** trail my fingertips along Korie's spine, enjoying the warmth of her skin pressed so intimately to mine. It's been a long couple of weeks without her. It's crazy how quickly I've grown addicted to this body and that smart mouth of hers.

"Well, good morning to you too." Yawning, she lifts her head and turns to prop her chin on top of her hands, which are folded across my chest. I still can't believe she's actually here. In my house. In my bed. Gloriously naked. And sporting some major bedhead. "Nothing that I know of…why? What's up?"

"Besides Ollie?" I waggle my brows, and her eyes sink to the appendage in question. Being the proud showoff that I am, I flex my groin, making my erection move.

She clears her throat, ogling the swaying tent in the sheets while I bite back a smirk. *Always so eager.*

"So…" I continue, as if I'm not lying here with a raging boner. "A guy who's friends with our stage manager is really good friends with one of the organizers of the Chicks with Tricks skate event going down that weekend in Mississippi. Pretty sure I can get you in as a wildcard."

"Shut up!" She slaps her palm on my chest, and her entire face glows with excitement. "Are you serious? Rhett, this is huge."

"That's what she said," I jest, joining my hands behind her back and rolling us over so I'm on top and nudging my cock between her legs.

"That too." Staring back at me through hooded lids, she takes a hard swallow. I can feel the pounding of her racing heart against my own. Her thighs part, and she shifts beneath me, lining up our centers. I'm a thrust away, seated right at her slick entrance, and it's sheer torture not to move.

"So, yes?" I ask, brushing my nose over hers, trying not to laugh at her irritated sigh and the blank look on her face as I needlessly draw this out, all for the sake of watching her squirm. She's completely lost sight of our conversation. "To the skate thing?" I remind her.

"Hell, yes," she growls, lacing her fingers behind my neck and lowering my mouth to hers. "To everything," she adds, her lips brushing over mine earnestly. Then she curls her legs around my waist and elevates her hips, forcing me inside.

"Goddamn, girl, I love the way you manhandle me..."

"This is amazing." Korie gazes around in awe as she follows me out to my private balcony overlooking the Malibu coast. Her bare feet make a light padding sound, keeping with the steady rhythm of the thumping of my heart, as she floats across the tile. "I didn't realize how spectacular the view was from your room when I got in last night. It was so late." She takes a deep inhale of the salty air, shutting her eyes and really letting it soak in.

"It's never looked quite this beautiful before." My eyes fix on hers, making no mistake of my meaning. She's leaning against the rail, my white button down hanging to her knees, with nothing underneath. The orange glow of the early morning sun highlights the silhouette of her naked form, and I find myself searching for breath. The way her long blonde hair looks whipping in the breeze against the turquoise backdrop of the waves is nothing short of majestic. So natural. Like she belongs in this scenery. In my life. If I could freeze this moment, it'd fuel a million love songs. "Now, this is a sight I wouldn't mind waking up to every morning, that's for sure."

Coming up behind her, I snake my arms around her waist, burying my lips in the crown of her hair. I'm a little taken back by how right this feels. All at once it hits me—I'm falling hard, and I'm falling fast. It's no longer about the challenge or wanting her for all of the things she isn't. I realize that, little by little, I've begun to fall in love with this woman for exactly who she is.

That she might never feel the same for me is fucking terrifying.

"Don't get ahead of yourself, mister."

"Can't help it," I say, tickling her side, to lighten the mood. "I've grown rather accustomed to getting what I want."

She giggles, wiggling in my hold. "So spoiled."

"Maybe," I admit with an unapologetic shrug. "But I think the bigger reason is that I'm not afraid to go after whatever my heart desires. Hard work and determination usually pay off."

"Well," she says, slinking out of my arms. "Hate to be the

bearer of bad news, but I think you may be overreaching this time, Hollywood."

Having her speak my fear aloud is a huge jolt to my ego. "Guess time will tell."

She moves to sit in a lounger. I get the feeling she's trying to put a little distance between us. Any talk beyond here and now makes her uncomfortable, but she motions for me to take the one beside it, so I do. When she gets like this, I'm learning not to push. There's a delicate balance between gently coaxing her out of her cocoon and sending her soaring right out of my life forever.

We sit in companionable silence for a long while, listening to the waves crash on the shoreline. "So, you all live here? The guys? *Anika?*"

"Yeah. This house was our first big purchase. We bought it together. Eventually when we start marrying off, we'll get our own places, and this'll become a vacation home."

She presses her lips together. "So, this isn't where you plan on settling down then?"

"Nah." I lay back, kicking my feet up, since it seems she's in no hurry to go back inside. "I'll be a gentleman and let you decide where we plant our roots."

"Rhett," she warns. Her cute little voice coming out all growly.

Throwing my hands out in submission, I let the subject die with a chuckle.

"Can I ask a question?" She rolls on her side, tucking an arm beneath her cheek to face me.

"Shoot."

"Will you tell me about your favorite memory with your mother?" She must recognize the look of surprise on my face because immediately she starts backpedaling. "I mean, it's okay if you don't want—"

"It's fine," I say, staring up at the clouds. "People just don't ever ask about her. I guess I don't get the opportunity to talk about Mom much." I flash her a wink to ease her nerves. "No passing, remember?"

"Sorry."

"Seriously, don't worry about it. Ummm..." I drum my hands on my cargo shorts. "Favorite memory..." My chest grows taut. "When I think of my mom, the first thing that always comes to mind is music."

"So, she's where you inherited your insane talent?"

"Yeah, I guess so. God, Stick, she was *incredible*. Better than I could ever dream to be. She used to sing at our church. I remember being just a little boy, not more than three or maybe four. I'd watch her up there on the altar from the first pew every Saturday and Sunday. Just my mother and her guitar, surrounded by the colorful rays of light that filtered in through the stained glass windows. I truly believed that woman was an angel."

"I bet she was gorgeous."

"She was. Tall and sort of willowy. She had really thick, long, dark hair. Her eyes were unnaturally blue." I get a flash of her smiling face, leaning in to kiss me good night, and it shakes me to my core. "I can still smell her—jasmine powder and mint. She had an addiction to Doublemint Gum." I laugh. "The nasty one in the green package."

Korie cringes. "That stuff's the worst."

"Our house was always filled with music. We'd wake up to it, go to bed to it. She loved classic country most: Reba, Patsy, Dolly...but she could belt out a good Whitney or Mariah ballad like nobody's business too."

"How old were you when she taught you to play?"

"I started off just singing along with her...girly shit." I scoff. "My first performance in front of a crowd was fucking, 'Somewhere Over the Rainbow.' I was six. Pretty sure Dad still has it lying around on video somewhere, even though I demanded he burn it. If that shit ever got out..." I wince.

She cracks a smile, and I can tell she's imagining it. "I think you should sing that for me right now," she taunts.

"Not a chance." I give her a hard look, letting her know I'm serious. "Anyway, we never had much money, and the guitar she played with belonged to the church. When she realized I could actually sing, she pawned the jewelry she'd inherited from my grandmother to get the money to buy me one. I was too young to realize the sacrifice she was making. I still have it," I say, rising from my seat and wandering inside to retrieve it from the leather case in my closet, suddenly having the urge to strum its tattered strings.

I sit sideways on the lounge chair, propping the old guitar on my knee, and tuning it by ear. After I'm done, Korie holds her arms out, wiggling her fingers in the space between us, like she just can't wait to touch it.

My heart swells, filling up the entirety of my chest as she runs her small hands over the oiled wood, examining the instrument as if it were an ancient artifact. I'm moved by the way she takes her time, fully appreciating how special it is. "There's an inscription," she says, eyes glistening as she reads it silently to herself.

I nod, staring off in the distance to avoid the sudden onset of emotion.

"For my sweet boy, Rhett. One of these days I just know you're gonna be a big ol' star. Let this inscription serve as my, 'I told ya so.' I love you, Boogy, always, forever, and big like the sky. Love, Mom." As she finishes reading out loud, the tears fall unchecked in a steady stream down her cheeks. It's a silent cry, like the one crippling me inside. My well dried up long ago, and while I may have gotten good at hiding any outward signs of grief, I have yet to discover a way to condition my heart not to feel the immense pain of her loss.

"Argh," I growl, shaking away the moisture that's building behind my eyes. "Yeah. So, she told me so."

"Jesus, Rhett. She has to be so proud, looking down on her little boy and all that you've accomplished."

"I sure hope so," I say, taking the guitar back and settling it in my lap.

Korie's tear-soaked face splits into a wide grin when she recognizes the beginning chords to "Somewhere Over the Rainbow."

Chapter 28

KORIE

"**W**HY EVEN BOTHER WRITING YOUR OWN SONGS? **Y**OU COULD just stand up there on stage, singing nursery rhymes, and women would still throw their panties at you."

As if the boy could possibly get any cuter, his cheeks flush with a rosy shade of embarrassment. He props the guitar against the outer wall of the house, leaning forward with his elbows resting on his knees—his face now mere inches away. "You think?"

"Oh, I know. I'd throw mine, but they're lost somewhere in your room." His nearness causes my throat to dry and my words come out gravelly. I swear, the man keeps me in a constant state of arousal. I'm not even sure this is healthy.

His answering grin is predatory as he lifts both of his hands to cup my sticky cheeks. Goosebumps ripple across my skin in waves, while his fingers gently progress to the nape of my neck. My body trembles as the pads of his thumbs brush my ear lobes, and he leans closer still. Starting from the corner of my right eye, he begins peppering whisper soft kisses, blazing a path over every inch of my overheated skin. Then he's hovering near my mouth, staring so deeply into my eyes that I feel naked and exposed. I swear he can see right into the very heart of my soul.

I wish that I could read his thoughts—to know exactly what's going through his mind—as he stares at me with such intensity that I feel it in my marrow.

Motionless but for the heavy rise and fall of my chest, I await his next move.

Rhett's tongue takes a leisurely stroll across his lips, like he's savoring the flavor of something sinfully delicious. "I don't think I've ever tasted anything sweeter..." he rasps before clamping his lower lip between his teeth.

My tears. Dear God in heaven, he is *licking* my tears off his lips!

"...than the taste of your empathy, Korie Potter," he continues, rendering me speechless.

What does one say to that?

Nothing. There is no appropriate way to respond. I don't know whether to feel embarrassed or disturbed by what's just happened, or to swoon into a freaking puddle at his feet.

Thankfully, he doesn't give me long to worry over the matter. With my chin gripped between Rhett's thumb and forefinger, he brings my mouth to his, pulling me in for a long, sensual kiss. We take our time pouring our heightened emotions into each stroke of our tongues, every brush of our lips.

I don't know where this is going or what these intense feelings swirling around inside of me might mean, but I do know for certain, whatever happens between us, I'll never visit the ocean again without reliving every detail of this perfect moment. Never will the sea breeze whip through my hair without reminding me of the way his hands feel fisted tightly in the strands. And when I hear the steady rhythm of the waves crashing the shores, I'll recall the way they synced seamlessly with the beating of my heart. For as long as I live, when I taste the ocean water, it'll be the salt from my eyes to his lips.

"Y'all need to calm it down," Aiden growls, pointing the slice of cold pizza he just took a bite from our way as we enter the kitchen. "I didn't appreciate being woken up to the headboard knocking against the wall. Some of us need our beauty rest."

My cheeks flush ten shades of red. I hope he couldn't hear *me*. Oh, God…

"Fuck off, Aid." Rhett gives him the finger. "Don't listen to him, Stick. His room's on the other side of the damn house."

"Just like fucking with ya," the lanky brunet says with a snicker, dropping his food on the paper plate in front of him and pushing back from the table to greet me with a hug. His gray sweats are hung low on his hips, his tatted chest on full display. I have the sudden urge to tug on the little bars speared through his nipples. *Ouch.* "Welcome to our humble abode."

I glance around the stark white kitchen: white granite countertops with flecks of black and gray throughout, white cabinets, white- and gray-swirled marble tile floors. The appliances are top of the line black stainless steel, without a print on them. I don't think Raven and I have ever seen our kitchen so clean. The ceiling is dome-shaped and made of gray brick with pendant lights dangling over the island. A rectangular crystal chandelier lights an eight-seater weathered wood table with ten white pin-tucked chairs surrounding it. Floor to ceiling windows make up the wall behind the table, framing a breathtaking view of the ocean as far as the eye can see. This house is anything but humble. It's rich. Immaculate. Daunting.

"Korie…" Rhett snaps his fingers to draw me back to the land of the living. "Would you like me to whip you up some eggs and bacon?"

"You actually cook in here?"

The boys both look at me like I've sprouted a horn, or wings, or maybe both.

"You don't use your kitchen to cook?" Rhett asks, half joking.

"Of course, but it doesn't look like anyone's ever used this one. Everything is so white and pristine and…perfect." There's literally nothing out of place. No piles of bills, no basket with keys and fingernail clippers, and other odds and ends. There's no can opener, toaster, or coffee pot littering the counters. No phone charger wires laying around. Not one thing that makes this place look lived in.

"We use the kitchen," he laughs. "We just have the world's best housekeeper, Rosy. You'll see her lurking about. Short little Latina lady that follows us around tidying up. Anika brought her in after less than a week of living with four guys."

"Rosy is a lifesaver! My favorite human." Speak of the devil. Anika promenades into the kitchen, already dressed in a beige pencil skirt, four-inch nude heels, and a teal blouse. It's not even nine a.m. and her long, dark hair is braided down the side, and she's wearing a full face of makeup.

Her put-together state has me examining my own ensemble: Rhett's faded navy Fender tee and a pair of his boxers, aqua with big purple eggplants, rolled at the waist. My hair is sex tousled and windblown, piled on top of my head in the messiest of buns. At least I put on a bra.

"'Morning, Anika," I greet, smiling despite the lingering tension between us.

Her face splits into a huge, unexpected smile. "Korie." She nods, like she's actually happy to see me, which I know is bullshit and all for the boys' benefit. "I've taken the liberty of purchasing a few items of clothing for you. They're hanging in the far right of Rhett's closet in case you feel like dressing up or anything. Not sure what y'all's plans are."

Fucking snake.

"That's so sweet," I grit through a smile. "You shouldn't have." And I fucking mean it. How dare she try to dress me? *Cunt.*

"Annie is the best." Rhett grins at his manager and longtime friend.

"Anything for my boys," she says, walking over to the corner cabinet and retrieving a Keurig. From the door above, she grabs a mug, and in the drawer beneath is a vast array of pods.

Coffee. Thank God.

"I'll just have a coffee, and maybe we can go out for pancakes?"

Rhett gasps. "You that scared of my culinary skills, Stick?"

"No, I just don't really like eggs…or bacon."

"Say no more," he says, flinging various cabinets around the room open and littering the island with ingredients. "Who doesn't like bacon?" he mutters, throwing a lace-trimmed floral apron on over his wife beater, tying it around his waist. Then, he begins measuring out the milk, oil, flour, sugar, baking powder, and salt.

I post up on a stool, resting my elbows on the cool granite, my cheeks in my hands and observe him as he works. There's something unbelievably sexy about watching this muscly man, in his girly apron, cracking eggs with delicate precision. The way the veins protrude on his forearms as he whisks it all into a fluffy batter is whipping something up in me.

He puts a skillet on the stove then cuts a bowl of fresh strawberries and fills another with blueberries. Finally, he grabs a bag of miniature chocolate chips from the pantry and pours them into an identical bowl.

Nick chooses that moment to trudge into the room, still wiping the sleep from his eyes. It's like he smelled the food that's not yet cooking. "Morning fuckers…Annie," he says, nodding to where she's scrolling on her iPad across the room. "Cuz." He nods. "You sleep okay?"

I nod, giving him a one-armed hug as he takes the stool beside me. We chat while Rhett busies himself making three platters of pancakes. One plain, one with blueberries, and one chocolate chip. I can barely focus on Nick's chatter as I watch my *boyfriend* maneuver his way around the kitchen. It's still crazy to think of this thing between us as anything other than pretend. But this is real. He's mine for as long as I want him— or until he moves on.

Life is weird.

"Ladies first!" Rhett orders when Aiden creeps up behind him, trying to load his plate.

He hands me a real plate, rather than the disposable ones, which I wouldn't have minded eating off of at all. It's what Rave and I use at home. But he's trying to impress me, and it's cute. "Thanks," I say, taking it from his hand and serving myself two chocolate chip cakes with a dollop of whipped cream and a cherry, and douse it in all maple syrup. Finally, I sprinkle a light dusting of powdered sugar over the top. It's beautiful, and my mouth fills with saliva as I inhale the sweet aroma while making my way back to my seat.

Anika, on the other hand, fills a small bowl with the strawberries and blueberries, and cuts herself half a pancake with no syrup. Half. A . Pancake! Just one more thing about the girl to drive me batty.

"That's my cousin," Nick shouts, clapping me on the back. "She knows how to eat."

"*She's* going to give herself heart disease," the bitchy brunette snaps before taking her food out to the patio. I can't be more relieved to see her go. I don't know why she hates me so much, but I'm beginning to suspect she may have feelings for Rhett. The fact that they live together and work together...that they have more history than we'll ever have with each other...well, I can't say it doesn't make me feel some kind of jealous.

I don't like it.

Chapter 29

RHETT

MY DICK TWITCHES AS I WATCH STICK FORK A GIANT BLOB OF cream-covered pancake into her mouth. I shift in my seat. Giggling, she brings a napkin to her chin to swipe at the syrup that's leaking down her face. If we were alone, I might have licked it off myself.

I find it incredibly sexy, the way Korie lives her life without conforming to anyone else's expectations. She's a total badass at a sport that's very male-dominated. The girl wears a T-shirt and jeans better than most women do a cocktail dress. And here she is in a house full of men, stuffing her face full of sugary goodness, moaning and sighing with contentment at every bite, not giving a damn who's watching.

"Good morning, boys!" Rosa slips in like a ninja, getting to work on the disaster I just made. I feel bad. It looks like a damn batter bomb went off in here.

"Wait, I'll help—"

"No, ma'am," our housekeeper orders, lightly swatting

Korie's hand away from the mixing bowl she was about to pick up. "I've got this. You go enjoy yourself."

"I really don't mind…"

"Give it up, girl," Lyle says, laughing as he finally joins us at the table with a loaded plate. "Rosa has her own way of doing shit around here."

"Mr. Lyle is right. I do shit my way." Rosa winks at Korie as she piles the soiled dishes in her arms to let her know it's nothing personal. "I am very OCD."

With a little hesitation, Korie nods, sinking back down into her seat.

"Let's get out of here?" I suggest once she has all but licked her plate clean.

"Sure. Where're we going?"

"It's a surprise."

"Ugh," she scowls. "You and your damn surprises. You know how much I hate them."

"Well, you're gonna love this one," I say, guiding her up the winding staircase and back to my room to get changed. "Bring enough clothes for a few days."

"Watch your step." Alex, our charter captain, takes Korie's hand and helps her from the dinghy into the boat.

He's a few years older than me, tall, with a shaggy dirty-blond mullet and deep blue eyes. He dresses like he stepped right off the set of Gilligan's Island, with his floral button downs and sandals, but he's a cool guy. The band and I have sailed with him in the past, so I know that he's trustworthy and discreet. He's also one of the few private charters with access to some of the most beautiful protected islands off the California coast.

Before setting sail, Captain Alex gives us a quick tour of the upper deck of the Catamaran, introducing us first to our chef, Mal, a leggy brunette with kinky curls and tanned leathery skin. She's already busy preparing our dinner in the kitchen, located at the center of the ship. The scent of sizzling onions and garlic makes my stomach growl. I have no idea what she's cooking up, but it already smells delicious.

On the rear deck is a covered outdoor seating area with a square table at the center and benches on each side. At the front of the ship is a white leather sectional and tanning deck, where we meet his first mate, John.

John can't be but twenty at most. He's buff, dressed in a muscle shirt and khaki cargo shorts. His brown hair is clipped in a short fade, and his dark brown eyes are wide with wonderment. I'm used to people's initial reaction to meeting a celebrity, but it surprises me that Korie isn't giving him shit over being starstruck.

Alex then takes us back through the kitchen, where I'm again assaulted with the tantalizing aromas. We continue down a narrow stairway leading to our cabin. There's a small bathroom with a stand-up shower, toilet, and sink to the left, and a closet to the right. The rest of the room is largely taken up by a queen-sized bed made up with plush sea green linens and nautical-themed throw pillows. After depositing our weekend bags in the closet, we complete our tour with a quick view of the crew's cabin, consisting of four bunks and a bathroom of their own.

"Rhett, this is incredible." I watch her wide-eyed smile grow impossibly broader.

"Wait till you see our first stop," I tease, linking my fingers with hers to help keep her balance as the motor roars to life and the boat begins to pull away from the dock.

After nearly two hours on the water, John finally joins us on the deck with snorkeling gear in hand and a smile to rival that of the Cheshire Cat. The guy's a looker. I'll have to keep my eye on him. "Hey, guys. We're almost to Mystic Cove. I wanted to bring out your gear and go over a few things before we drop anchor."

"Snorkeling?" Korie shields her eyes, grinning up at me from where her head's been resting in my lap. "I've never been." After adjusting the top of her black bikini, she pops up, eager to hear what John has to say.

"Okay, so this is a private tour. There shouldn't be any overzealous fans or paparazzi lurking in the shadows. We have the island for three hours. After that, all bets are off."

"You *rented* an island!" Her nails dig into my knee, and she's literally bouncing with excitement.

I wrap an arm around her middle, pulling her body flush against mine. Her bare skin is warm and slick from the sunscreen I've had the pleasure of rubbing all over her. She smells of coconuts and wet dreams, and I have to cough to conceal a growl. "Yes," I mutter into her ear. "Pay attention."

After John has explained how to use the gear and the dos and don'ts of the island, he hands us each a packet of waiver forms, relinquishing them from any responsibility if we should be injured or worse by any marine wildlife or washed away in a riptide. Or a number of other hypotheticals equally as horrifying.

"This sounds serious." She looks up at me, tapping the back of her pen against the stack of forms. "You sure this is okay?"

I shake my head. "No...but if you want to swim with the seals and sea lions, it's mandatory."

Without another word, she scrawls her name across the

dotted line.

We drop anchor about thirty feet off the coast, where Stick and I don our wetsuits, flippers, and headgear, and drop into the cool, sparkling blue water.

"Do you hear that?" she asks, looking around anxiously before popping her mouthpiece in.

"Sea lions...look up on the rocks."

"Holy shit!" she garbles. Her eyes light up as she stares at me in awe through the mask, before turning her attention back to the cliffs at the dozens of sea mammals sprawled out in the hot sun.

"Come on." I dip my head toward the shore and take her hand in mine. Together we swim along the surface, squeezing each other's fingers and pointing when something cool turns up.

Schools of silver, yellow-finned fish swim right in front of us while thick, lime green seagrass blankets the reefs below.

"Look," I mumble, but I'm underwater with a mouth full of plastic, so it just sounds like gibberish. Either way, it gets her attention, and together we watch in wonderment as a large brown sea turtle lurks around in a patch of red kelp just beneath us. When he begins swimming up to the surface, I remember my GoPro camera and start snapping pictures.

Korie releases my hand, going out a few feet. She points to the turtle and then to herself and gives me a thumbs up. I swear I must take a hundred or more pictures of her swimming around with this turtle. With her flippers and long blonde hair floating in all directions, she looks like a mermaid. The entire encounter is surreal.

When our four-legged friend swims off, we pop up out of the water. "Rhettttt!" Stick squeals, panting as she yanks the snorkel from her mouth. "Did that really just happen?"

My heart is pounding something fierce, so I can only imagine the adrenaline rush she's experiencing having been close enough to touch it. "Fucking amazing."

"Thank you so much for this." I know that I would do just about anything to keep the look of pure joy on her face. I tug her closer and wrap an arm around her waist, treading water to keep us both afloat.

"It's funny because I feel like I'm the one who should be thanking you," I admit, brushing a wet clump of hair from in front of her eyes.

"Oh, yeah?" she asks. "Why's that?"

"Because when I'm with you I just...I don't know. I feel like me...like a real person."

Her lips start to dip into a frown, then she reaches out and twists my nipple through the wetsuit.

Holy fuck that hurt!

"That's cuz you *are* just a person, Rhett Taylor, even though you think you're something extraordinary." She pokes out her tongue, and I trap it between my teeth, before twining my own around it. We really get into it, licking and nibbling, then our fogged-up masks collide, and our first kiss in our private alcove ends in a fit of laughter.

"Let's go, brat. Time's a tickin'."

Chapter 30

KORIE

I'VE NEVER SEEN ANYTHING SO MAGICAL IN ALL MY LIFE. WHO knew Rhett could be spontaneous and romantic? Or how freaking hot he'd look in a sleek black wetsuit? Okay, so that's really no surprise; he'd look hot in a dang trash bag. But, hey, it's a definite perk!

More and more he's breaking down all the preconceived notions I had about who he is, and most importantly, teaching me who I truly am. I feel stronger and more confident, and probably the biggest surprise of all, less guarded. I trust him, and with my past and the walls I've built around my heart, that's huge. And just a bit frightening.

There's a perma-smile on my face as I watch him from behind the lens, swimming in circles with a pair of sea lions, clicking away like a proud mama, or fiancée...girlfriend... *whatever*.

He waves me over, and I shake my head. They're beautiful and all, but bigger than he is. I don't know if I'm feeling quite that adventurous. Rhett steeples his hands in front of his face, begging me to join, and again I refuse. Then that fucker tucks his fists beneath his arms and starts flapping like a chicken, leaving me with no choice but to go.

There are worse ways to die than being drowned by a two hundred fifty-pound sea lion, right? *Oh, God.*

Rhett extends his hand for mine once I finally locate my lady balls and swim over to join him. He pulls me close, and I have to admit that at first I'm terrified as the two wild animals begin to circle around me. They're checking me out. I can't help but wonder if they really are like dogs and can sense my fear.

What if they decide they don't like me? Would my prima donna country star rescue me, or save his own ass while the beasts snack on my carcass?

There's a tug on my hair, and my head jerks back. Then another. At first, I think Rhett's messing with me, and then I realize the smaller of the two brown-speckled sea lions is playing with my hair.

She's beautiful, with big round eyes and whiskers that remind me of a kitten. The little girl that still lives in me adopts this stray animal and names her Molly. If I could do so without being arrested, I'd bring her home to live with me forever. I swear she smiles at me every time she comes back to chomp at the blonde strands floating around my head. When she dives back down into the deep, dark water, I look over to Rhett, who at first I think is being mauled by the other one, but it turns out she's only trying to *hug* him. This could be the cutest thing I've ever seen.

He rubs the top of her head, and she presses her mouth to the front of his mask. The whole time, I'm taking pictures. They really are like little sea puppies. They bark, even while under the water, and they're desperate for attention. I half expect Bertha's tongue to come out and lick his face. *Yeah, I named his too.*

My heart soars when Molly returns, bringing with her three friends. As they get closer, they become clearer and it looks like she's wrangled up a few dolphins!

Giddy with excitement, I'm waving around, trying to get Rhett's attention, when they finally come close enough to see fully, and my delight is replaced by blind fear. My heart begins to pound deep in my chest. I hear it in my ears, drowning out every other sound. An ice-cold chill trickles down my spine as the beating grows louder. Forgetting my snorkel, I scream, "Shark!" and my mask begins to fill with water.

Let me just stop right here and tell you, Rhett is no fucking Prince Charming. I'm practically drowning myself trying to save his ass, and he's staring at me like I've lost my ever-loving mind. Maybe he doesn't see them or doesn't care, but I will live easier knowing I tried. I'm not sticking around to be eaten by a herd or whatever you call a group of fucking sharks.

Oh, and my new "puppies?" They're on my shit list too. What happened to protecting your owner? Man's best friend? Traitors. That's what they are. Molly, that bitch. She gained my trust then went to round up her friends and led them right to us!

I spit out the mouthpiece and throw off my mask, swimming for dear life. The whole time I'm swimming, my thoughts are racing. *Are they right behind me? Under me? Is Rhett coming?* Surely, he sees me haul-assing toward the shore and followed, right? It's what any sane person would do.

When I finally reach land, I crawl up the bank and fall to my back, panting and heaving for air. I'm flooded with relief when I see my boyfriend walking out of the ocean a few yards down the beach. That is until he comes close enough for me to see that the asshole is in hysterics.

"What the hell are you laughing at?" I sit up in the sand, still feeling dizzy and on the verge of a heart attack.

He can't stop laughing long enough to speak.

"Now I see why they make you sign all those damn waivers. Do you even realize how close we came to becoming shark food just now? What is the matter with you? Are you delirious?"

He plops down beside me, holding his chest. Still. Fucking. Laughing. "You—you should have seen yourself."

I cross my arms over my bent knees giving him a laser-sharp glare. I am wholly unamused.

"They were leopard sharks."

"Okay…"

"They don't bite. Friendly as can be."

Smoke billows from my ears as I climb on top of him, punching him repeatedly in the chest.

Laughing, he blocks his face with his forearms dodging my blows.

"You don't think you should have maybe warned me about friendly sharks? My entire life just flashed before my eyes, you ass!" I'm so angry and embarrassed, yet at the same time just relieved to still be alive.

Once he's endured enough of my abuse, he rolls us over, so his big body is smooshing mine. He takes my wrists into his hands, holding them down in the sand above my head.

I'm trapped, but I make no attempt to escape, as the warmth of his breath surrounds me, pulling me under his spell.

Baby blues irises stare deep into mine, and his teeth bite into his lip, doing a shit job of concealing a smirk.

"That was mean," I rasp, my chest still heaving, but no longer in fear.

"I'm sorry." He nudges my nose with the tip of his, and a swarm of butterflies flutter in my tummy. I can hardly remember to breathe when he's this close.

A drop of saltwater falls from his lashes to my lips and without hesitation, I lick it away. "Liar."

My captor shrugs before clearing his throat. His eyes become bedroom heavy and hooded with lust. Without another word, he dips down, running the tip of his tongue along the seam of my mouth. "I've wanted to taste these lips all day."

"Mmm," I moan, nipping back at his. "I've sort of alternated between wanting to do the same and the desire to kick you in the balls, myself."

"I'm glad you were able to refrain." He releases my wrists, clutching my chin in his thumb and forefinger. "I have every intention of busting a nut tonight, and that's not at all what I have in mind."

I snort at his blunt honesty, then squirm when he cups my breast through the thin rubbery material, the pad of his thumb brushing over the hardening bud. The echoes of barking seals and squawking seagulls fade into the distance as once again the thumping of my own racing heart rushes to the forefront. With the afternoon sun beating down on my face and the fire raging between the two of us, I'm feeling flushed and feverish. And horny. So fucking horny.

"God, I want you." My choked plea is rewarded with a ravenous kiss. We're all lips and tongues and teeth. His hands are cupping my face, then tangled in my hair—mine tracing the rippling muscles not at all concealed beneath the fabric of his wetsuit.

"That's impossible in these suits, but I'll make you feel good," he says, clasping the zipper at my neck and lowering it to where it stops at my navel. My pulse races at the promise of his skin on mine.

He slips inside my bikini top, palming my breast with a

wet, sand-covered hand. With a yelp, my back arches off the ground and my nails dig into his back. The intense friction is unlike anything I've experienced, a sensation so good it's nearly too much.

"Does it hurt?" he asks, careful not to be overly rough with me, his face constantly searching mine for a reaction.

I can't even speak I'm so lost in the sparks firing off inside of me, so I shake my head. The pleasure is now bordering pain, but still so exquisite, I'd rather die than ask him to stop.

Rhett seals his lips to mine, and I rake my fingers through his damp hair, pulling him impossibly closer. I've never felt more desperate for a man than I do for this one. Right here. Right now.

While still gently massaging my breast, he shifts forward, wedging a knee between my thighs, right where I need him most. Wantonly, I grind my swollen sex against him, riding this wave of ecstasy. Desire pools in my core. Every nerve ending in my body is rushing to the center, preparing for the inevitable rush.

His teeth clamp down on my nipple, and my limbs start to tremble. My entire body breaks out in a light sweat and I freefall—tumbling down an endless ravine. My vision fades to black, and the world falls into complete silence. For this brief moment in time, nothing at all exists but this feeling of euphoria. Immense relief floods my body, like a waterfall bursting over a cliff. Wave after wave of pleasure shoots through me, slowly fading to a steady pulse.

When I open my eyes, I find him gazing wordlessly down at my face. His ravenous blue orbs slowly peruse my body, his lower lip gripped between his teeth.

I reach out to touch the side of his face, and he nuzzles into my hand before guiding my fingers to his lips and kissing the tips.

"We have to go," Rhett says with a regretful sigh. He pulls me tightly to his chest, pressing his lips to my forehead. "Captain's been blowing the horn for at least five minutes."

Chapter 31

RHETT

OUR RETURN TO THE SHIP IS FAIRLY UNEVENTFUL. KORI REFUSES to put her snorkel back on or to even look below the water's surface. We don't really have time to lollygag anyway, if we're going to get out of here before tourists start arriving on other charters.

We take turns showering off the sand and dressing for dinner. I opt for a white linen button down, sleeves rolled to my elbows, and teal cotton shorts. I spritz a little sea salt spray in my hair and muss it with my fingers before slipping into a pair of leather Sperrys and taking myself above deck to wait for my date.

Korie surprises me, choosing one of the dresses Anika picked out for her. It's emerald green, almost identical to the shade of her irises. The fabric is light and silky, brushing against the peaks of her breasts whenever she moves. It's tied at the neck, leaving her sun-kissed shoulders bare. Her hair is loose, in beach waves stopping just above the curve of her ass. Her skin is already noticeably bronzed, the apples of her cheeks tinged pink from the sun. One look and my heart leaps to my throat. *I'm gone.*

"Can we skip right to dessert?" I ask, rising from the couch to meet her when she steps out onto the deck. I bury my nose in the curve of her neck, inhaling the scent of coconuts and roses.

Lovely, I'm sporting a semi already and the night's only just begun. But I've pretty much been at half-mast since getting her off on the beach earlier.

She squirms in my hold as I nip at her collarbone, throwing her head back, inviting me to feast upon her throat. I am all too happy to oblige. With my hands fisted in her hair, I trail my tongue in the dip between her breasts, dragging my lower lip along the center of her throat. I nip playfully at her chin, then nibble on her pouty lips. I want to taste every inch of her smooth skin.

Her hands link behind my neck, fingers playing in the short hair at my nape, causing a chill to travel down my spine. When the first sultry notes to "Senorita" by Shawn Mendes and Camila Cabello float through the overhead speakers, she becomes a livewire in my arms, her hips swaying in perfect time with the beat. Memories of dancing around the fire at camp come flooding back.

I turn her in my arms so her back is to my front, the way we were that night. Her ass rolls against my erection in a deliberate tease. My hands trace the curves of her body as she shimmies down low before working her way back up, her movements fluid as the music travels through her.

I take her hands in mine, guiding them above her head to rest on my shoulders and lightly brush the sensitive skin from the inside of her wrists to beneath her arms with my knuckles.

Her body tenses, and I watch her breasts rise and fall with each heavy intake of breath. The tips of her fingers trail down the center of her chest, finding mine fisted in the fabric at her waist. She laces her fingers with mine and nuzzles into me. I place a kiss at her temple before swinging her out and reeling her back in. When her body slams back into mine, my lips find the delicate skin behind her ear. I pepper soft kisses then bite down gently on her lobe with a growl.

The blonde beauty melts in my arms, a soft moan barely heard above the music floating from her lips as she presses her ass into my hips.

Desire radiates between us like a living, breathing thing, heating my blood, stifling my breathing.

"Sorry to interrupt," Mal says, stepping through the sliding glass doors connecting the front deck to the kitchen with a silver-domed tray in hand. John follows closely behind with an identical tray balanced on one hand and a bottle of champagne on ice in the other. "Just wanted to bring your dinner out before it gets cold." She blushes, obviously uncomfortable intruding on our intimate moment. She sets it on the table in front of the couch, then lifts the lid on the first tray. "To start we have a creamy lobster bisque." She lifts the other. "And homemade French bread with butter."

"Oh, this looks amazing," Korie says, running her hands over the front of her dress to smooth it back into place as she takes her seat. Her chest is red and splotchy. She's visibly flustered, and that observation sends a jolt right to my dick. *As if Ollie needs any more encouragement.* "Thank you, Mal," she says, lifting her hair over one shoulder and lightly fanning her neck with the other hand.

"You're welcome. We'll be out in about thirty minutes with the main course."

"Perfect. Thank you." I nod to both Mal and John, who swiftly disappear back the way they came. I've requested complete privacy for the two of us tonight. They'll be making themselves scarce unless called upon.

"Perrier-Jouët?" I ask, removing the foil from the top of the bottle.

"Never had it. I'm more of a mixed drinks girl, but I'm willing to give it a try." She jumps back when the cork pops, probably anticipating a shower like she's seen on television. Laughing, I bring her glass under the bottle, which is lightly overflowing with bubbles, and fill her champagne flute before filling my own.

"Mmm," she moans, dabbing her cloth napkin to catch the soup that stayed stuck to her lips. "Jesus…this is delicious."

I fall back in my seat, exhaling dramatically with the back of my hand pressed to my forehead. "So, you do eat more than ice cream and candy."

The glare she aims at me from across the table is lethal. "Don't make fun of my sweet tooth, mister."

"Oh, I'm fairly certain you have more than one." I'm not kidding. I had to call Raven to find out what to feed her that wasn't comprised of primarily sugar. I was assured that seafood and carbs were a relatively safe bet.

She takes a sip of champagne, holding it briefly in her mouth before swallowing it down with a smile and a nod of approval.

"To falling in love," I say, holding my glass up to hers.

She purses her lips, running the champagne flute back and forth beneath her nose. "To protecting our hearts," she counters, tapping the rim of her glass to mine.

We each drink to our toasts, that I'm fairly certain just canceled each other out, then dive into our food.

She's right. The soup is divine—rich and creamy with the perfect blend of spices. "Thought you liked it?" I ask when I've drained my bowl and find Stick leaned back with her arms crossed watching me—her own still half full.

"Oh, I did." She sends me a coy smile. "Leaving room for dessert." She pats her flat stomach.

"Of course."

Our next course arrives as soon as I set my spoon down—an impressive array of oysters on the half shell and a side dish of grilled asparagus.

"Bon appétit!" Mal chimes with a wave of her hand, already on her way back to the kitchen.

Stick's brows knit as she examines the spread. "Not a fan of oysters?" I ask, fully prepared to have it taken back and something else brought in its place.

She scrapes her lower lip through her teeth. "I love oysters, actually." Scowling, she picks up an asparagus with two fingers and dangles it over her plate. "But what the hell is this green, phallic looking thing?"

I choke. "It's asparagus, and delicious. And my phallus is nothing like that."

After placing the object of her revulsion back on the plate, she covers it with a napkin and shudders. "I don't eat green things."

"What? Are you five?"

"Pretty sure you know that I'm not, considering you're feeding me a meal of aphrodisiacs." She narrows her seductive eyes my way.

"Oh, you caught that, huh?" I raise a brow, not even trying to deny it.

Stick reaches forward, taking a shell into her palm and loosening the meat with a cocktail fork. She squeezes a lemon wedge, dripping the juice over the top, and then adds a little spoon of mignonette sauce. Bringing the wide end of the shell to her lips, she makes a show of tipping her head back and slurping the oyster into her mouth. I watch with rapt fascination, unsure of why I'm so eager to learn whether she swallows it whole or savors the natural flavors. She bites down, chewing once...twice. Then her head rolls back in pure ecstasy, and she purrs her delight.

I gulp hard, reaching below the table to adjust my now rock-hard cock. I feel like I'm back in high school, with no control over myself. She's just given a whole new meaning to the term food porn.

Following her lead, I pick up an asparagus spear and roll the head around my tongue before sucking it into my mouth. Moaning dramatically, I chew it to a pulp and swallow. She's not the only one who can put on a performance.

The look of disgust on Stick's face is worth the humiliation I should feel over that erotic spectacle. If I were one inclined to feel embarrassment, that is.

"If sexy is what you're going for, Hollywood, you're failing miserably."

I shrug. "There's still time to redeem myself," I say with a wink, leaning forward to prepare my own oyster.

Korie has two more, leaving the rest of the dozen for me, again claiming she doesn't want to spoil her dessert. Once I've devoured the remainder of our meal, Mal returns one last time, with a platter of chocolate-covered strawberries and a hot fudge brownie sundae for my girl.

"You didn't disappoint, Hollywood," she announces, bringing the first loaded spoon of ice cream to her mouth. "Well," she corrects, talking with her mouth full. "Besides the asparagus."

While she satisfies her sweet *teeth*, I refill our glasses and sip on champagne.

"Dance with me?" she asks, pushing the other half of her dessert away. She rises to her feet, wobbling a little. She steadies herself by holding on to the table and slipping out of her shoes.

I remove mine, too, not wanting to accidently smash her toes. Then with her hand in mine, I lead the way to our makeshift dance floor.

The song is slow—"Don't Close Your Eyes" by Keith Whitley. I pull her close, resting one hand just above the curve of her ass and splaying the other across her bare back. She buries her face in my shoulder, her warm, alcohol-soaked breath completely overwhelming my senses—making me wild with want. We move in rhythmic circles, swaying in time to the music, both caught up in the emotion of the lyrics. In the beauty of the setting sun. In the magic of this moment.

Chapter 32

KORIE

NO FEELING COMPARES TO THAT OF BEING WRAPPED UP IN THIS man's arms. There's nothing more exhilarating or more frightening than the way my body responds to his. How my breathing suddenly quickens and my blood heats. The way my skin tingles at the slightest brush of our skin.

The familiar scent of his spicy cologne sends my pulse racing as I hug him close.

It's a night fit for the movies—fancy food, bubbly drinks, and romantic music, the sky lit up with orange and purple rays as the sun sinks down over the horizon. My inhibitions are lowered, thanks to the three glasses of champagne I had with dinner, allowing me the freedom to truly revel in this moment. To feel every exquisite touch without the constant worry over what's to come.

I forget to be cautious. Forget all the reasons this is a terrible idea. I forget the pain my father caused, the games, and Rhett's sordid past. I forget everything but the way I feel right here. Right now. The tickling of butterflies fluttering in my stomach. The rush of heat spreading through my veins. The lump of emotion I can't seem to dislodge from my throat.

Rhett's hands lift to cup my face, forcing my eyes from the ocean to his. I swear my heart stops beating when I see the way he's looking at me—with hunger, with adoration…with *more*. His fingers massage behind my ears while his thumbs delicately brush my cheeks. I swallow hard as a wave of emotion washes over me.

He brings my mouth to his, brushing his lips lightly over my own. Then his tongue slips between them, dancing with mine in a slow and sensual rhythm. I'm not sure if it's the champagne clouding my judgment or the romantic atmosphere making me swoon, but this kiss somehow feels more intimate—more meaningful—than any other thus far.

He pulls away, swiping the back of his hand over his mouth, staring at me with a stunned look on his face.

Guess I'm not the only one feeling confused and utterly overwhelmed.

"Korie, I—" He starts to speak then seems to think better of it, giving his head a slight shake.

"Yeah?" I whisper, wanting and also maybe not *really* wanting him to finish whatever it is that he was about to say.

He clears his throat, "I, uh. I need a drink."

With a nod, I follow him back to the table, where we feed each other chocolate-covered strawberries and finish off another bottle of champagne.

I'm now well past tipsy and feeling brave enough to continue our little game. "So," I slur, "What's with you and Anika?"

"What do you mean?" he asks.

"Well, it's obvious she doesn't like me, and I think it's maybe because she has feelings for you. I was just wondering if you two ever dated or..." I trail off, mumbling the end of my question, because even three sheets to the wind, I feel uncomfortable asking it. "If you've *slept* together?"

His Adam's apple bobs with a hard swallow, and a pit forms in my stomach, because his reaction gives me the feeling I'm not going to like his answer. "We're um—we're just friends. Never been anything more."

I nod, feeling more relief than I care to admit.

"There aren't many people I can trust. She's one of the few." He scrubs a hand over his chin. "And I'm sure she doesn't dislike you. Anika is just very protective of the band. She'll warm up eventually."

"Fair enough," I say, feeling satisfied with that answer. "Do you want to ask me anything?"

"Nah. I'm saving mine up for something special. You go ahead."

My face flames crimson before the burning question has even passed my lips. "Will you let me watch you—umm... *pleasure* yourself?"

Oh, my God. Did I really just ask him that? Drunk Korie needs a fucking muzzle.

A cocky smile curls his lip. Without a word, he bunches the tails of his shirt around his waist and unfastens his shorts. My mouth salivates as I watch him lower them along with his boxer briefs, and his thick cock springs free.

I'm in a drunken, trancelike state as I watch his strong hand fist the base of his erection and slowly begin to slide up and down in a twisting motion. "This what you want?" His raspy tone has me clenching my thighs together and breathing heavy.

With a throat that feels as if it's been brushed with sandpaper, I nod. "God, yes. Just like that."

Eyes fixed on mine, he continues to stroke himself. My stare volleys between the massive cock thickening in his hand

and his dilated pupils and flushed cheeks. His sexy grunts and thrusting hips have me wet with desire.

When his face tenses, I know it means he's close. Suddenly there's nothing I want more than to wrap my lips around that glorious appendage. To be the one responsible for the sexy little sounds he's making.

"Rhett," I whimper, dropping to my knees and crawling between his parted legs. I rest one hand on his thigh and the other replaces his. When I lower my head to take him into my mouth, he growls his approval. His hands fist my hair as he drives into my mouth hard and fast. I pump my fist at the base to match his stride.

Hollowing out my cheeks, I suck him off like a woman starved and searching for sustenance.

When his cock spasms in my mouth, I become ravenous for it. Bobbing my head, I take his full length, base to tip, and suck him harder, while reaching between my own legs to ease the throbbing ache. With the pads of my first two fingers, I massage my clit, coming almost instantly. My mouth constricts with the force of my orgasm, compelling his release to follow. A stream of warm cum shoots to the back of my throat and greedily I drink every drop.

A pained cry jars me from a dead sleep, and I'm not sure whether I actually heard the agonizing sound or possibly dreamed it. It takes a moment for me to remember where I am, why the room is swaying, and the mattress feels like it's been carved from stone. This isn't my bed. Rhett's scent lingers on the pillow beside me. Along with the pungent smell of stale alcohol floating in the air, it's a recipe for disaster.

I reach for him on the other side of the bed, but come up with nothing more than a fistful of sheets and blankets.

The loud retching sound coming from the direction of the closet-sized bathroom tells me where I can find him.

"You okay?" I yell from where I lay on the bed, afraid to get up and have to fight him for the bathroom. All I get in return is a series of groans followed by more vomit. He sounds pitiful. He must've drunk more than I thought, because I've never known him to have a hangover before.

After this goes on for at least an hour, I decide I should probably check on him. Apart from a little dizziness, I make it to the bathroom just fine. "Rhett?" I whisper, rapping my knuckle lightly on the door. "Hey...I'm coming in."

When he doesn't respond, I shove the door open with my hip and find him bent over the toilet, his hair wet with sweat and sticking to his forehead. I lift the front of my tee to shield my nose, the odor in the tiny room rancid, like spoiled milk.

With extreme effort, he turns to face me. He's pale and also a little green. One look tells me this is more than a hangover.

"You look like hell."

He gives me a thumbs up before clutching the seat in both hands and dry heaving into the bowl, his body convulsing as it rejects everything and anything.

I wet a washcloth in the sink and wipe down his face and his neck like my mom used to when I had a virus. It always made me feel a little less revolting. "Thanks," he rasps, his voice weak and shredded.

"Don't mention it." I wave him off like it's no big deal, even though I should win the best girlfriend award ever for enduring this torture. I slink down, making myself as comfortable as I can beside him on the floor.

"You—you don't have to stay." He tries to wave me away before he's hit with another bout of heaving.

"I'm not leaving you alone," I insist, rubbing a hand in slow circles on his back.

We spend hours on that smelly bathroom floor, him teetering on the edge of death and me trying not to become sick myself. Not that I think he's contagious—I know food poisoning when I see it—but because it's just fucking gross. I don't know how we ate the same thing and I managed to escape the plague, but I'm counting my blessings, believe me. Once he's finally gone half an hour without gagging, I manage to get him into the shower and cleaned up.

"Here." I hand him a towel to dry off. "Your bag is on the bed. Go get dressed and lie down. I'll phone up to the kitchen and have someone bring you a large bowl in case it comes back. Then you and I are gonna get some much-needed sleep!" I feel like I haven't slept in weeks. Tired from such a long day yesterday, sluggish from an evening of too much drinking, and exhausted from playing nurse all night.

"I'm so sorry, Stick. This wasn't at all how I'd planned to spend our weekend together. It was supposed to be fun and romantic." He shrugs, wrapping the towel around his waist. "You were supposed to fall in love with me."

I snort at his boyish grin and shake my head. "How sexy have those oysters got you feeling now, Casanova?"

"Probably not my best idea."

"Meh," I shrug. "I've come to expect it by now."

Chapter 33

KORIE

"Hello, skate fans, and welcome to Cottonwood, Mississippi! We're thrilled you've come out to celebrate our first ever Chicks with Tricks, females-only skate park competition."

My skin buzzes when the one-and-only Melanie Binx addresses the crowd. It's been a hot minute since my last competition, and I'd almost forgotten how much I thrive on this feeling. The adrenaline has me bouncing in my shoes. I glance over to my section, where Raven, my mom, and my cousin Abby Jane, who's actually from Cottonwood, are right behind the barricade, ready to cheer me on. I'm trying not to dwell on the fact that Rhett isn't here. The band has to perform at some festival in Santa Monica tonight. It sucks, but it is what it is. I can't expect him to drop everything for me.

Today's competition is being judged on overall impression. It's broken into four heats of six skaters each. The top three from each heat will compete in two heats of six women this afternoon, and the top three skaters from each of those will make it to the final, which takes place tomorrow morning. In addition to prize money, placing also secures a sponsorship from Vortex energy drinks and an invitation to the Vortex Energy Pro Series.

That's the real prize. It's an international tour that would put me in front of all the right people. If I can earn a spot on the tour and skate well, *and* this publicity thing with Rhett really works out, I'll have my shot. No pressure or anything.

"Drawing third in the lineup in our first heat of the day, we have Korie Potter. At twenty-one, she's the second oldest competitor here today." When I hear my name, I stop daydreaming and pay attention to the announcers.

"Isn't she the one dating that country singer. What's his name? Ryan, Rex, Reese—"

"Rhett. It's Rhett Taylor," Melanie supplies, helping her cohost, Duncan, out.

"Jesus, they make me sound ancient," I grumble to no one in particular. The competition just keeps getting younger and younger, with an average age of only fourteen.

"Don't let them get to you," Yoko, the ten-year-old prodigy from Japan, offers. "They act like I'm still in diapers."

She's so tiny and cute, but I don't dare treat her as anything less than an equal. She skates with power and a finesse unlike anyone else out here, and has a damn good shot at winning not only this heat, but the entire competition.

"Good luck out there today."

"Thanks," she says, snapping her helmet beneath her chin as she prepares to drop into the bowl for her run. "Same to you."

The crowd goes wild when little Yoko lands a freaking frontside 540 at the buzzer. That full turn and a half on the board makes the 360 I've been working so hard on look like child's play.

I congratulate her when she passes by. She's positively beaming with pride, as she should be. Not many female skaters have that trick in their arsenal, and I'll have to take comfort in that as the next skater, Rylie Jean, wraps up her first run, signaling the start of my own.

I pop my ear buds in to drown out the noise. Music's always been instrumental in helping me find my flow. I start off with a nose grind and follow it up with a boardslide along the rail. I keep my first run relatively safe, putting in as many technical tricks as I can, but nothing I'm not confident won't land me on my ass. I'll pull out the big guns in my third and final run. Forty seconds passes by in a flash, and with adrenaline bursting through my veins, I'm on my way out to await my next turn.

Rhett: So proud of you!

Me: Thanks...but how are you watching?

My eyes wander to my section, selfishly hoping that somehow the concert got canceled and he managed to make it out here after all.

Rhett: Raven went live on your Instagram.

Me: Oh.

Poop!

Rhett: btw. You look hot.

Me: Phew! Thank God.

Rhett: Prettiest girl out there.

I can't help but blush down at the phone in my hand.

Me: Thanks.

In a huge stroke of luck, two of the three girls after me can't manage to stay on their boards, and I'm officially in third place after the first round.

Our second run starts immediately. One by one, we drop in and do our best to excite the judges. I repeat some of the same tricks from my first attempt, giving them more air and throw in a backside kick flip at the end.

A text alert chimes in my ear just as I'm climbing out of the bowl.

Rhett: I'd hit it.

Me: Shouldn't you be getting ready to perform?

Rhett: Gonna finish watching porn first.

Me: Oh, does this turn you on?

Rhett: Everything you do turns me on.

Me: So smooth.

With bated breath, I watch my competition slay some of the toughest tricks in the sport, inwardly cheering each time one of them falls off because it means I'm that much closer to achieving this crazy dream of mine.

On my third run, I really turn up the heat. If they're judging on overall impression, I'm going to leave them with the best I've got. This time, I begin with my 360, which increases my difficulty level because of the risky landing. The stars align and I land it flawlessly, then pretty much nail the rest of my run.

Rhett: I just splooged.

When I hear my mom and Raven screaming at the top of their lungs, I steal a glance over to the leader board, where I've now jumped into second place.

Me: I think I did too.

Ilsa, a seventeen-year-old badass from Russia, knocks me back into third, but I can't even be mad about it because I've advanced to the evening round.

For the next few hours, I scope out the competition, plotting my runs for the semifinals. My plan is very similar to the way I ran my earlier rounds, but with a few new tricks thrown in to show variety.

This time I draw first in the second heat. It gives me a little more time to observe, but also ample time for my nerves to go haywire.

Rhett: About to hit the stage. Just wanted to wish you the best of luck. Not that you need it. No matter what happens, just remember, you're still pretty.

Me: Dude, I can't even with you.

Rhett: Aren't you going to tell me how pretty I am?

Me: No.

Rhett: *gasp*

Me: I don't want to make your head any bigger.

Rhett: Too late. It's already straining against my zipper.

Me: Oh my God. Go away.

Rhett: Seriously though. Deep breaths. Don't be nervous. Just picture me naked. You're going to kick ass. I'll check in after the show.

Me: Knock 'em dead.

Before long, the first heat is over, and I'm up. I pop my ear buds in, take in a deep cleansing breath, crack my knuckles, and I'm off. Halfway through my run, I misjudge the landing on a kick flip and lose my board, ending my turn. On a simple fucking trick that I land every damn day.

Raven: Shake it off. You have two more chances to make up for it.

I'm so pissed with myself that I can't even respond. I'm just so thankful Rhett was on stage and didn't see me fall. At the end of the first round, I'm one of only two who didn't complete their runs and sitting in fourth place.

Knowing I need to make up for that last ride in a big way, I change things up and start off with the exact kick flip that tripped me up, to prove to the judges that I can land it. I follow it up with a nose grind and bring that straight into a huge eggplant invert.

When the buzzer sounds, I exit the bowl feeling really fucking good about myself.

With my confidence restored and one round to go, I observe the rest of the girls from the sidelines, some having killer runs and others crumbling under the pressure.

At the start of the final run, I'm still in fourth. My chance at tomorrow's final comes down to this. I have literally everything to lose. It's time to go big or go home, and I'm sure as shit not ready to go home.

Once again, I begin with a huge 360. It's my most difficult skill, and thankfully I land it without issue. The adrenaline of making that trick fuels me through the rest of the run with more speed and air than I've had in any other so far today. When I climb out of that bowl, I know that whatever happens, I gave it my absolute best.

Chapter 34

RHETT

"OH MY GOD, WHAT THE HELL ARE YOU GUYS DOING HERE?"
"Shhh." Nick cups his palm over Raven's mouth. "We're incognito."

Her dark eyes take in our latest attempt at hiding in plain sight. We're all wearing various ridiculous tees from Hot Topic, cargo shorts, Vans, ball caps, and of course, can't go anywhere without the sunglasses.

"Hey, Aunt DeeDee." Nicholas wraps the petite blonde in his arms. "Been a while."

DeeDee Potter assesses me from over her nephew's shoulder. "It's so good to see you, Nicky." Her hands comb through his hair in a motherly gesture.

After a few minutes of small talk, he introduces my future mother-in-law to Aiden and Lyle, and then finally to me.

"Rhett Taylor." She smiles, but it's a smile that undeniably doesn't reach her eyes. To say the least, she is not impressed. I've got my work cut out for me with this one. "I've heard so much about you."

"Likewise," I say, shaking her hand, and then lifting it to my lips where I place a light kiss. "Big fan of your work," I add, eying Korie in the lineup with a waggle of my brows.

"Dude…" Lyle groans, shaking his head, and for a moment he has me thinking that maybe it was a mistake, and my little attempt at humor is going to backfire—until DeeDee spits out a laugh.

See, I've got this. I'm so fucking charming. Women can't resist me. I could win Momma Potter over in my sleep.

"Ahem." She winds down, clearing her throat. "Yeah, well, she's definitely the best thing to ever happen to me." Her fingers tighten around mine. "So, don't destroy her." She pulls her hand back to her side, her piece said.

I swallow hard and nod. "Wouldn't dream of it, ma'am."

Thankfully, the announcer's voice interrupts our awkward exchange, introducing the six girls who are competing in the Chicks with Tricks final this morning.

The guys and I took the red-eye to get here because I really wanted to surprise Stick. My pulse escalates when I take out my phone to send her a message. I've been looking forward to her reaction since we decided to come last night.

Me: You're looking especially beautiful this morning.

Stick: You're so full of shit. I haven't even had my first run yet, so I know you can't see me.

Me: I'm especially fond of the way that white fitted tank hugs my favorite girls like a second skin.

She looks down at her chest then jerks her head up and scours the crowd. When her eyes meet mine, I *feel* the weight of her smile in the center of my chest.

Stick: You came!

Me: All that porn yesterday made me really fucking horny. What time's this thing over with?

Stick: Stop it. I can't think of sex right now. I have to skate.

Me: Fine. You skate. I'll think of sex.

She shakes her head, shoving the phone into her back pocket to give her undivided attention to the announcers. She drew fifth out of six. Not too shabby.

From the moment the buzzer sounds, everything happens so fast. One girl after the next drops in, all with the same goal: to make their best impression in under forty seconds. It's absolute insanity.

I haven't ever felt stage fright as strong as the nerves that cripple me when Korie takes her run. I can't move. I'm not even sure I'm breathing when she takes off, flipping upside down and balancing on one hand at the top of the ramp.

I must make a panicked sound because her mom chuckles. "She's got this, just watch."

She follows that up with a few smaller tricks, things I've watched her do at the park. Things that don't make my heart feel like it's hurdling right out of my fucking chest. Then just before her turn ends, she gets massive air, spinning around in a complete circle before landing on her board and pumping a fist into the air.

"Yeah!" I shout, jumping up and down. "That's my girl!"

"Rad, right?" Raven slaps my shoulder before throwing her arms around DeeDee's neck. "That's got to be her best run yet."

Once the last girl has finished her turn, the leader board finally appears.

"What?" I shout when Korie's name comes up in second. "Bullshit! Are they serious?"

"Shhh," Raven hisses, looking around. "Stop it. This isn't a fucking football game. There's no heckling the refs."

I bite my tongue, not wanting to get thrown out, and decide to send her a message to cheer her up...you know, just in case she's feeling as slighted as I am on her behalf.

Me: You're still the prettiest.

Stick: Thank you.

Me: That was scary.

Stick: That was everything!

Me: You're kind of a badass.

Stick: That's what I've been telling you...

At the start of the next run, she shoves her phone back into her pocket, keeping her eyes on the competition. She's all business.

"How old is that little girl?" I ask, indignant, when a kid who can't be more than sixty pounds soaking wet soars into the air.

"She's ten...holds the record for youngest female competitor," Korie's cousin, AJ, answers.

It's so different being here and watching this all go down live. It's more real. More exciting. And more dangerous. "Yeah, well. Korie better not get any ideas with our kids. This is giving me heart palpitations."

"Such a puss—" Lyle starts, stopping dry when DeeDee glares her momma eyes his way.

"She's up," Raven announces, silencing our group.

My damn heart climbs into my throat when Stick soars through the air, doing some fancy flip trick. She grinds her board the length of the rail and transitions right into a nose grind at the top of the wall. On the way down, she loses her balance, skidding on her back in one direction while her board roles in the other.

"Oh...she's pissed," I mutter when I see the puckered look on her face as she exits to the side wall.

Stick: Don't.

Her threat comes before I even have the chance to get my phone out from my pocket.

Me: I wasn't gonna say anything. But since you brought it up...still so pretty.

I'm not positive, but I think I catch a glimpse of a smirk before she darkens the screen and readies herself for round three.

At the start of the final run, she's dropped into third. All she has to do is at least maintain her current position, and she's in.

Me: No matter what happens...

Stick: Don't you dare.

Me: Just fuckin' with ya. I'd like to ask a question though.

Stick: Now?

Me: Now. It's of the utmost importance.

Stick: You're such a pain in my ass. What?

Me: Do you love me yet?

Stick: No.

Me: Not even a little?

Stick: A little less no than the last time you asked. Now I have to go.

Me: Knock 'em dead, beautiful.

She looks up from her phone, grinning ear to ear, then scratches her temple with her left middle finger before kissing her fingertips and blowing it my way.

Yeah. She's totally in denial about this whole love thing.

All of the girls really bring it in the final round. I feel bad for the little bitty one when she has a huge fall on her first trick, but she's been holding tight to first, so I'm ashamed to admit I'm also a little relieved.

"That's my baby!" I shout when Korie wraps up an amazing run. Our whole little group is jumping and screaming. The girls have tears lining their cheeks, and the guys' fists all pumping in the air. The official results haven't been announced, and there's still one girl currently in the middle of a run, but there's no way she's not ending up on that podium after what I just witnessed.

Korie climbs out of the bowl and rushes straight to our little cheering section, throwing her arms around my neck. I lift her into the air, burying my face in her sweaty hair. "I'm so fucking proud of you, Stick." I feel her nod, but she's so filled with emotion, she just squeezes me tighter. "No matter what happens..."

"Oh, for fuck's sake," she pants, pulling back to make sure I see her eyes roll back in her head. "Pretty doesn't win medals."

"Maybe not," I admit, watching the final scores pop up on the leader board over her shoulder, "but second place sure as fuck does!"

"What?" She whips around, turning to see for herself, and that's when her tears come. "We did it…Oh my God, Rhett. We're doing it!"

"*You* did it!"

Almost immediately after the winners are announced, a reporter is in her face with a camera. "Ms. Potter, you've just secured your spot in the Vortex Energy Pro Series. How are you feeling right now?"

She sniffs, clearing her throat. "So happy. Amazing!"

"I bet. You were one of the wildcards of this competition. I think it's safe to say you took us all by surprise. What made you decide to get back into the fold?"

"This guy right here," she says, reaching for my arm behind the barricade. "My fiancé is a huge believer in chasing your dreams."

"Rhett Taylor," the reporter croons, moving the mic to my mouth. "How are you feeling right now?"

"I'm just really fucking proud. She's amazing."

"That she is," she agrees. "We'll see you on the podium, Ms. Potter."

Chapter 35

KORIE

AFTER THE MEDALS CEREMONY, I RUSH BACK TO THE HOTEL
room to get cleaned up. I don a pair of fresh skinny jeans and
black fitted tee with black and white chucks.

"You're wearing *that*?" AJ asks, clearly appalled. I mean, the
girl has her nerve judging anyone, with her rainbow-colored
hair and black leather bondage dress. Don't know where the
hell she thinks we're headed, but I was under the impression we
were going out for beer and pizza. I think I look fine.

"Uhhh, yes?" Standing in front of the full-length mirror, I
rotate side to side, trying to decide what's so wrong with this
outfit.

"No offense, cuz." She wanders to my suitcase and starts
rifling through it. "But tonight is the last night with your hot
as fuck celebrity boyfriend for who knows how long?" She pulls
out a short, red, strapless dress—one of Anika's purchases—
and tosses it my way. "Leave the man something worth
remembering, huh?" She waggles her brows.

"How'd that get in my bag?"

"You're welcome," Raven pipes in, with the straps to a pair of black heels hooked around her pointer finger, another *gift* from Rhett's manager.

"For heaven's sake, child. Listen to your friends." I narrow my eyes at my mother. She always wished I'd let her dress me up like a little china doll. Of course she'd side with the fashion police. "At least if you get caught off-guard by the paparazzi, you'll look decent."

"I'd just like you all to know, I'm feeling hella judged right now."

But it is three against one, so I point an angry finger at each of them before moseying my ass into the bathroom. I remove my comfy clothes and proceed to stuff myself into the red sausage casing.

"It feels like my ass cheeks are hanging out," I gripe, tugging it down as I wobble back into the firing squad feeling like a total imposter.

"Just don't bend over," Abby Jane says, circling around me like she's inspecting a classic car she's considering for purchase. "You'll be fine."

"Hot dayum," Raven whistles. "Who are you and what have you done with my drab friend?"

"Let's go," I grumble, grabbing my phone from the night stand. "We're gonna be late."

Raven comes at me twisting up a tube of lipstick in her hand. I throw my palms into the air, backing away like an animal bracing itself for attack.

"Don't push it," I warn. *Dude, I will fuck her up. That lipstick will look awesome shoved up her—*

"Just a little?" She steeples her hands in front of her face, hanging her lip. "You're already wearing the dress and shoes.

Might as well go all the way."

When I find myself literally backed into a corner, I finally concede to mascara, eyeliner, and a nude gloss. "Now if y'all are done playing dress up, I haven't eaten all day and I'm freaking starving."

"Wait. Just one more thing." Mom shoves the three of us together, pulling out her phone for a photo op. "Look at my girls." She brings her fingers to her lips, her eyes shining. "You look like Charlie's Angels." Pretty sure we look more like Charlie's Hookers, but I keep that comment to myself.

Mom, Raven, and I ride with Abby Jane in her car to some local pizza joint called Vinney's. AJ's husband, Brock, called ahead and secured their private party room, so we'll be able to enjoy our dinner with the rock stars in peace.

Vinney's is a quaint restaurant, a little neglected on the outside with cracked paint and whatnot, but the inside is charming, with vintage wood tables and chairs. The chandeliers dangling over said tables are designed in the shape of wine bottles and cheese graters.

Like I said, adorable.

Small it may be, but the place is packed, a true testament to how good the food must be. But the huge crowd instantly has me on guard, hoping like hell no one recognizes me.

"Right this way," the hostess says, when she spots Abby Jane.

I'm relieved not to have to announce our party aloud. One person catching wind of Rhett's name could turn this evening into complete chaos.

She leads us down a little hall, past the bathrooms, to a closed off area. "Make yourselves comfortable. We've laid out some chips and salsa and cheese sticks with marinara to get you started while waiting for the rest of your party to arrive. A server will be with you all shortly."

"Thanks so much, Trudy," AJ says, giving the pretty redhead a hug. "We really appreciate it."

We aren't there long when Rhett and the guys are brought in through a back entrance, completely bypassing the throngs of people out front. My heartrate escalates the minute he steps into the room, my body instantly aware of his presence.

Heavenly mother of all that is holy, he looks divine, clad in a pair of dark, distressed jeans and two-toned blue plaid button down, cuffed at the elbows. Just the front of his shirt is tucked in behind a thick brown leather belt. The toes of his matching cowboy boots are visible sticking out from beneath the hem of his jeans.

"Stick?" He shields his eyes with a hand, like he's searching for someone...*me.* "Is that you?" His eyes widen then trail up and down my body. "I'm sorry," he says dropping his arm to his side. "I must've come to the wrong place." He turns on his heels like he's about to walk back out to the parking lot.

"Haha, really funny." I grip his shoulder then pull him around to face me.

Arms held up in a show of surrender, he slowly backs away. "I'm sorry, miss. Hands off...I'm engaged."

"You're such a dick."

"Oh my God!" he shouts, cupping his mouth in feigned surprise. "It *is* you!"

"Are you trying to embarrass me?" I grit, while attempting to shimmy the bottom of my skirt down a bit. "AJ and Raven dressed me in *Anika's clothes.*"

"I'm just fuckin' with ya, babe. You look amazing." He slinks his arms around my waist, pulling me close. My hormones are firing on all synapses. "You always look amazing."

I quickly discover the one good thing about these monstrous

heels—the close proximity they provide to his heart-shaped lips, lips that swiftly descend upon mine, fusing our mouths together. Our tongues meet in tentative strokes before settling into a sensual rhythm.

Forget food. All I want in this moment is to nourish myself on the taste of his kiss.

Catcalls from our friends break through the haze of desire we've become lost in. A rumble of laughter vibrates against my lips. It's part embarrassment, part resignation.

"To be continued…" he whispers, giving the tip of my nose a lick before pulling away.

Rhett clears his throat, placing a hand at the small of my back. He guides me to the table, where everyone else has already claimed their seats and begun diving into appetizers.

I'm seated between Rhett and my mother. *Oh, this won't be awkward at all,* I think to myself as my boyfriend's hand grips my thigh and slowly inches higher.

"I'd like to make a toast," Raven announces, distracting Rhett just as I catch myself about to whimper.

We each take a champagne flute from the server's tray. She waits patiently until everyone has a glass before tapping a spoon to the top of hers to grab everyone's attention.

"To Rhett and Korie, who haven't had a chance to celebrate their engagement yet. To true love, fairytale romances, and happily ever afters. I've never known a couple more deserving." She holds up her glass, and I want to crawl under the table and kick her in the shin for carrying on like this, being one of the only people in the room in on the charade.

I feel the heat of my mother's glare and concentrate hard on a bunch of plastic grapes wound into a light fixture as we all bring our glasses to the center of the table, clinking them together with a resounding, "Cheers!"

"My turn," Rhett says, pushing back from the table. "To going after what you want and not accepting no for an answer." He glances my way with a subtle wink, and I'm fully aware of the double entendre. Everyone else assumes he's referencing my dream to skate in the games, but I know he's also referring to his own persistence in getting me to date him despite the many times I thwarted his advances.

Chapter 36

RHETT

"**Wear something you don't mind getting dirty.**" She comes out of the bathroom of my suite in skintight jeans and a camouflage tank. She's got knee-length black rubber boots like the shit you see on *Swamp People*. Her wavy blonde hair is in a ponytail, pulled through the back of a ballcap.

"You taking me fishing?" I ask, raking my eyes over her body. It doesn't matter if she's in a dress or jeans, hair styled or ratty as fuck. Every damn time I see her, she makes my heart skip a beat and my dick stand at attention. I want to strip her down and take her again on the rumpled bed taunting me across the room, but AJ and Brock'll be here any minute.

"Nope," she says popping the P. "For real. Don't wear that shirt. It'll get ruined." She's having a little too much fun turning the tables on me with this mystery date.

"I'm only here for two days. It's all I brought."

"Ah, well…" She shrugs. "You can always go shirtless." She waggles her brows.

"Paintball?" I ask, still trying to guess where she's taking me. I can't help but smile at the fond memories of the last time. You know, minus the whole bullet to the balls part.

"Nuh-uhn." Her ass sways side to side as she goes to answer the knock at the door. "Aren't surprises so much fun?" she asks sarcastically.

"Y'all ready?" AJ steps into the room, glances at me, and snorts. "Where's he think he's going?" Her rainbow hair is knotted on top of her head, and she's dressed similarly to Korie.

"He has no idea." Stick takes the plastic shopping bags from her hands. "It's a surprise."

"These are for you, country boy. Catch!" AJ tosses me a pair of white rubber boots. "Brock's making a delivery to the guys in the other room."

I slide my designer jean clad legs into the shit-kickers, examining myself in the full-length mirror.

Anika would die. She'd never let me out in public like this.

"Here. Put this on." Korie pulls a plain white tee from the packaging.

"An undershirt?" I'm laughing inside, anticipating my manager's reaction when she sees the pictures on my Instagram tomorrow.

"Or ruin yours. Makes no difference to me…just figured you might want to blend in with the crowd. You're not in Hollywood anymore, Toto."

"Oooh," Abby Jane hoots when I shrug out of my shirt. "You done real nice, cousin." She rolls her tongue over her lips. "I approve…"

The two of them stand there ogling my chest while I pop my head through the neck of the cheap Hanes tee and roll it down my abs. "I'm feeling a little objectified."

"Good." Korie stalks over, rubbing her hands through my

hair. "Then you should feel right at home."

An hour later, after driving out to the middle of nowhere, we park our caravan of pickups in a gravel lot. My boots crunch on the rocks when I jump down from Brock's jacked-up truck. Off in the distance is a wood sign that says, "Cottonwood Creek Off-Road."

"Ever been mud riding?" Stick asks, her eyes glowing with excitement.

I swear to Jesus, I have the best fake fiancée that ever existed.

Ethan, one of the owners and a good friend of Brock's, meets us at a covered pavilion that we've apparently rented for the day. It's closed on three sides, with a built-in kitchen and bathroom. It's about as fancy as what you'd find at an old campground, with doors barely hanging on the hinges and cracked Formica countertops. Its simplicity is a breath of fresh air.

We fill out the mandatory waivers then snap a few pictures with Ethan. He assures us he won't post them until we're long gone, as to not reveal our whereabouts.

"We have six ATVs," Brock says, leading us down to where the rented quads are lined up at the start of a trail. "AJ and I will ride together. Korie and Rhett." His eyes move to Nick. "You and Raven can share one." Then he turns to the singles, Lyle and Aiden. "You two get your own."

"What's with the snorkels?" I've ridden four-wheelers back when I was in high school plenty of times, but never with PVC pipes sticking out of the hood.

"Stops it from flooding out in the water," Brock answers. "Motor's got to breathe."

"Hop on," Stick orders, taking control of the handle bars. "You can drive on the way back."

"You just love choppin' off my balls, don't you?"

Her shoulders lift and fall in an unapologetic shrug. Without even waiting until I've sat all the way on the seat, she takes off flying down the path. "Eat my dust," she yells as she passes the rest of our group, who are still mounting their rides.

The scent of gas and mud fills the air as we soar over the bumpy terrain leading to a creek. Without slowing down, she dives in. The thick brown water, tire deep, splashes our bodies. Her carefree laughter causes my chest to swell. My adrenaline is at an all-time high from the rush of the wind in my face and having this girl back in my arms.

The deeper we get, the slower our four-wheeler moves. Now waist deep, AJ and Brock speed by, hugging the water's edge. When they've made it a good distance ahead, they pull their souped-up ATV in front of ours. Brock leans back, riding a wheelie with AJ clinging to his waist for dear life.

"Oh, fuck no," I hear, just before Stick floors the gas. "Showoff," she mutters.

"Don't even think a—Shit!" I shout, gripping her waist with one hand and reaching around to clutch the front of the seat with the other as she climbs back on two wheels.

"Whooo!" she screams, pumping a fist in the air. She glances over her shoulder briefly, her eyes connecting with mine. I feel the ATV jerk back with her movement, but don't even have time to react before it flips, submerging us both. Thankfully the water is deep enough in this spot that we can slide out from under it without being crushed by its weight.

Korie slips a little, trying to get to her feet. She's laughing hysterically as she wipes the thick sludge from her face with the back of her hand. "You okay?"

"Yeah," I nod, spitting the grime from my tongue. I pull her to my chest, running my hands over her body, assessing for damages. My damn heart is in my throat. If anything had happened to her...

"I'm fine." Her wet hands cup my face and she leans in close. My pulse leaps. Just before her lips connect with mine, she takes advantage of my distracted state pushing me head first back under.

I come up choking and laughing so hard I can't catch my breath. Her playful nature is such a turn on. "That was dirty," I say, wading toward her retreating form.

"Literally..." She's backing away, hands out in a show of surrender, when lucky for her, Aiden pulls up beside us, cutting his engine.

"What the hell happened?"

"Stick, here," I say, motioning her direction, "thought she was Evel Knievel for a second there and flipped us."

He hisses, assessing the situation. "Lucky y'all didn't get killed." He chuckles to himself. "Wait till Anika finds out."

"I mean, you don't like...*have* to tell her about this part, right?" She steeples her hands, giving him puppy dog eyes.

"You're lucky I like you." Aiden points at her, shaking his head. "Cuz watching her chew his ass out would have been the highlight of my week."

He and I flip the ATV back on its tires. Korie's able to start it up without issue, but when she tries to climb out of the water, the damn thing won't budge. She jumps on top of the seat, leaning over, with her ass in the air. Rocking side to side, she gives it gas, trying to dislodge it.

"Think y'all could maybe give me a push?" she asks, looking back at us over her shoulder. Her eyes roll and she lets out a frustrated breath when she finds us both just standing there, arms crossed on our chests, watching her little show.

"I don't know…I think maybe if you shake that ass just a little harder, you'll get it." I pinch my chin, looking to Aiden for confirmation.

"Definitely," he agrees. "Twerk a little harder." He turns around facing his backside toward Stick. Bent over with his hands on his knees, he starts popping it. "Shake whatcha mama gave ya!"

"You can do it," I sing. "Put dat ass into it."

"Ha. Ha." She drops down, straddling the seat. "Come on before they send a search party out for us."

Aiden and I relent, each taking a side.

"Give it some gas," he shouts, slapping the back of the seat like it's the ass of a horse. She nods, the engine revs and the tires spin, once again coating our faces in mud. The cackle coming from her thrown-back head tells me she did that shit on purpose.

By the time we get the damn vehicle out of the water, I swear I've got an inch of sludge covering my eyelids. Korie rushes over, scooping it away with her fingertips.

Once Aiden's rinsed himself off in the creek, he hauls off to catch up with the rest of the pack.

"My turn," I say, straddling the seat before she can claim the wheel a second time.

My throat swells, right along with something else, when she clutches the hem of her shirt and her arms rise into the air, leaving her in a black bikini top, jeans, and boots.

She's a redneck's wet dream.

Korie rinses her top in the water before wringing it out, then climbs on in front of me, with her face toward mine. Her dirt-covered legs wrap around my waist, and with her wadded-up shirt, she scrubs my face clean.

I barely hear the thud when the wet fabric lands on the seat behind me. As her lips meld to mine, I slip the hat from her head, then the elastic from her hair. I cup the sides of her face, my thumbs stroking her temples as our tongues grapple with each other for control.

"I'm so happy you showed up," she pants into my mouth, her chest heaving. "I've missed this."

"Missed you too." I nip at her lips when she smirks at my response. "So much."

"I wish you didn't have to leave already in the morning."

"Me too," I say, gripping her chin in my thumb and forefinger and placing a tender kiss at the corner of her mouth. "You'll be so busy competing that you won't even have time to miss me." I drag my lips across hers to kiss the other corner, then clear my throat. "We'll be together in Nashville before you know it."

Her eyes glisten in the setting sun as she leans back against the handlebars, trying to catch her breath.

"Come on," I say, gripping her around the waist. "Let's go find the others. We can pick this back up in the shower at the hotel."

Chapter 37

RHETT

"Dayum."

Stick's lips quirk at the hissed expletive as she descends the winding staircase. Her honey-colored locks are a mass of curls cascading down her bare back. My breathing halts somewhere between ogling the plunging neckline that dips between her perky breasts, stopping just above her bellybutton, and the slit in the black-sequined number that is bordering on scandalous.

"Ohh." An embarrassed laugh pushes past her ruby red lips when she loses footing in the heels Anika chose to compliment her dress. With a firm grip on the railing, she rights herself. "This isn't going to end well."

With the swipe of a finger, I loosen the bow tie that's suddenly suffocating me. "Oh, I'll see to it that this night ends really, *really* well." I give her a thorough onceover, starting with the crown of her head all the way to the tips of her red-painted toes. I don't even attempt to hide the effect she's having on me. That smoky eye paired with her barely-there dress has transformed my gorgeous, no fuss girl into a seductress. I'd love nothing more than to carry her sexy ass right back up those stairs and keep her all to myself, but I'm already on shaky ground with the label. They, along with the rest of the band, would have my head if I didn't show up to perform tonight.

"Not if I trip over my own feet trying to walk in these things on the red carpet." She takes my offered hand, concentrating hard to make it safely down the last five steps. "Is it really that big of a deal for me to just wear flats?"

"Absolutely not." Anika barges in from the living area of our Airbnb, where she's been busying herself with setting the scene for pre-show publicity photos. "No one with any class attends a red-carpet event in anything other than a sexy pair of heels. You'll be fine."

With the back of my hand, I brush the hair from her shoulder and lean in close. I allow myself a moment to breathe in the scent of her feminine perfume. "You look incredible."

She shivers when the heat of my breath brushes the bend of her neck, where I press a tender kiss. "If it'll make you more comfortable to change into flats—or hell, even chucks—go for it. You'll still be the hottest woman in that building."

She clutches the lapels of my jacket, pulling me closer. I watch as she chews her lip for a moment before her mossy eyes drift back to where Anika's still looming. "Just don't let go of me, okay?" Her grip tightens. "Don't let me fall."

"Wouldn't dream of it."

Nick bursts our bubble with an outraged huff. "We're gonna discuss adding a jacket to that sorry excuse of an outfit just as soon as—" Nick ends his rant when Raven appears near the top of the staircase in a sapphire two-piece that leaves her midriff bare.

"You were saying?" Korie snickers, applying pressure to my

chest to move us further into the foyer and out of their space.

"Holy mother..." Nicholas brings a fist to his mouth, biting the knuckle of his first finger.

I can't hold back my laughter. "Whoa, Nick...Never knew you to be a religious man."

"Yeah, okay...pretty sure if I were, the thoughts running through my head right now would land me a one-way ticket to hell."

"I don't understand why you lovebirds don't make it official already." Korie turns to watch her girl's grand entrance, slipping an arm around my waist. "Everyone within a mile radius can feel the lust emanating from you two."

Nicholas glares at his cousin over his date's shoulder. "Nothin' wrong with two people having a little fun."

Raven's spine visibly stiffens, and I take that as my cue to lead Korie to the living room for our photo op.

"What's his damn deal, anyway?" I've been looking forward to this night for weeks now and hate that she's letting their situation sully her mood.

"He's just not ready to settle down. Nick's been completely open with her. If Raven doesn't have an issue with it, why should you?"

She slows her gate, gawking up at me. "For the same reason I should have followed my gut and stayed far away from you." She swallows hard. "He's going to hurt her, Rhett."

Ouch. "What's it gonna take?"

"For what?" She turns to face me when she realizes I've stopped moving, linking her hands around my neck. Her sparkling green eyes are almost level with mine as she rocks back on her heels, giving me her full attention.

A lump forms in my throat, and I attempt to swallow it down. "For you to finally realize how fucking crazy I am about you?"

"Oh, I don't doubt that you are…" The pads of her thumbs rub back and forth on the nape of my neck, sending a jolt of desire rushing through me. "For now." With that her hold loosens and her hands trail lightly over my shoulders, finally resting on my chest.

"This rock says forever." Her stance wavers as I twist the diamond around the ring finger of her left hand, now clutched in mine.

"You and I both know this is nothing but a lie."

I lace my fingers with hers, tugging to get her moving again. "I prefer to think of it as a practice round." That earns me a genuine smile.

"You're relentless, Rhett Taylor."

"Only when I know what I want."

When our limo arrives at the arena, the girls grow uncharacteristically silent, and Korie's palm starts to sweat in mine. Me being the front man of the band, we're out first, and I find myself feeling anxious on her behalf. It'll be our first red-carpet event together, and I hope the attention doesn't discourage her from ever wanting to accompany me again.

As soon as Reginald pulls the door open, the blinding flashes of lights start, following us all the way down the never-ending carpet. I try to hurry by without being noticed, but despite my best efforts, we're stopped by none other than Joan Brooks, the fashion police.

The notoriously nervy woman shoves a mic in my face. "Mr. Taylor, you're looking quite dashing tonight. Who are you wearing?"

"Thanks, Joan. You look lovely as well. The suit is courtesy of Prada."

Korie's fingers tighten around mine when Joan moves on to her. "And aren't you a sight...it's Korie, right?"

She clears her throat. "Yes. Korie Potter."

"That's right...the skater girl. Well, don't you clean up nice? Who had the honor of dressing you tonight, love?"

I can't help the laughter that bursts out of my chest when my oblivious date answers simply, "Myself."

The reporter's head jerks back with surprise.

"Well," Korie adds, "that's not entirely true. A lovely stylist by the name of Simon is responsible for my hair and makeup. He was fantastic." She smiles at the camera. "Thanks so much for everything, Simon!"

Normally ready and waiting to bust everyone's chops, Joan appears flustered and completely at a loss for how to respond. She rolls her shoulders, straitening her spine. "Would you mind telling us about your shoes?"

"They're a death trap," she whispers. "Most uncomfortable thing I've ever had the displeasure of wearing."

Everyone within earshot erupts into hysterics, including the wicked witch herself. "Thank you, darling." She waves us off. "Enjoy your evening."

"Was it something I said?"

"And now the nominees for male vocalist of the year," Tinley Tucker announces, motioning to the screen behind her, where the names are revealed, followed by a short clip of each of our most popular songs in the year 2019.

I knew well in advance I was nominated in this category, but it doesn't make the nerves churning in the pit of my stomach any less. My heart leaps into my throat when the video montage comes to an end and Tinley slowly unfolds the sealed envelope in her hand. A huge grin splits her face. "Congratulations to our male vocalist of the year, Mr. Rhett Taylor!"

Korie squeals, flying to her feet and throwing her arms around my neck. While holding her close and breathing in the comforting scent of her perfume, I feel the shoulder and back slaps from the band. Their congratulations all meld together, getting lost in the erratic beating of my heart. The applause is deafening as I place a brief kiss to my girl's lips and make my way up to the podium, completely shell-shocked, and not at all prepared.

"Wow," I say, taking the award from Tinley and positioning myself behind the mic. "This is truly an honor. I'm a fly by the seat of my pants kind of guy and honestly didn't expect to win, so please bear with me while I try to gather my thoughts." My eyes slowly scan the crowd, stopping on my crew. "First of all, I want to thank my fans for making this dream of mine possible. My bandmates, Nick, Lyle, and Aiden…without y'all I am nothing. Thank you to Anika, my manager and childhood friend, for handling this bunch of misfit guys with a heavy hand and loads of grace. You keep us all in line and are more vital than you could ever know."

Her big eyes well with tears. She kisses her first two fingers, extending them in the air toward me, mouthing the words, *I love you.*

"Love you too, Annie. Thanks to my pops, and my sister, Judy, who couldn't be here tonight. Your love and support keep me going. My little niece, Princess Autumn. Uncle Rhett loves you to the moon and stars, baby girl." My eyes finally land on my date, and my chest swells to nearly bursting because somehow this award feels more than the rest, just for having this woman by my side. "I promise I'm almost done. There's one more person I need to thank. Korie Potter, thank you for keeping me humble. For refusing to allow me to get a big head. For reminding me daily that I am simply a man who's been blessed immensely in both my professional and now my personal life. You ground me. You center me. You make me a better man."

Chapter 38

KORIE

Rｈｅｔｔ ｄｏｅｓｎ'ｔ ｒｅｔｕｒｎ ａｆｔｅｒ ｈｉｓ ｓｐｅｅｃｈ, ｗｈｉｃｈ ｌｅｆｔ ｍｅ feeling some kind of way. The rest of the guys have all disappeared as well, joining him in the back to prepare for their upcoming performance.

Raven holds my trembling hand in hers, lightly stroking her palm over my forearm in soothing strokes. I'm a mess. Truthfully, I don't know how I'd have handled this night without her by my side, always aware of exactly what I need. She probably has a better idea of what's got me so riled up than I do.

Could I actually be jealous over the words exchanged between him and Anika? He assured me they were no more than friends, and I completely believe him. So, why did those three words feel like a dagger stabbing repeatedly into my chest?

At the same time, I'm touched by the way he thought to acknowledge me at all and reeling over the heartfelt proclamations he made.

To top it all off, I'm confused, because it could have been a ploy to further our cause, but it didn't feel like a performance. It felt real. It felt honest. It felt *good*.

The lights dim, and Jim Walters, the host, is lit by a spotlight. "Up next we have The Rhett Taylor Band performing their first single from their upcoming album, Think Hard."

Every hair on my body stands on end as the lights move, illuminating the stage, and the man occupying my every thought is there, front and center, and looking like a snack.

His Prada suit has been replaced by tight jeans and a fitted dark gray tee. He's wearing his signature boots and backward cap.

I gasp when I see the guitar his momma gave him, slung over his shoulder. He grips the neck, looking up and pointing a finger to the sky, a silent tribute to his dead mother that steals my breath.

Nick beats his drum sticks together once, twice, three times…

All at once the room is filled with infectious energy. I can't take my eyes off of Rhett as he alternates between strumming his guitar and gripping that mic in his fist. From way out here I can see the veins cording his neck while he belts out the lyrics with passion and impeccable skill.

We've been together for a few months now, but this is the first time I've witnessed him performing live. Our busy schedules haven't allowed for it before now. Every note is pitch perfect and stirring a fire in my blood.

Is every woman in here flushed and slick with desire, or is it my intimate knowledge of what he's capable of with that bulge in his pants that has me squirming where I sit?

Every thrust of his hips has my core clenching with need.

By the time the song ends and the lights darken, I'm panting and fighting the urge to chase him down backstage and finish what he's unknowingly just started.

"Hey, sugar. Come give your old man a hug." My blood runs cold, and every muscle in my body stiffens.

I haven't seen my sperm donor since he showed up uninvited to my high school graduation, but that gruff voice of his is one I'd recognize anywhere. I was sure after the way I laid into him, followed by ignoring his calls until they eventually stopped altogether, he'd finally gotten the message. But here he is—the bane of my existence—approaching our group as we make for the limo that'll take us to the after party.

The first thing I notice, when I can finally bring myself to look at him, is his haggard appearance. He hasn't aged well at all and somehow that feels like a victory. He may have used her up like yesterday's trash, but despite the years of torment, my mother is still as beautiful as ever. Too beautiful for the likes of him. The knowledge that she'd take him back in a heartbeat snuffs out that short-lived moment of triumph. I will never understand what she sees in him.

Have I fallen prey to the same fate? Surpassed the point of no return?

No, I finally decide with a side glance at my date. There's something here. I feel it growing stronger every day, and I'd definitely be sad to lose him...but it can't be love. At least, not yet. This unexpected encounter puts that much into perspective. I'm sure I'd feel relief if I could feel anything over the disgust that's descended upon me.

His tattooed arms swing open wide. Much like his face, they're covered in wrinkles, prematurely aged by years of drug use and neglect. The snide smile that curls his lips says he knows he has me right where he wants me. Always playing games. There's no way I can deny him without embarrassing Rhett, and he's ready to take full advantage.

My fists clench, nails cutting into Rhett's palm as I steel my emotions, swallow the vomit rising in my throat, and stretch the taut muscles in my cheeks into what I hope comes off as a passable smile. Every ounce of elation, the cloud I've been floating on since this fairy tale of a night started, is gone like some distant memory.

Like it never happened at all.

"Father," I choke, leaning in and placing a limp arm around his back as he squeezes me to his chest.

"Knew you'd come around eventually." The scent of his smoke-filled breath has me battling the urge to gag. "I've missed you, sweet girl."

Pulse racing, my stomach sinks into a bottomless pit. I'm so close to losing it when Rhett's hand curls around my waist, and he tugs me back to his side. "Hey now. Don't be trying to steal my arm candy."

Jax Potter has the audacity to offer a genuine laugh, throwing his hands up in mock surrender.

What alternate reality is this man living in? Can he not see what his being here is doing to me? *Of course not.* That would mean he'd have to care, and my father cares for no one but himself.

"You have my blessing," the old bastard offers, eyes volleying between Rhett and me like a proud papa. As if I'd ever want or need his approval. I'm going to come unglued.

"Smile and nod." Raven's hushed whisper pulls me from my

murderous thoughts. "Think of the band—of Rhett."

"Thank you, sir." The lingering respect toward the man to which he feels he owes his career is obvious and has me feeling unjustly betrayed by my boyfriend.

Try as I might, I can't utter a sound. Not without exploding. So, I stand stalk-still, betraying all that I stand for by remaining silent for a man. One I'm not quite sure deserves my loyalty at this point.

"Uncle Jax." Nicholas steps around us, pulling my father into a one-armed hug and saving me from causing a scene.

"Get her out of here, if you know what's good for you." Raven hisses at Rhett as her fingers close tightly around mine in an offer of comfort.

The walk to the limo is a blur. Completely checked out, I allow my date to guide me through the throngs of people, pausing and smiling for the cameras when instructed, like a good little fiancée.

My mind won't stop racing, replaying every word of our encounter and filling me with regret. I'm not this meek, pushover of a girl. I should storm right back in there and tell that man exactly what I think of him and just where he can shove his blessing.

"I'm so sorry." Rhett's voice pierces through my whirling thoughts once the door shuts and we're safely inside the car.

"Don't." I snap, sliding across the leather bench seat with moisture building behind my eyes. I'll be damned if I allow myself to shed one more fucking tear over that deadbeat. "Did you—" I shake my head, praying for an answer I know isn't coming. "Did you know?"

The panicked look in his eyes says it all. "Know what?"

"That Jax would be here?"

Rhett's face screws up, a further admission of guilt, but I

need to hear the words. "I want complete honesty."

His broad shoulders slump. Intense blue eyes—which usually shine so bright—dim, offering up an apology before the words cross his lips. "I didn't think..." A hand covers his face trailing down to scrub over his freshly shaved chin, and I can hardly breathe from the punch to my gut. "I mean, he's usually at these things. But, babe, I swear, I wasn't trying to force you into seeing him. It just never crossed my mind that the two of you would end up in the same place."

He moves closer, his hand reaching for mine.

I swat it away. "I said *don't*. Dammit, don't touch me." The tears I'm barely holding at bay wouldn't survive it.

Rhett's elbows move to rest on his knees. Head hung, he angles his stricken face toward mine. "I'm sorry. I don't know what else to say."

Deep down I realize he didn't plan for this to happen—that he doesn't deserve my wrath—so I try to pull away to keep myself from directing it where it doesn't belong. My self-control is hanging by the thinnest of threads. "I know." With my knees tucked into my chest, I throw off my heels and curl into the window, so I no longer have to see the look of desperation on his face.

"Tell me what I can do to fix this."

I shrug, making circles with my finger in the condensation on the glass. "How do you do it?"

"Do what?"

"Live a lie for the cameras...cuz I'm telling you right now, I'm not sure I could do that again." I take a deep, somewhat calming breath. "You should—No." My head spins back to face him before continuing, so he fully grasps the gravity of what I'm about to say. "You *need* to get out now before I ruin your career."

"If the things I've done haven't destroyed it yet, I think it's pretty safe to say we'll get through it."

My head whips back and forth. "You don't understand. I'm so angry. That man fills me with blind rage. I just..." I shudder. "I want to break something...preferably his face." My cheeks flush crimson, and my hands instinctively ball into tight fists. I hate the way he still gets to me. The way he reduces me to that little girl who wished and waited for her daddy to come home. Who watched her mother cry into her palms day after day and never knew why she was always so sad. Who eventually grew up to learn of all his indiscretions from kids at school and the *National Enquirer* or whatever other gossip magazine he was plastered on that day. The sense of betrayal. The shame. It lingers. It festers. And seeing him tonight's brought it all back tenfold.

And here's this beautiful man with the patience of a saint, holding me with his intense stare, trying to decide what to do with the mess before him. "Come here." His voice is warm and tender as he beckons me over with the crook of a finger.

"I can't." My own is small and strained.

Without a word, he rises from his seat, moving to crouch before me. He places a hand around each of my ankles and guides my feet to rest on the floor on either side of him. Then he takes my hands into his, pulling them away from my face, refusing to let me hide. "Let me have it."

The pounding of my heart grows louder. Struggling to free my wrists from his hold, my anger boils to the surface, and I can't hold back any longer. "Have what?" I shout. "What more do you want from me?"

"Everything."

My God, he's so serious with his confession that I want with every fiber of my being to believe him. To throw caution to the wind and trust that I could actually be enough for this man.

"But for now," he continues, clearing his throat. "What I really want more than anything else is to take away the pain I've caused you." Rhett guides my hands to his mussed sandy blond hair. "Let it all out, baby." His teeth scrape over his lower lip and he nudges my chin with the tip of his nose, so our eyes meet. "Don't hold back." He balls my fingers to fist the strands and with a little hesitation at first, I pull. Barely registering the hiss that escapes his lips, I pull again as hard as I can. Once I start, I can't seem to stop the assault. My angry fists pound against his hard chest, and for a moment I forget he's here at all, unleashing every ounce of pent-up aggression until I'm spent. Until I'm panting and disoriented. *Until I'm filled with shame.*

"That's it," he says, swiping his calloused thumbs beneath my eyes. "There's my girl. You're so goddamned beautiful, Korie." The gentleness in his touch, in his tone, have me burning with a new fervor. "Both inside and out."

Consumed by the heat that's pulsing in my veins, I yank the bow tie from around his neck, tossing it to the floor. A handful of buttons swiftly join it when I rip the front of his shirt open. "I need you."

"I'm yours." I can't look him in the eye nor dare to think of all that those two words imply, because I know he's referring to more than just sex. And I just can't go there at the moment.

"Don't be gentle with me, Hollywood," I order as I guide him to the seat and get to work on his pants.

A flicker of something resembling pain flashes in his eyes before he reaches between our bodies, pushing my fumbling hands to the side to unfasten his slacks freeing his erection.

My already throbbing core clenches in anticipation for the

relief I know he's capable of delivering. Standing between his parted legs, I wait for him to make the next move. Rhett slips a hand through the slit in my dress and hooks his finger in the elastic band of my panties. With one firm tug, it snaps, falling to my feet. I kick it away to join the rest of our mounting pile of discarded clothes.

I waste no time in hiking my dress and mounting him. There's nothing slow or delicate in what follows. No gentle touches. No whispered words of affection. I want none of it.

The sexiest moan escapes his lips as I impale myself on his cock.

His hands trail softly. *Too softly,* up my back. So, I grab them, pulling them around to cup my tits through the plunging neckline of this ridiculous dress.

"This was your idea," I remind him, squeezing his hands around the sensitive mounds of flesh.

He nods and his expert fingers find my pert nipples, pinching to the point of pain. "Yes," I moan, leaning in to his touch. It's exactly what I need as I ride him hard and fast. The mingled sounds of our moans and panting breaths fill the cab, spurring me on.

I fuck him with wild abandon.

I fuck him like a woman possessed.

I fuck him like I hate him.

With every downward thrust, I let go of a little more of the heaviness that's been sitting in my chest, until I'm weightless and soaring.

Until I'm free.

My mouth crashes against his, and our tongues join in the battle. I am nothing but sensation. But wanton and desperate. *And so completely lost to this man.*

Tears freely trail my cheeks as Rhett makes love to my

mouth with a tenderness that steals my breath away. He holds me cradled against his chest, kissing me so thoroughly I lose all sense of time and place.

I lose what's left of my heart.

Chapter 39

RHETT

WE DECIDE TO SKIP OUT ON THE AFTER PARTY, NEITHER OF US in the mood any longer. I just fucked the woman I love like she meant less than nothing. The experience, while something she might have needed at the time, leaves me feeling dirty and hollow inside.

The only way I know to rectify the regret consuming me is to show her. To finally tell her exactly what she's come to mean to my life.

All of the stolen dates between performances and skate competitions. The late-night phone calls and flirty texts. For me, they've become something real. They've become the best part of my days. The thing I look forward to most. I can only hope she feels the same.

Regardless, tonight is the night I come clean.

When we arrive back at the rented house, I run her a bath in the oversized Jacuzzi tub, adding lavender bubbles, bath salts, and lighting the candles scattered throughout the bathroom.

"This for me?" she asks, leaning against the doorframe in her disheveled dress, with my suit jacket layered on top. With makeup streaked across her face and her hair in complete disarray, she's never looked more delicate—more alluring. More *mine*.

"Yeah." I cross the room, slipping the coat from her shoulders and tossing it to the chair in the corner. "Figured you could use a warm bath to unwind."

"You're perfect." Her hands frame my face as she stares into my eyes briefly before hooking her thumbs in the thin straps at her shoulders and slinking out of what remains of her dress. She stands before me, completely bare, without an ounce of shame.

Speechless, I slowly take in every delicate inch of her creamy white skin. The rosy buds hardening on her chest. The light mound of curls between her legs. My pulse escalates as I scan each subtle dip and curve of her body.

Korie closes the space between us, sneaking her hands through the opening in my shirt. She lightly skims her fingertips over my chest to my shoulders, where she shoves the sleeves down the length of my arms, dropping the offensive material to the floor. "Join me?" she rasps, reaching lower to unfasten the button on my dress pants. "Please." Her long lashes flutter seductively.

"Okay." I place a chaste kiss on her forehead before stepping out of my pants and boxer briefs and following her over to the tub.

I take her hand, helping her in behind me. She settles between my legs, her back resting against my chest, her long hair tickling where it brushes my nose. The water line reaches to just above her breasts, blanketing us in a cloud of thick bubbles, the soothing aroma wafting into the warm, humid air.

While the jets massage our bodies, we lie limp in each other's arms, content to just be with one another.

"I'm sorry about earlier," she finally says, after a long period of silence. "I can't believe I behaved like that." Shame floods her cheeks.

"You don't have to apologize." I brush the hair back from her face with a wet, soapy hand. "You needed a release. I'm just glad I could provide it."

She snorts. "Well, you sort of provided two."

My chest clenches up at the mention of what went down in the limo this afternoon. "Yeah, well *I'm* sorry about that. I never meant to let it go that far. What happened between us was savage and…" I cringe. "It was cold." I gulp hard, trying to swallow past the guilt lodged in my throat. "I don't want sex between us to be a means to an end."

"What are you talking about, crazy man?" She twists in my arms, looking up at me with her mossy bedroom eyes. "It was so fucking good." She sighs her contentment.

"I will give you sex any way you want it—hard…soft…fast…slow…but never…" I shake my head. "Never while you're emotionally detached from me like that again."

Her eyes glisten in the candlelight as she begins to understand.

"Don't close off your heart to me."

"I won't," she whispers into the corner of my mouth before pressing her lips to mine. Slowly she turns in my arms, and what starts as a gentle and languid kiss becomes fueled with fiery passion, the chemistry between us burning with the heat of a thousand blazing suns.

"Take me to bed," she growls, nipping at my lips while her hands comb frantically through my hair. "Now."

"Yes, ma'am."

I step out from behind her, quickly drying off before binding the towel around my waist and retrieving another from the shelf for Stick. She wraps it around her body, tucking the end between her breasts to keep it in place. Before she's even lifted a leg over the side of the tub, I scoop her into my arms, carrying her bridal style to the massive king-sized four-poster bed.

Our lips fuse together, never parting as I gently place her in the center of the bed, my body hovering over hers. For a brief moment I just look at her, my heart speeding up at the range of emotion passing between us. There's no way possible she doesn't feel what I'm feeling…at least to some degree. This overwhelming urge to make her mine. To be connected to her not just sexually, but on a spiritual level.

Her fingers begin exploring the lines of my chest, stirring up a frenzy of electricity in my groin.

Resting all of my weight on one arm, I use the hand of the other to unwrap the terrycloth that's concealing her body from view. She follows my lead, reaching between us to tug my towel away and toss it across the room. I sink down on top of her, relishing the feel of her warm skin on my skin, of her heartbeat drumming against my own.

I cup her right breast in my hand, rolling my thumb over the nipple, teasing it into a hard bud, eliciting a sexy little whimper. Then, I rub harder, tweaking the sensitive flesh between my fingers. She hisses into my mouth, her back arching off of the mattress. I bite down gently on her lower lip before pulling away and lowering my mouth to cover the soft globe, flicking my tongue rapidly while she writhes beneath me, moaning her pleasure.

I move to her other breast, lavishing it with the same attention, my cock thickening as she begins to lose control, her nails scoring my back while her head whips side to side.

Liquid heat fills my shaft, the pressure building more with every erotic noise she makes.

"Rhett," she hisses, gripping my hair and pulling my mouth back to hers. "I want you, please."

"Look at me." I nudge her nose with the tip of my own, encouraging her eyes to connect with mine. They're hooded—dilated, and wild with desire. "Do you feel this, Stick?"

She nods, lifting her hips seeking relief. "Please..."

"I've had plenty of meaningless sex, but not with you." I say, prodding the tip of my erection into her slick opening. "Never again with you."

"Never a—ohhh," she moans, her head flung back in pleasure as I slide all the way in, burying my cock to the hilt. With deliberate slowness, I rock in and out of her warm, wet, heat, giving her every hard inch before slowly withdrawing and then doing it all over again. As her mounting climax builds, I feel her body trembling beneath me—an occasional spasm rocking her core. Her hungry pussy squeezes my shaft, bringing me to the brink. When I know that I can't hold back any longer, I pick up the pace. Gripping the back of her head in my hand, I bring her mouth to mine, thrusting my tongue inside. I devour her like a man starved while plunging in and out—my groin tensing as the pressure mounts with each stroke.

"Now," she begs, her walls clenching tight around my cock. "I'm—I'm coming..."

My entire body locks up as wave after wave of intense pleasure rockets between us. My release shoots out in warm spurts, each one eliciting a full body spasm from her. Korie's orgasm intensifies with each burst, continuing long after mine finishes.

Not until her body goes limp do I fall to my back beside her, completely exhausted and in a state of total bliss. She curls

254 HEATHER M. ORGERON

onto her side, resting her head on my chest, her leg flung over my thigh. I run my fingers lightly along her spine while we lay wrapped around each other, reveling in the afterglow.

When the numbness wears off, my mind starts to race with this overwhelming need to tell her how I feel. I tuck a finger beneath her chin, turning her face to mine, my heart beating so fast.

Her eyes are heavy, her body in a state of full contentment. Her kiss-swollen lips spread into a lazy smile. "You were right," she whispers into the darkness. "That was much better."

I kiss the tip of her nose, tracing the side of her face with my knuckle. "That was love."

Her body lightly tenses in my hold. I cup the side of her face, gently stroking her cheek with the pad of my thumb. I feel her throat constrict with a hard swallow, her fears creeping in.

"I love you, Korie. You don't have to say it back or even say anything at all. I just needed you to know—I'm all in."

Wordlessly her lips meet mine. She kisses me slowly, tenderly, *lovingly*. She may not be ready to say the words, but her body tells me everything I need to know. So, while she battles with her demons, figuring it all out, I'll be here loving her, anxiously waiting for the day her mind catches up to her heart.

Chapter 40

KORIE

"YOU NO-GOOD, LYING BASTARD!" I STORM INTO RHETT'S room with fire rushing through my veins and throw the paper I just found lying next to the coffee pot at his chest. I have no doubt the bitch left it there for me to find.

The surprise on his face when he looks at the article is unmistakable. *So is his guilt.*

"How could you?" I swipe my hand along the top of the dresser in a rage, sending all of its contents crashing to the floor.

"Stop." He lets the newspaper drop and charges across the room. "Would you stop throwing things and just give me a second to explain?" After a brief struggle, he grips me by the wrists, pulling me inches from his face. His guilt-ridden eyes are wild and wet with mounting tears. It's almost enough for me to believe whatever bullshit excuse he has for this picture... this picture that's just shattered my fucking soul. Because I want more than anything for there to be a logical explanation.

For him to give me any reason that would make it acceptable to stay. But I'm also not so naive that I don't trust what I can see clearly with my own eyes.

"Explain?" I scoff. "You actually think there's something to explain?"

"I know…Look, I know this looks bad, but it's not what you think." There's a desperation in his voice I've never heard. Maybe he meant what he said last night, but even if he did, it's not enough. If what he felt for me wasn't enough to keep him faithful, then he can rot with his *feelings*.

I shrug out of his hold, my hands clutching my chest, trying to squeeze away the throbbing ache where my heart once beat. "Not what I think?" I snatch the paper up off of the floor. "So, you're going to tell me this isn't you lying naked in *your* bed?" I screech, my mind drifting to the many times we made love, tangled up in those same sheets. Nausea pools in my stomach when my eyes roam to the disheveled bed where he professed his love for me just last night.

Oh God, I'm going to be sick.

"Yes, but…"

"And this," I say, jabbing my finger at the naked brunette draped across his chest. "This isn't Anika?"

"Fuck." His hands knot in his hair and he pulls, releasing a feral growl, as he paces back and forth in front of me. His fist crashes through the drywall, and I flinch, stumbling back toward the door.

"I trusted you, Rhett."

"It was before we ever met." *That's his excuse?*

I don't bring up the night I asked him if they'd ever slept together on the boat, because it won't change a thing.

He'll still be a fraud, and I'm still a fool.

I nod, as a torrent of tears stream down my cheeks. "Maybe,

but this one—" I point to the photo beside it. The photo where she's in his arms, her lips not an inch from his on the dance floor of some club. The date stamped in the lower left corner. "This was taken two months ago, while we were together."

"We were dancing. That's all. I swear to you that nothing else happened. We had just finished the album and gone out to celebrate. Ask Nick if you don't believe me. We were all there." His hands are on my shoulders. His face crumbling. "Baby, please believe me."

"There is no possible explanation," I say, standing my ground. "No excuse for you to have a woman you've been intimate with in your arms, with her lips a breath away from yours, dancing or otherwise."

He starts to speak, and the anger blistering inside of me takes control. My hand flies straight for his face. Immediately I hate myself for striking him, but not as much as I hate what I've allowed this man to do to me. Because now I know without a doubt that I've fallen head over heels in love with a liar. A cheat.

He's no better than my father, and I'm as reckless as my mother.

Rhett stares at me with his hands balled at his sides. He sucks his lips to his teeth, and I watch his tongue glide across the inside of the cheek where I've just hit him. "Feel better?" he asks.

I swallow hard, locking eyes with the man who I know will haunt my heart until my dying day, and I give him honesty he doesn't deserve. "No." With the same hand that just struck him, I reach for his face, tenderly gliding my thumb back and forth over the heated flesh, every part of me fighting the urge to fall into his arms. To seek comfort in the man who's just destroyed me.

A tear slips out from the corner of his eye, landing on my palm. I pull back, staring at the warm droplet. I swirl my thumb in it, until it's no more, gone like whatever *this* was between us.

Without another word, I turn on my heels and walk away.

I'm at the gate, waiting for a flight home when a familiar face—angry, hurt, and filled with concern—appears crouched in front of me. Raven lowers my hands from my eyes, sees my tears, and instantly throws her arms around me.

"Oh, Kore…I was ready to kick your ass for leaving without me, but I can see someone else has gotten to you first." She smooths the hair that's sticking to my wet face. "What the hell happened? Why aren't you answering your phone?"

"I turned it off," I say, retrieving the folded-up article where it's tucked beneath my thigh on the seat beside me. I don't know why I took it with me. I guess maybe I need the visual reminder for why I'm running against the tide—running from the only place my heart wants to be. "He wouldn't stop calling."

Leaving feels wrong, but staying…well, that would be worse.

"What the fuck?" Raven's face contorts with anger. It was my initial reaction too, but now…now, I'm just filled with the overwhelming feelings of betrayal and heartbreak. Consumed by a sadness I could never have imagined possible.

"I don't know what to do," I confess.

Her eyes narrow. "What do you mean?"

"Where do I go?"

"Home. We go home and burn everything that reminds you of him and gorge on Ben and Jerry's. You take a day or two to mourn, and then you pick your ass back up and move the fuck on. You didn't need him before. You sure as shit don't need him now."

I giggle at the thoughts going through my head, even though this situation is anything but funny. "So, we torch the place?"

Raven finally seats herself in the chair beside me. "What place?"

"We live in *his* house, Raven. I'm competing for the chance to skate at the X games in a tour *he's* responsible for...I don't know how to erase him."

"Oh, no, baby girl," my best friend says, waving her bossy finger in the air. "First of all, you *earned* a spot on that tour. That two-timing prick may have opened a door, but you put in the work. You deserve that spot."

She's right. Hearing her put it that way, I'm relieved I at least still have my outlet.

"And as for the house...I mean, he really hasn't spent all that much time in it...we can keep it, right? It was a gift...and I'm rather fond of the place."

I snort. "I never wanted him to buy me a house. I just knew something like this would end up happening."

"Consider it pain and suffering...payment for the hell he's putting you through. For the embarrassment of making you look like a side piece." She snarls. "You ain't no side-hoe, bestie."

"We'll see," I answer, not ready to commit to anything. "Mom and I leave for Japan in a few days. I'll just go stay with her til then and decide what to do about the house after the tour."

"Hey, baby. I wasn't expecting you till tomorrow," Momma says, greeting me at the door in a bathing suit with a pink lace coverup, her freshly bleached hair piled in a topknot at the crown of her head. "To what do I owe this surprise?"

"You were right," I say, dropping my bags to the floor and throwing my arms around my mother's neck.

"Oh no." She holds me close, circling her fingers in soothing strokes at the center of my back. "I saw the article, but I really hoped it was from before…"

I shrug, my lower lip quivering. "The one in the bed was… the other wasn't."

"Are you sure there's not an—"

I shake my head. "When we went sailing, I asked if he and Anika had ever been more, and he said no." The back of my eyes burn with tears. "He lied. No matter what he says now…" I shrug, pulling out of her embrace. "Better now than later, right?"

"I'm so sorry. I really hoped…"

"Just tell me it gets easier?" I beg, clutching my chest when the cursed tears start to fall.

"You love him." It's a statement, one I don't confirm or deny with a noncommittal shrug. "With time," she finally answers. "Just give it time."

"Can I stay here with you for a while? The house…" I trail off. "I can't bring myself to stay there. I didn't know where else to go."

"Of course, you can. This will always be your home. Stay as long as you need. Hell, stay forever." She winks. "Never wanted you to leave in the first place."

I smile, sniffling as I swipe the moisture from my face. "Thanks, Ma. You're the best."

Chapter 41

RHETT

THE SOUND OF STILETTOS CLICKING ON TILE ALERT ME TO HER
presence before the light knock on the frame to my open
balcony door. I took the first flight out of Nashville after Stick
left, not ready to face Anika or the band. For two days I've been
holed up alone in my room, drinking myself into oblivion.

"Not now, Anika." I don't look back, keeping my eyes on the
rolling waves.

She joins me anyway, taking a seat on the chair opposite
mine. "I need you to know that it wasn't me. I—I didn't release
those pictures."

I send her a weak smile before taking another long pull
from my beer. "I know."

"I have no idea where they came from, but I swear to you,
I'm going to do my damnedest to find out."

"Won't make a difference." I scrub a hand over my face,
blowing out a long breath. "It won't erase them—won't bring
her back."

The guilt swirling in her big brown eyes is uncharacteristic and painful to see. "What do we do?"

Well, fuck. If Anika doesn't know what to do, there really is no hope.

"You're asking me?" *That's a first.*

"They're all saying we're romantically involved..." She tugs at the neck of her blouse, nervously running a finger back and forth along her throat. "You and I know that's not true, but I don't know how to make them believe it."

"So, do nothing." I set the Bud Light bottle down harder than necessary in front of me and begin picking at the label.

Her head jerks back. "But what about Korie?"

I shrug. "Nothing will change her mind. I could give a fuck about everyone else. In a week they'll move on to the next thing, and this will be forgotten." A sinister laugh escapes. "By everyone but Stick...and me. Ain't that some shit, Annie?"

Weeks have passed since the mystery photos of Anika and I leaked, and I haven't heard one word from Stick. Not for lack of trying. She won't take my calls. My texts go completely unanswered.

Nick is only just starting to speak to me again, but our friendship is suffering bigtime. This shitstorm has put a strain on the entire band. Thank God we're in between tours at the moment, only playing a few festivals and smaller venues while our Think Hard tour is in the works.

Just as I suspected, the alleged love triangle between my manager, Korie, and me is yesterday's news. A couple of days following the release of the photos, I gave a vague statement apologizing for hurting the woman I love and assuring my fans that despite how bad it looks, my manager and I are not and never have been romantically involved.

I doubt anyone believed it, but despite what I told Anika, to say nothing at all would have been as bad as an admittance of guilt.

I've been keeping tabs on her from a distance. Unsurprisingly, she's making waves in the circuit. There's not a competition she hasn't medaled in. Tonight is the Vortex Energy Final taking place in Long Beach, mere miles away from my home. If she medals, she'll secure her shot at the games. Even if she doesn't, the girl has made such a name for herself that I'd be surprised if she didn't receive an invitation due to her popularity alone.

"You're not going," Nick says, when I walk down the stairs dressed in a Hawaiian button down, khakis, and dark sunglasses with a floppy hat. "So, you can just march your ass right back up those stairs."

"You can't expect me to keep sitting around here doing nothing."

"That is *exactly* what you're going to do." He stuffs his finger in my face, his big chest heaving. "What do you think's gonna happen if she recognizes you? Huh? I'll tell you...she will fall a-fucking-part and so will her chance at the games."

"Goddamn it," I growl, knowing he's right but also that I can't have her so close and not at least try to reach out. "Will you just tell me where she's staying then?"

"No."

I shrug, slipping my feet into a pair of leather flip-flops. "Then you leave me no choice. I'll take my chances."

Smoke billows from his ears. "Why do you need to know where she's staying? You planning on showing up?"

"I want to send something to her room, delivered by courier.

I promise to personally stay away. I won't even send it 'til after the competition, so she isn't shaken up."

Nick studies my face for a long time before nodding and jotting the name of her hotel and room number on the back of a receipt. He shoves the slip of paper into my palm. "Do not make me regret this."

Chapter 42

KORIE

"**W**HY ARE YOU SO NERVOUS?" Raven asks, fanning me with a stack of tourist pamphlets she picked up at the airport. It's not even ten in the morning and already the sun is beating down. It's hot as freaking Hades.

"He's so close," I admit, feeling a bit shaken. "Rhett's still calling and leaving messages daily. What if he shows up here?"

"He won't," Nick says, walking up from the direction of the parking lot. He wraps me in a bear hug, rocking back and lifting my feet from the ground. "I made sure of it. Just go out there and do your thing. We'll be here with Aunt DeeDee, cheering you on."

He's just told me exactly what I wanted to hear, so why do I feel the opposite of relieved? It's almost as if I want him to show up…

Yeah, you're an idiot, Korie.

"Great," I say, forcing a smile. "Thank you for handling that, Nick. I owe you."

"You can pay up right now with a win," he says, pushing the brim of my Vans ballcap down over my eyes. "Kick ass, Potthead."

I burst out laughing. He hasn't called me that since high school. "Takes one to know one."

Chuckling, he takes Raven's hand and begins leading her toward my section with a shrug. He points his finger back at me and clucks his tongue. "I resemble that remark."

Yeah, he does...

There are eight girls competing tonight, all of whom I've become rather friendly with over the course of this tour. Well, as friendly as you can be when you want everyone to do their best, just not quite as well you.

I draw fifth in tonight's lineup, giving me time to scope some of my competition before my run. At least that's what I should be doing...

But instead, I find myself scanning the crowd, in search of Rhett. I can't be with him—have cut him out of my life completely. And yet I still hope to see him out there lurking in the crowd, because if he truly loved me like he says...where else would he be? If I'm still hurting this fucking bad, I want to know he's just as miserable. That he can't stay away.

My preoccupation with a certain country star is showing in my runs. I don't have any major falls, but everything's a little small and wobbly. I just can't seem to stay focused on my routine. When it's time to announce the winners, I honestly have no idea which way it'll go.

While waiting for the scores to appear on the leader board, I look over to Mom, Rave, and Nick. They give me a reassuring thumbs up. I smile back, but my pulse is skyrocketing because I can't help thinking I just blew my shot. Every second we wait feels like an eternity.

"We did it!" Yoko yells, throwing her arms around my back. I can't believe my eyes. Somehow despite my shoddy runs, I managed third place. Little Yoko takes first, a position she's more than earned.

After the medals are awarded, we're each handed our ticket to participate in the X Games. It's such an emotional moment for all of us. The games are something I've dreamed about since I was a little girl, but it felt as likely to happen as taking a rocket to the moon. Yet here I am, holding the ticket in my hand. And all I can think is that I wouldn't be here at all if a certain someone hadn't pushed me into it.

"Do you want me to get him out here?" Nicholas asks when we're on our way out to the car.

"Pshh. No, why?"

"Because you look ready to burst into tears, and not the happy kind. You fucking earned a spot to compete in the X Games, Kore, and you just don't look happy at all."

"I am happy," I tell him. "It's just a little bittersweet, you know?"

"I guess," he says, holding open the door to the Uber. "Sure you aren't in the mood to go out and celebrate?"

Rising up to my toes, I place a kiss on his cheek. "I'm just really exhausted. You are more than welcome to take Rave though."

As I fold into the seat, he dips his head inside. "You sure?"

"Positive. I'm just gonna go have a hot shower and pass out anyway."

Raven's hesitant, but I can see in her eyes that she really wants to go.

"Get out of here," I tell her. "You're in California with the opportunity to hang out with your rock star." I give her shoulder a good shove. "Go do fun things."

"You're sure?"

"She's positive," Mom says, reaching over to Raven's side and flicking the door handle. Then her eyes are on Nick. "You take care of my girl, Nicholas Potter."

"Will do." He gives Mom a Boy Scout salute, giving us all a good chuckle.

"I saw you looking for him," Mom says once the other two have taken off and we're pulling onto the highway.

"I don't wanna talk about it." I rest my head on the cool glass of the window, closing my eyes.

Mom lets out a long-frustrated breath but allows the conversation to drop. The next thing I know, she's jostling me awake and I'm wiping drool off my chin, as we pull up to the front of the hotel.

On our walk through the lobby, we're stopped by the front desk. "Korie Potter?"

"Yeah?" I look back at the dark-skinned woman with the most gorgeous golden springy curls. She's carrying a large white box as she rushes toward me from around the counter.

"This came for you while you were out."

"Oh," I say, taking it from her arms, surprised by how heavy it is. "Thanks so much."

"What's that?" Mom asks as we start for the elevators.

"No clue...I bet it's something from Vortex."

Once we're inside of the room, I set the box on the edge of the bed and flip open the top. The first thing I pull out and unwrap is a bottle of Perrier-Jouët. It must be a coincidence that it's the same gold foil, floral-accented bottle Rhett and I shared on the boat. A cruel coincidence.

"Champagne!" Mom claps, taking the bottle from my hand. "And it's the good stuff."

Reaching back into the box, I grab the next item, removing

it from the pink tissue paper. My throat caves in. Big, round brown eyes and whiskers. She looks just like Molly, and I know exactly who sent the box.

"Maybe they mixed up yours and Yoko's?" Mom giggles. "You haven't played with stuffed animals in over a decade."

"It's a umm...It's a sea lion." I can hardly breathe as I stroke it's fluff. "It's from Rhett. Has to be..."

The last item is a box of chocolate-dipped strawberries and a card with a handwritten note.

> Stick,
>
> CONGRATULATIONS! You did it!
>
> I just wanted the chance to tell you how proud I am of all that you've accomplished. You are so talented and so deserving. And so goddamn beautiful it hurts my heart.
>
> Please accept this bottle of champagne and chocolate-coated strawberries to celebrate your big win. I briefly considered tossing a few oysters into the box, but well, we both know how that turned out last time. I hope they took you out for dinner and drinks and spoiled you rotten. You deserve it.
>
> Seriously though, I saw you scanning the crowd, and I know you were looking for me. I can't begin to tell you the way that shredded me. I have no right to ask anything of you, but I'd appreciate it if you didn't tell Nicholas I was there. I promised to stay away, but how could I when you're all I think about both night and day?
>
> I love you, Korie Potter—today, tomorrow, and all the days of my life.
> Forever yours,
> Rhett

"Well," Mom asks, peeking over my shoulder. "What's it say?"

Quickly I fold the note in half and shove it into my bag. "It just said congratulations and he's proud of me."

"Mmmhmm," she mumbles knowingly. "That was awful

nice of him."

"I guess."

"You guess?"

I place everything back into the box. Everything but the stuffed Molly, who I toss on the bed. With the heaviest of hearts, I seal it up and place it on the dresser. "Doesn't change anything, Mom."

"Well, I think he's really sorry." Since when does she side with Rhett?

"Mmmhmm, well, you also thought Dad was really sorry like a billion times and fat lotta good that did you."

"We're not talking about me and your father."

I nod, pulling back the covers. "We're not talking about me and Rhett either."

"Fair enough." My mother walks over to the bed, tucking me in like she did when I was a little girl. She places a kiss to the center of my forehead. "I'm so proud of you, baby girl." Her warm hand cups my cheek before she shuts out the lights and climbs into the other bed.

In no time, I drift off to sleep, cuddling the stuffed sealion to my chest, and I swear she smells like coconuts and salty air.

Chapter 43

RHETT

"SHE GOT THE DAMN BOX," NICK GROWLS, FED UP WITH MY constant nagging.

"You're sure?" I'm truly baffled as to why I haven't heard a peep from her. Not a thank you, a fuck off, a flaming bag of shit on the front steps. Just nothing.

"I know this is going to come as a shock, but the girl really is trying to get over you. To make contact would be a little counterproductive."

"I guess."

"Look, Rhett. I really think it's time for you to give it up. Move on. I told you from the start this life wasn't for her, but you just had to be *you* and go after her anyway." He gets up from the armchair where he's been watching a *CSI* marathon, and clicks the power button on the remote.

"It was working between us…"

"Yeah," he agrees. "Til it wasn't."

"I didn't cheat on her."

272 HEATHER M. ORGERON

He steps in close. "Then explain the picture."

My hands clench into tight fists. "I already told you...I can't do that."

"Then you don't deserve her. Plain and simple. Move the hell on, fuckboy." With that he disappears from the living room, leaving me to marinate in my misery alone.

"Rhett!" Judy exclaims when she answers the door, drying her hands on the front of her apron. She wraps me in a hug then kisses each of my cheeks. "What're you doing here?"

"You, uh—you read those romance books, right?"

She squints, side-eying me as I push past her into the house. "*Yes*...you came all the way to Texas to talk about romance novels?"

"Sort of...where's the midget?"

"She's napping."

I follow my sister into the kitchen and take a seat at the breakfast table, rearranging the salt and pepper shakers and napkin holder. I can't seem to stop fidgeting.

"What's going on?"

"So, I was thinking of sending Korie a few books."

"Uh-huh," Judy says, pulling up the chair across from mine. "I think it might be time to let this go, little brother."

"I can't." I'm so tired of everyone advising me to give up. I'm a fighter. It's not in my nature. She, of all people, should know this. "Judy, I didn't sleep with Anika. I have no way of proving it. It's...well, it's complicated. But I didn't do it."

"Okay," she says, steepling her fingers beneath her chin. "If you say you didn't, I believe you, but it looks really, *really* bad.

You have to know that."

"I'm aware."

"So, we're gonna send her some books?"

"Yeah. She loves romance novels. So, I figure if I send her a couple, maybe it'll remind her how much she misses me. It'll also show that I paid attention, right?"

She nods, slinking out of her chair. "Alright, then..." My sister holds up a finger then begins walking toward the living room. "Be right back."

When she returns, she has a stack of books clutched to her chest. "These are three of my recent favorites." She hands me one with a pretty blonde on the cover, *Center of Gravity* by K.K. Allen. "This one's about a girl moving to LA to chase her dreams of becoming a professional dancer. I think it's something she can definitely relate to, with the whole skate thing."

"That's perfect." I knew I could count on her.

The next book has a kissing couple on the cover. "*Best Laid Plans* by LK Farlow is a really sweet romance," Judy says, holding it out to me. "I chose it because it centers around a big secret and lots of miscommunication. Anyway, sounded like something that fit the bill. There's also a really cute kid, and she loves kids, right?"

"Right. Great." I rub my hands together, excited. "And that one?" I'm a little more hesitant when I see the bare-chested dude on the cover.

My sister notices the grimace on my face and giggles. "Calm down. Women like this stuff, trust me. *Ask Me Why* by Harloe Rae is my most recent read. It's about a single father with a cute as a button little boy who basically brings the two together through his love of candy. What could be more perfect?"

"This has to work, right?"

"Well...it won't hurt. It'll let her know you're still thinking about her, but you need to do something epic. Think big."

"Uncle Rhett!" Autumn screams when she plods into the kitchen in her unicorn footy pajamas, rubbing sleep from her eyes. "When did you getted here?"

"Hey, princess." I pick her up, situating her on my lap. Like always, her hands go right to the scruff on my chin. "I got here a few minutes ago...was missing my favorite girls."

"We been missin' you too." She gives me a tight squeeze then looks around the room, confused. "Where's your girl?"

Judy gives me an apologetic shrug.

"It's just me this time."

Autumn's lip hangs to the floor. "I guess that's okay," she finally grumbles.

"You guess it's okay?" I shout, poking my fingers into her sides.

She wriggles around, laughing and screaming. When she can't catch her breath, I relent.

"Wanna have a tea party?" she asks once she's calmed down.

"Actually, I'm going to send Miss Korie a present, and I was hoping you might want to help me decorate the box?"

Whenever my sister sends me anything, the box is always covered in stickers and jewels and little doodles from my niece. She enjoys it, and truth be told, so do I. Korie thought it was the cutest thing ever.

"Duh!" she shouts, slithering out of my lap and running for her room. "I'm going get my stuff!"

"Please tell me you have a box?"

"Duh!" Judy says, imitating her daughter, before walking to the pantry to retrieve a flat, plain white box, which she quickly assembles.

When Autumn returns, she goes to work bedazzling the box with sticky jewels, half of which will fall off in the mail, but I don't tell her that. She draws a rainbow on one side, a little house on another. Then she makes two stick figures with long blonde hair. "Dis is me and Miss Korie, and dis," she says, pointing to the blobs in their hands, "is our tea cups."

"Of course," I say, stuffing the bubble-wrapped books along with a folded-up note inside. "She's going to love your drawings."

"Wait," Autumn instructs before running back toward her room. "I'll be right back. Don't cwose it yet."

She returns toting her favorite book, *Pinkalicious*. It's one I've read to her more times than I can count. "I wanna give her one of my books too. I bet her likes dis one the best."

"Something tells me you're probably right, little bit." I laugh. "Here, write your name inside so she knows it's from you."

Autumn draws a lopsided heart and scrawls her name across the inside cover. I have to say, it's not too shabby for a three-year-old.

"You're staying, right?" my sister asks, taping the box shut. "Dad's coming for dinner."

"Yeah. I was gonna spend a few days, if that's okay?"

"Yippee!" Autumn does a little victory dance. "Dis is the best day ever!"

I address the box to Korie's mother's house, which is where I've discovered she's been staying. Then, I take Autumn with me to the post office, followed by an ice cream date at a repulsive little local place that she's currently obsessed with. Korie would love it. That thought stings.

Autumn fills a bowl with strawberry soft serve—"because it's pink. Duh!"—and I choose a pineapple and vanilla swirl. Then we head over to the buffet bar of toppings, which I wouldn't touch with a ten-foot pole.

Few things gross me out more than watching little kids

stick their grubby fingers in all the candy buckets, like they have no clue what the little spoon is there for. Their parents pretend not to see, but I'm on to their lazy asses. My niece has been taught to use utensils, because I refuse to allow her to be a savage.

"Help me up!" She can barely see over the bar. With my ice cream in one hand, I hoist her up with the other, and she proceeds to litter perfectly good strawberry ice cream with a scoop of damn near everything on the menu.

"You know those other kids were sticking their dirty hands in these buckets."

She gives me her mother's side-eye. "And?"

I can't help but laugh. "And nothing, princess. Carry on."

If she doesn't mind eating after booger-picking, butt-scratching, non-hand-washing demons, who am I to be the one to stop her?

"Now, tell me what's wrong," the very wise beyond her years threenager demands, climbing into the booth across from me.

"What're you talking about? Nothing's wrong."

She looks up at me in disbelief. "Daddy only buys Mommy special presents when he's a jerk and makes her cry. Or it's her birfday or Chritmas."

I gulp. Perceptive little shit.

"So," she says. "Is it her birfday? Cuz our tree isn't up, and I didn't get no presents."

"I came here for ice cream, not a therapy session."

She shrugs before taking a heaping bite of her dessert. "I don't know what dat means," she garbles around the food in her mouth. "I juss wanna know what you did to Miss Korie, cuz I like her."

"Well," I say, unable to believe I'm actually about to talk to a toddler about my problems. "You're right. Miss Korie is very angry with me right now."

She nods knowingly. "Did you say sorry?"

"Why do you automatically assume it's my fault?"

"Cuz you're a boy. Duh. Dat's why they make flowers, so boys can apologize to girls when you do dumb stuff."

This kid. "What if it was her fault?"

She actually drops her spoon and crosses her arms on her chest. "Well, was it?"

"No…but it could have been."

"You're reflecting, Uncle Rhett."

"I'm what?"

"Dat's what Mommy says when me or daddy tries to change the subject when we're in trouble. And it is *not* a good thing."

"I believe the word you're looking for is *de*flecting." Are they making kids smarter these days? Geez.

She rolls her eyes and begins drumming her chubby fingers on the tabletop. "You're doing it again…"

"You're right. It's my fault. She won't answer my calls or messages. I've sent presents, and I just don't know what else to do. Got any advice, since you seem to know it all?"

"Hmm…" She taps her pointer finger against her lips. "Okay, so here's what you gotta do." She pushes her snack to the side, all business. "Are you listening?"

I rest my arms on the table, leaning closer. "All ears."

"First you gotta get a horse. It hasta be a white one."

I suck in my lips, trying not to laugh. "White horse. Got it."

"Then you gotta show up and do something really dumb, so she can see she still loves you and saves your life."

That is not where I saw this going. "Do what?"

"Listen, it happens in all the movies. Ariel saves Prince Eric when he's drowning. The princess has to kiss the frog, and he gets to be a prince. Nala goes to get Simba at Timone's house.

And the bestest one is when Belle kisses Beast, and he turns handsome."

"You're giving me dating advice based on Disney movies?"

"Take it or leave it, dude." She snatches a gummy worm off the top of her ice cream and pops it into her mouth. "Who knows, maybe she will kiss you, and you can get handsome too."

Chapter 44

KORIE

"Hey, honey," Mom calls when I return from a visit with the kids at the hospital. I can't wait to finish with the games and finally start my new job. I didn't realize how much I'd miss them with all this traveling. There's nothing like spending time with sick children to bring life into perspective. Suddenly my problems don't seem so bad.

"Hey, Momma." I drop my keys in the glass bowl on the console table near the door and find her in the kitchen. She's got a steaming mug of coffee cupped in two hands and, as always, a welcoming smile.

Gosh, that smells delightful.

"How was it?"

"Good. They're just so sweet and innocent, you know?" I walk over to the pot and pour myself a cup, adding two spoons of sugar and two scoops of creamer.

She nods. "Oh, speaking of kids. A box came for you today. I put it on your bed. Really cute. Looks like a little girl colored all over it."

"Oh?" *It can't be.* "I'll go check it out. Be right back." I abandon my coffee mid-stir.

The whole way up to my room, my heart is racing. When I burst through the door and see the box, my eyes start to sting.

Oh, Rhett Taylor, you fight dirty.

I sit cross-legged in the center of the full-sized bed, examining Autumn's artwork. She's got real talent for a kid her age. I run my fingers over the jewels before bringing them to the ends to unfasten the tape, careful not to destroy any of her drawings.

The first thing I see is a kids' book. *Pinkalicious.* I open the cover and find Autumn's little name written in her wiggly print and lose it. I spend a few minutes reading the book before placing it on my nightstand and fishing through the box to see what else is inside.

I pull out three books and a folded-up note.

Hey Pretty Girl,

I miss you. God, I miss you so damn much. Not being able to talk to you. To see you. To touch you. It's killing me.

I hate myself for doing the one thing I promised I wouldn't. I embarrassed you. Brought all your worst fears to light. I know you probably won't ever believe me, but for what it's worth, I swear to you that Anika and I have never been intimate, despite what the picture suggests. I can't elaborate more, and I know how guilty that makes me look. But my word is my bond, and unfortunately, it's cost me you.

Anyway, I'm not writing to beat a dead horse. Just wanted to say I'm sorry.

I was thinking about the day you told me how much you liked to read romance, and then I remembered that Judy is a huge fan too. These three come highly recommended. I hope they'll occupy you on your travels and help keep your mind off the games.

You know Autumn couldn't be outdone and had to send a present of her own. I'm afraid she's outdone me with Pinkalicious. She says hi, and that she misses you.

Good luck next week in Minneapolis. I'm still here rooting for you. If you ever want to talk, I'm here for that too.

Love always,
Rhett

He *can't* elaborate? What a crock of shit. More like he won't. I wish his words didn't affect me. That I didn't have the urge to pick up the phone and hear his voice.

Instead, I flip through the stack of books, reading the blurbs on the back covers. I haven't read an actual paperback in so long, usually reading in the Kindle app on my phone. I decide to start with *Center of Gravity*. I stack two pillows behind my head, snuggle into the covers and crack the spine. There's something about the scent of printed paper that takes the experience to another level.

I step out onto the hotel balcony, breathing in the morning air. The sun is barely over the horizon, and it's already sweltering. I'm so thankful we're skating on an indoor course.

As soon as I sit in the wooden patio chair, my phone dings.

Rhett: Today's the day! Just wanted to say how proud I am of you. Kick ass out there. This is your moment. You've earned it. No matter what happens, enjoy the experience.

I can't help but chuckle to myself. I swear I thought he was going to say I'm still—

Rhett: Still the prettiest.

Damn him.

I stare at his messages for a few minutes before darkening the screen and setting my phone face down on the little table. It's taken a long ass time, but I can finally hear from him without wanting to curl into a ball and drown in a pool of my own tears. I never respond. I'm in no way immune to his charm, and I refuse to allow myself to be sucked back in. But it does feel good to know he's still thinking about me too. No one wants to be alone in their solitude, right?

I spend the day lazing around, watching Netflix with Raven and Mom. A lot of the girls are out getting practice runs in, but I know at this point I've done all I can. I've been practicing like it's my job. Knowing tonight will be exhausting enough, I've chosen to conserve my energy and veg out with my bestie.

Around four o'clock, we get our things together and head to the arena. The competition starts promptly at seven. Just like at the Chicks with Tricks competition, there will be two heats of six. But instead of waiting until the next morning, the top three from each immediately compete in the final. I feel extremely lucky to have drawn the first. At least if I place and make it to the final, I'll have a little time to rest before my next set of runs. The girls in the second heat will have to compete back to back.

After I've signed in and taken care of all the procedural stuff, I get the chance to warm up. It's a steep course, with high walls and a really dope grind rail on top of a plateau in the center. The feeling of being in here, seeing the X Games signs plastered on every wall, is just surreal.

An eerie calm washes over me when they call our names over the speaker. Time to line up. I expected to feel nervous, nauseous, terrified. But surprisingly I don't feel much of anything. It's almost as if I'm having an out of body experience, watching from the outside.

When my turn comes, I pop my earbuds in and let the

music lead me where it will. I come out guns blazing with my 360. Then, I climb the high wall and do a one-handed invert. I cross the bowl, pumping my knees to pick up speed and then glide clean across the grind rail. I give them a few technical tricks and end with a sweet kick flip.

Having drawn second, there are still four girls to go after me. I sit back and watch with such a mixture of emotions. These women have all become my friends, but they are still my competition, too.

Yoko is the last to compete in our heat, and despite the fact that I know she's just outskated me, I can't help but feel like a proud big sister. Of all the girls I've met, she and I have become the closest.

As she's climbing out, and Pippy Rain is dropping in, the scores appear: Yoko in first, and me in second. My little friend rushes over to high-five me before I've got to drop in for my second run.

"We did it, Korie!"

I pull her in for a one-armed hug. "So proud of you!"

"Same," she says, before waving me off.

I put on a really high energy track and take off full steam. Mixing up my tricks to show a little versatility, I stick my 360 in the middle and add a nose grind and a few other technical tricks I didn't use in my first run. Just before the buzzer, I make my first public attempt at the 540 I've been working on all summer. My landing is a tad wobbly, but holy fuck. *Oh my God.* I just did a fucking 540 in the X Games!

I climb out of the bowl with my heart racing a million miles an hour, finally feeling present and like I've busted out of the haze I've been in since arriving. I look over to my mom and Rave who are screaming their freaking heads off and give my fist a few pumps in the air.

Immediately following my second run, I've jumped into first, but once the rest of the girls have skated their last run, I fall into second, once again behind Yoko.

I rush over to my mom, hugging her above the rail. She's been with me to every single competition. Skating was far from her thing—Mom was more of the cheerleader type—but when she saw the passion I had for the sport, she made it her thing.

During the second heat, I rehydrate and watch with nervous energy, anticipating what's to come.

It's not long before they're announcing the winners and calling us all back to compete in the final. Three out of the six of us will go home with X Games medals. I have a fifty percent chance of taking home a medal. What is this life?

Of course, I drew the dreaded first spot. You can't win 'em all, right? As soon as the first buzzer sounds, I dive in and give it all I've got. I begin with the 540, which thankfully, I land, then I go up the opposite ramp and into a nosegrind. I throw in another 360 but overshoot the landing. I see stars as my ass hits concrete and my board rolls away. But above all else, I feel disappointment.

Rhett: Shake it off, babe. You're doing great.

I didn't realize how much I'd missed his mid-competition messages, but it brings a smile to my face.

Raven: Girl, pick that lip up. You did amazing. Didn't fall till the end. Don't let it fuck with you.

Me: Love you, girl.

Raven: Love you back. Now, go make some bitches cry.

When it's time for my last run, I give myself a little pep talk and take off, knowing whatever happens, I'm skating in the freaking X Games, and I'm going to enjoy this experience. I block out the crowd and throw my planned run out the window. With the beat of the music pumping in my veins, I glide across the course, doing whatever feels natural. I nail everything. My 540, textbook perfect. My 360, child's play. I nail a huge eggplant invert and various nose and board grinds. Before I know it, the buzzer sounds, and I climb out to await my fate.

Chapter 45

RHETT

I'M HIDING IN THE WINGS, WATCHING FROM A SECLUDED SPOT my buddy, Tommy, managed to secure for me, when the final scores appear on the leaderboard.

Gold.

She fucking earned X Games gold.

My chest swells with pride as I watch the megawatt smile that spreads across her face. She's jumping around, wrapped up in her mother and Raven's arms, and I want so badly to be down there. To hold her close and tell her how fucking amazing she is.

Me: CONGRATULATIONS!!! I knew you could do it.

For the first time since the picture scandal, I get a response.

Stick: Thanks. For everything.

That message supplies the fuel I need to go through with my plan.

Once the medals are awarded and a million pictures have been taken, and interviews have been conducted, I'm escorted out to the podium and handed a mic. People have already started to disperse. Those who are still hanging around freeze in the stands. I hear my name whispered repeatedly throughout the crowd.

A million thoughts rush through my mind when I look up and my eyes connect with hers for the first time in so long. "Stick." Her name comes out a hoarse whisper. My heart leaps into my throat. Being this close to her...it literally steals my breath.

Korie's eyes widen, and her hands visibly start to shake. "What are you doing here?" she grits out, looking around briefly to see who's watching.

"A very wise woman...well, it was a three-year-old little girl, actually, told me in not so many words that I needed to fight for the woman I love."

A chorus of awes can be heard among the crowd, but my girl stands stalk-still, like she's staring at a ghost. It feels as if she's looking right through me. Her lower lip starts to quiver, and it takes all of my strength not to climb up on that podium and suck it into my mouth. To kiss her with all the pent-up desire bursting inside me.

"She told me if I made a fool of myself, you'd realize you loved me back and save me like the princesses save the princes in her movies." I smile nervously and shrug, then drop to my knees. "So, here I am. An absolute fucking fool for ever hurting you, begging for the chance to make things right between us."

"Get up," she growls. "Please don't do this."

"I have a question, Stick. One question then I'll go." The weight of her rejection sits like a boulder in my chest.

The tip of her tongue wets the corner of her mouth and she

nods. "What?" Her arms cross protectively over her chest as she stares down at me.

"Do you love me, Korie Potter?" When her face droops, my pulse beats out of control. I feel like I'm standing at the bottom of an avalanche and my feet won't move.

She turns her head up toward the sky, shaking it slightly, then looks directly at me. "Yeah," she says, her eyes glazing over. "But I wish like fucking hell I could stop."

The room falls pin-drop quiet. The last thing I wanted was to embarrass her, so I do what I can to lighten the mood which has suddenly become very, very heavy. "One more question?"

She sighs, but nods.

"If I'd shown up on a white horse, would it have made a difference?"

"Have you completely lost your mind?" she asks.

"A little more every day," I answer, away from the mic. Then I bring it back to my lips. "Congratulations on your win. You deserve it."

"Oh Rhett...what the hell have I done to you?"

Slowly I peel my bloodshot eyes open, trying to focus on Anika's face. "Huh?" I really wish she'd stop swaying like that, it's making me nauseated.

"What on earth possessed you to approach her with a mic at the fucking X Games?" The familiar sound of heels hitting tile echoes through the room. She's the only woman I know who walks around her own house in stilettos. I sort of have the urge to yank one off and stab her with it. Every clack grates my nerves more than the last.

"You saw that, huh?" I hiccup, turning to my side in hopes that everything will stop spinning. "Judy said, *think big.*"

She nods. "And the white horse? The Disney princesses? You're taking relationship advice from a toddler now...that's just great."

"She won't talk to me, Annie," I groan. "What the hell else can I do? I n—need her." I take a few deep breaths, trying to ward off the bile rising in my throat.

"You really do love her." Why does she look so shocked? Haven't I made that abundantly clear?

"Well, no fucking shit." I sit up, leaning back on my elbows.

"It's all over the internet," she says sheepishly. "I mean *everywhere.*"

"So? I don't care." And I don't. I would make an ass of myself a hundred times over if it'd bring her back to me.

"What did you think would happen?" She sits at the foot of my bed, stroking my calf over the covers.

"I honestly didn't know. But I had to see her. I had to try. Didn't go over so well," I slur.

"Definitely could've gone better..." she agrees. Then her eyes meet mine and get all shiny and concerned looking. I blink a few times to make sure I'm still talking to Anika. Because the Annie I know, rarely shows emotion, and this one looks like she's drowning in it. "You just gonna drink yourself to death now? Is that the plan?" She gets up and walks around my room, tossing empty beer bottles into the can. All the movement and clanking bottles has me feeling dizzy. "Get up and get into the shower. I'm getting Rosa in here to clean this place up."

"Just get out," I groan, falling back onto the pillow and pulling the covers to my neck.

The air turns thick. "What?" Her brows dip inward.

"I want you to go. I don't want anyone to clean up my mess.

I just want to drink in fucking peace."

Her lip trembles, making me feel like an ass, but fuck. This whole mess is, while not intentional, to some degree her fault. I'm trying not to blame her, but I just fucking *can't* right now. I can't be responsible for her guilt when I'm barely holding my own head above water.

"You're angry with me..." she mutters, stroking her own hand up and down the opposite forearm.

"I'm not angry with you...I'm angry with *life*, Annie."

Chapter 46

KORIE

"OH, HELL NO," I SAY, SLAMMING THE DOOR I'VE JUST OPENED in the prissy brunette's face. How dare she show up at my front door in her pencil skirt and blazer with her expensive, red-bottomed heels?

And smiling at me, like we're friends…This shitshow just keeps getting better. I'm waiting to find out I'm being filmed for a reality TV special against my knowledge. The drama just keeps unfolding.

The door pushes back, and I'm ready to lose it when I hear Nick's voice. "You want to hear what she has to say, Kore. Open up."

"Great. You two here to tag-team me now?" I toss my hands into the air, defeated, and move out of his way.

Nick takes Anika's hand and guides her past me into the foyer. "I'm on your side, cousin. Always on your side. Just here to help right a wrong. I knew you wouldn't give her the time of day without me vouching for her. I promise, she's not here to make trouble."

Hugging my chest, I nod and walk toward the living room, motioning for them to have a seat on the couch, while I take the recliner. "I'm listening."

"I haven't been very nice to you," she starts.

No shit.

"And I want to apologize." She pauses, smoothing down her pristine skirt anxiously. "I just…the boys, they mean a lot to me and I knew the engagement was all a ploy for your skating thing. I didn't trust you. Rhett has a huge heart, and I just knew he'd end up hurt when all of this was said and done. Right from the start he was so sure you were *the one…*"

"So, you released those pictures to get rid of me?" I ask, the hair standing on the back of my neck like a feral cat.

"No." She sighs. "I finally traced the pictures back to an ex of his, Ana Michelle. She'd planted a camera in his room to get photos of the two of them together to sell to the tabloids, back when they were messing around. Apparently, she got the one of the two of us, as well, and has been holding on to it all this time."

The acid in my stomach churns. Hollywood is such a fucking shady place. I'm livid on Rhett's behalf at the invasion of his privacy, and I'm still so angry at him. "Great, so the mystery of where the picture came from is explained," I snap. "But the fact remains, Anika, that the picture *exists*. I don't care if it was before the two of us were together. He. Lied. To. Me." My blood pressure spikes as I stab my thumb at my own chest to punctuate each word. I spring to my feet. "I asked him. I asked him if you two had ever been more than friends and he said *no*."

"Let her finish." Nick motions with his hand for me to sit back down. "There's more."

So, fighting every urge I have to toss this bitch out of my

house, I sit and nod for her to go ahead.

"This is really hard...bear with me, please?" She smiles nervously, and I force myself not to roll my eyes. "So, all my life I've been one of the guys. I hung out in their smoky rooms, playing video games and watching them make music, but nothing more. Everyone thought I was sleeping with all of them. But the thought never crossed my mind. The temptation...it wasn't there." She shrugs. "With any boy. I mean, I dated, of course. It's just, none of them really did anything for me."

She bites her lip then rises to pace the living room. "The night that picture was taken, we'd gone to a party thrown by Ana Michelle's agent. We were drinking and dancing, a whole group of us, and next thing I know this model—she kissed me." Anika's face turns beet red. "I, uh...I kissed her back." She covers her own mouth like she can't believe she's just admitted that aloud. "I'd never felt a buzz like I felt from that kiss with any guy, and it scared me." Her whole body starts to shake.

I suddenly have the urge to wrap this poor girl in my arms because I can see the truth in her eyes. Feel the pain in her stance.

"So, I rushed home and I drank, and I drank some more, and I cried more tears than I thought possible. Later, when the boys were home and had all gone to bed, I went to Rhett." A huge tear drips down her cheek. "I knew if I could ever love a man, it'd be him." She shrugs. "So, I went into his room and I—I took my clothes off, and I threw myself at him." She laughs, a dry humorless sound. "But he stopped me. God, the look on his face...he was so confused. He didn't kiss me back—didn't touch me the way he did all those other girls. He just—he held me in his arms and stroked my hair and asked me what was wrong."

I reach for her hand and she takes it, sitting on the coffee table in front of my chair.

"I told him everything, and I made him swear he would never tell a soul. My family is...they're super religious, and they'd never understand. Hell, I'm still coming to grips with it myself."

"And that's why he couldn't explain." It all makes sense, her attitude toward me. His secrecy.

She nods, dabbing her tears with a tissue Nicholas hands her. "But I can't let him do this. He's so in love with you, Korie...It's not right. I've never seen him this miserable. He–he deserves to be happy. The band's suffered. I told Nicholas, Lyle, and Aiden last night. I wanted to tell you before it hits, so you understand everything and don't have to read it first in the papers. I'm going to come out. I'm going to clear this whole mess up."

I rise from my chair and pull her into my arms. "Shhh," I whisper against her ear. "Don't. You don't have to do that." I smooth her long brown hair down her back and suddenly I'm crying with her. "It's enough for me, knowing the truth." I shake my head. There's no way I'll be responsible for forcing her to take that step before she's ready. "Thank you for telling me. But you wait until it feels right for *you*. No one else."

"Th–thank you," she sniffs. "So...you'll talk to Rhett?"

"Yeah," I say, my mind spinning like I'm riding a Tilt-A-Whirl. "I just need to figure out my next move."

"Okay, you guys, everyone find a seat, and my friend Anika is going to pass out snacks. I'll be around behind her with drinks."

Probably my absolute favorite part of my new job is arranging entertainment for the children in the pediatric unit. From visits with Mickey Mouse and Cinderella for the little ones, to meet and greets with movie stars and musicians for the big kids, I just want to do anything I can to make these babies smile.

"Who is it?" Shelly, a fourteen-year-old girl with sickle cell asks, dragging her IV pole behind her. She's here for her monthly blood transfusion, along with quite a few others suffering from the same terrible disease. I do love that they schedule the kids in the same age group together, so they have friends during their stays. It gives them something to look forward to in all of this, and it's got to help having people to talk to who truly understand what you're going through.

"You'll find out in just a—"

At that moment Rhett walks out, with Nick, Lyle, and Aiden closely behind. My heart jolts. He looks so good in his faded jeans and dark gray V-neck. His hair is perfectly messy, and his dimpled smile sends my pulse racing. Just breathing the same air has me tingly from head to foot.

"And here they are," I laugh. "Kiddos, please welcome our very special guests, The Rhett Taylor Band."

The look of pure joy on their faces and the sound of teenage girl squeals fills me with immeasurable pride. To look at all these babies in their hospital gowns, toting IV poles, some even on oxygen. The shiny bald heads of our cancer patients, with their steroid-puffed cheeks spread wide with smiles. Gah…It's almost too much to bear.

"Thank you, guys, so much, for being here to entertain my friends," I say, turning to address the band. "It means the world to us."

"We're excited to be here," Nick says, waving at a little

blonde in the front row.

"Shhhhh," I say, holding my pointer to my lips. "Let's quiet down for a minute. They're gonna play their new single for you, Think Hard. After that you can meet and take pictures. Don't be shy. Their sole purpose in being here is so you can post all the selfies on Instagram and make your school friends super jealous!" I wink, then move aside while the boys take to the four stools. Rhett has an acoustic guitar strapped around his chest. Aiden's got his bass, and Lyle has a small keyboard with a stand. The drums would have been too much, so Nick is just there with a mic to help sing a little back up.

"Thanks for having us," Rhett says into the mic, his face slowly scanning the crowd as he takes the time to really look at each one of the children. "It's an honor to be in the company of so many brave warriors." His Adam's apple bobs with a hard swallow.

As Rhett strums the first chords, his eyes bolt with mine. A current of electricity lights every cell of my body aflame. He gives me a small, sad smile that hurts my heart. Then the mask comes on and he's in performance mode.

Just like the last time, it's an unbelievably sexual experience for me, watching him perform. I imagine those manly hands on my body as he works his guitar with such skill. Sweat builds on his forehead just the way it would while we're tangled up in the sheets, and I can practically feel him rocking inside of me— filling parts of me I never knew existed. My breathing becomes erratic as the rough timbre of his voice hits me right at my core.

And then the music stops, and I barely register him thanking his audience. He gives them a wink and a smile, and my insides turn to goo. Anika helps them up one at a time to meet him, thankfully, because I'm stuck, rooted in one spot, my face flushed and my pulse racing. I'm fighting the urge to run into his arms. To cry a river of tears because I miss him so much that it's become unbearable.

If he doesn't want me back...

No, I can't even think that way. I won't.

Once all of the children have had their one-on-one time with the guys, Anika asks them to sit back in their seats for a moment. "Miss Korie would like you all to be a part of something very special."

Anxiously they await their next surprise and I. Can't. Breathe. Rhett looks completely bewildered as he, too, remains in his seat, staring right at me.

Here goes nothing.

With my heart climbing in my throat, I approach the "stage," and drop to my knees at Rhett's feet. If I thought he looked confused before, it was nothing on the way he's looking at me in this moment.

"Rhett," I croak, then clear my throat. "An incredibly handsome, talented, amazing man told me not too long ago that in order to make someone realize they love you back, you had to make a fool of yourself." I shake my head and smile. I can't believe I'm actually doing this. "So, here I am," I say, choking on my own tears. "Hoping you still love me back and that you'll save me from the pain of trying to navigate this life without you." I reach into my pocket and retrieve the platinum pick I had specially engraved with "Korie loves Rhett" on one side and "always and forever," on the other, and hold it out in two fingers like he once held a diamond ring to me. "Rhett, I'm sorry I didn't believe in you. I'm sorry I didn't listen. I'm sorry for all of the time we've missed. But if I've learned anything these past weeks, it's that I don't want to live another moment of this life without you by my side."

"Stick," he rasps, eyes welling with emotion.

I hold up one finger. "I have two questions left, and I put a lot of thought into what I wanted them to be. Number one," I say, staring into his crystal blue eyes, "Do you still love me, Rhett Taylor?"

He nods, clearing his throat, "More than ever." His right hand lowers to cup my cheek, and I want to melt into a puddle at his feet.

The first tear falls, and I don't swat it away. I wear it like a badge. Putting myself out here like this is hard. But this man is worth it, and I know that now, without doubt. "I love you so much," I say. "It makes me a little crazy…so crazy, in fact, that being together isn't enough. It could never be enough. So, that brings me to my second question." I hand him the pick and as he examines it, I deliver the single most important question of my life. "Rhett Taylor, I pick you. Today, tomorrow, and for the rest of my life. Will you marry me?"

Chapter 47

RHETT

"Good morning Rhett, Korie, and honored guests. Welcome to Camp Pour Judgment. It is with the utmost pleasure we open our doors to this special couple and all of you in celebration of their love. My wife, Essie, and I knew from the start that our last adventure with these two was the beginning of something very special. Very special indeed," Joe says, getting choked up. "We have two fun-filled days of action and adventure planned before the nuptials take place on Sunday evening at our grand pavilion."

Essie steps up, taking the mic from her husband. "Each of you have a packet with an itinerary and a stack of waivers, excusing us from liability due to any of your drunken debauchery," she laughs. "Please get those papers filled out with the pens in your bags and turn them in before leaving this cafeteria. We'll see you all in an hour for our first competition."

"One more thing..." Joe says, snatching the mic back. "On the far wall, you'll find a row of lockers in which you will place any and all electronic devices. Phones, iPad, laptops…all prohibited. What happens at Camp Pour Judgment," he starts.

"Stays at Camp Pour Judgment," his wife finishes with a familiar sly grin.

It's been a month since Stick got down on one knee and proposed with a room full of sick children to bear witness. How could I turn her down under those circumstances? Smart cookie, that girl.

To say I was shocked would be putting it mildly. I had no clue Anika had gone to talk to her. I hadn't even seen or heard from Korie since she shut me down at the games. When Nick approached with the offer to play for the children at the hospital she worked at, I didn't think twice. I knew how much those kids meant to her, and despite how screwed up things were between us, no one meant more to me than her.

I wouldn't be me if I simply said yes, without some sort of fuckery. So, I told her I'd marry her, but since she stole my balls out from under me *again* by proposing, I would be the one to plan the wedding.

This is gonna be the best fucking wedding to ever wedding. More guys should get in on the planning of these shindigs. Just saying, men, you're missing one hell of an opportunity here.

Nick, Lyle, Aiden, and I are sharing the same cabin from last time we were here. AJ's husband Brock is in the one next door with my dad, my brother-in-law, Ryan, and my buddy Tommy.

Korie is rooming with Raven, Anika, and AJ. Her mother, DeeDee, is in a cabin with my sister Judy, and Kline and Lisa.

After taking a few minutes to unpack our shit, we down a couple of shots at the open bar in our room and each grab a beer, then make our way out to the main field where we're meeting for the first event.

I can't help but lock eyes with my girl and tip my head toward the mud pit to the left of us. I cup my chest and shimmy, and she flips me off. I'll never forget her flashing us just to win a game of tug of war. From that moment on, I was titstruck.

"Hey you guys," Essie shouts into a megaphone. "You're probably wondering why the ground is littered with colored plastic balls, am I right?" She rests her foot on one of eight skateboards circling the pit and rolls it forward and back. "Today's ice breaker is Human Hungry Hippos. It's girls versus guys. Girls, you will pair up on the boards located on this side of the pit. Guys, you'll pair up where Joe is standing. A timer will be set for one minute, during which one partner will lie on their stomach long ways across the board, holding a pot in their hands while the other will grab their feet to roll them forward. When you reach the pit, drop your pot over the balls and pull as many as you can back with you behind the tape. You'll repeat this exercise as many times as possible before the buzzer goes off. The team with the most balls behind the line, wins."

"What's the wager?" Korie asks, tucking her tank into her shorts.

God, she's hot when she's all competitive. "Your birth control." I don't hesitate with my answer.

Our friends and family look on with curious smiles.

For a moment, my future wife looks as if she's swallowed shit. "Fine. If the guys win the weekend, I'll get off the pills. If I win, we wait a year, and no more hounding me," she qualifies, narrowing those green eyes my way.

"Deal." I smirk. "Can't wait to put my baby in your belly."

"You do know that's not how they get in there, right?" Aiden asks, laughing hysterically.

I pop him in the back of the head. "You do realize there's a lady present," I say motioning to my future mother-in-law. "So sorry, DeeDee, can't take these pigs anywhere."

"Hey," Raven snarls. "What about the other seven of us?" She looks around, and all of the girls are in agreement.

"I'm sorry. I'm not sure I understand the question."

"All right, ladies and gentlemen, now that we've determined what we're all playing for, pick a partner and get lined up behind the tape. Competition starts in thirty seconds."

Damn, Joe isn't fuckin' around.

"Face down, ass up," Nick says shoving me toward the board.

When the whistle sounds, complete chaos ensues. I probably shouldn't have downed my beer so fast because as he's rolling me back and forth in the field, I can feel it shifting in my stomach. Pots are crashing and there's so much yelling. I have no idea how I'm doing in comparison to the rest because I'm too focused on winning myself a baby to check.

"Time!" Joe shouts, after blowing his whistle.

"Mom!" Korie screeches, assessing each of her teammate's haul. "You didn't get a single ball!?"

DeeDee shrugs. "I ain't getting any younger, sweet girl."

She plops her hands on her hips. "Can we trade her for Nicholas?"

"Nope," I say, popping the P like she likes to do. "Girls versus guys. Don't be a sore loser, baby. It's unbecoming."

"Not so fast," Essie says, after tallying each sides total. "Even with DeeDee not retrieving a single one, the girls still beat y'all by seven."

Essie proudly walks over to the scoreboard, and as she slides the chalk in a line on the girl's side, I feel my dick shrivel a little in pain.

We have a few hours to blow before lunch, so we take everyone out to our favorite spot, the lake.

"Why do you want a baby so bad?" Korie asks, when we

paddle away from the dock in a purple kayak.

"Just do."

"That's not a real answer."

So, I think real hard before giving her the most honest answer I can formulate. "Because the thought of seeing your belly swell with my baby—our baby, a living representation of our love—would be the ultimate high. Because I see the way you love the children you work with, and I can't wait to witness you loving our own. And because I'm almost twenty-seven years old. If we're gonna have twelve kids, I'd like to get started right away."

Her face morphs from awe to shock and then horror. "We are not having a dozen kids," she assures me, her eyes widening. "I'm thinking two at most."

"Agree to disagree," I say, rowing faster.

When she starts to argue further, I "accidentally" flip the boat.

She comes up sputtering, cursing me to hell and back.

"I love you too," I say, cutting her off mid-tirade. I grip the front of her shirt in my hand and pull her against my chest in the shoulder-high water. Her eyes are still fuming when I lean in to capture her lips, but in no time the stiffness in her posture dissipates. She's a limp noodle in my hold. Her arms wrap around my neck, her fingers finding their favorite spot in my wet hair.

"That's enough of that, boy," my father shouts, laughing as he approaches in a yellow kayak with Ryan rowing behind him. "You're gonna drown that poor girl."

"Hey Dad," I say, swiping the back of my hand over my kiss-swollen lips. "Have you had the chance to meet Korie yet?"

"Nope." He smiles at my soon-to-be bride. "Was wondering when you'd get around to introducing us."

I can't believe it's two days before the wedding and Dad and Korie are only just meeting. But our lives have been a bit chaotic and our relationship a complete whirlwind. "Dad, this is Korie, your soon-to-be daughter-in-law. Korie," I say looking to my girl, "meet my pops, Cal Taylor."

"So nice to meet you," she says, her lips chattering from the cool water. "Your son's an ass."

My father's laugh booms across the manmade lake. "Girl, tell me something I don't know." His gray eyes connect with mine. "Son, get that girl out of the damn water before she freezes to death."

"I see what you're doing here," I say, hoisting her back into the boat.

"Really?" she says, innocently fluttering her lashes. "What is it you think I'm doing?"

I climb in from the pointed tip of the boat to keep the weight balanced, so we don't roll over again. "You think you're gonna use your feminine charm to get my dad on your side… you know, since your mom is on mine."

Her mouth opens wide in disbelief. "I'd ne—"

"Good," I say, cutting her off. "Cuz if there's one person who wants us to have a baby more than your mother, it's him."

Dad shrugs apologetically. "It's true. I rather enjoy being a grandpa. But you're still such a pretty little thing," he says, trying to save face.

"Oh, God," Stick says, rolling her eyes. "Not you too."

Chapter 48

KORIE

AFTER A LIGHT LUNCH CONSISTING OF FINGER FOODS, sandwiches, little meatballs, chips and dips, and mimosas, we meet in the field to see what our next competition will be.

"Oh, hell yes," AJ shouts, pumping her fist in the air. "I'm gonna fuck some shit up in archery."

That's when I see the targets and bows and arrows laid out in the grass ahead of us. I don't know how good the guys are, but archery was our grandfather's specialty. Abby Jane and I spent a few weeks out of every summer while growing up with him and Grams, and he taught us everything he knew.

"Welcome back, everyone. Hope y'all had a good lunch and didn't drink too much, because we're about to shoot some arrows, and I'd hate for anyone to lose an eye," Joe announces. "Standard distance for archery is seventy meters. Since we're not working with professionals here, we've shortened that to forty. Each team has eight members. Every person gets three shots. The scores from each team will be combined to determine a winner. May the best gender win."

Essie lines the girls up in front of one of the targets, and Joe does the same with the boys on the other. The center of the target is yellow and worth ten points. The next ring is red, which they have delegated five points. The teal ring is worth three points, black is worth two, and the outermost ring is white and valued at only one point.

We each get three practice shots before taking our real ones where Essie and Joe show us how to stand and fire the bow. Rhett and I are up first. On purpose, I miss every one of my practice shots. Rhett hits the target, but all of his arrows land in the two outer rings.

"Ready for the coochie doctor to be all up in your bidness, Stick?" he taunts. *Poor clueless idiot.*

"You go first," I say, feigning nerves.

Rhett's first arrow lands in the teal ring. The cheering from the guys behind us tells me they're probably not very good. His second shot lands in red, and his final shot also falls in the teal circle, giving him a total of eleven points.

"No matter what happens baby, you're still pretty." With a cocky smirk, his eyes rove over my body. "You'll be pretty pregnant, too. I can tell."

"Keep talkin' shit," I warn, holding the bow out in front of me. In rapid succession, I fire my three shots, landing each one in the center of the yellow bullseye. "Huh," I say, glancing at Rhett's stunned face. "Must be beginner's luck."

AJ and Brock are up next, but he must know how skilled his wife is because there is no shit talk coming from his end. My cousin struts up like a boss, taking the bow from Essie and pounding her shots right into the bullseye, bringing our total to sixty after only two rounds.

Brock appears nauseated but manages to land two in the red

zone and one in the yellow, earning his team another twenty points, bringing their total to thirty-one.

No one else has any skill worth mentioning, half of them missing the target completely. My mother, of course, misses every shot by a mile even though her father trained her up better than AJ and me. When the final scores are tallied, the girls have seventy-one and the guys have forty-seven.

"Another victory for the ladies!" Essie shouts, adding a mark on our side of the board.

My soon-to-be husband is looking pouty following his second loss of the day. "Aww, don't look so sad," I tell him, walking up and wrapping my arms around his waist. "At least you're still pretty."

"What in the world is Never Have I Ever?" my mother asks, studying the evening's itinerary as we walk the wooded path leading to the bonfire.

"It's a game," Raven explains, "where you go around in a circle and each person takes a turn saying something they've never done and then everyone who has done it takes a shot."

"There they are," Nicholas yells as we approach the fire. "Thought you ladies chickened out."

"Pshh, you wish," Raven taunts, plopping down on the log beside her fuck buddy.

"Welcome, ladies," counselor Joe, says, passing us each a stick with a marshmallow at the end while Essie sets a plate on our laps with graham crackers and chocolate squares already prepared for our s'mores. Apparently, the boys have already demolished theirs. "While you roast your marshmallows, I'll go over the rules…" He proceeds to explain the game in almost the exact fashion Raven just did for my mother.

There's a folding table off to the side where Essie is filling disposable shot glasses with Fireball. "After three each, I'm cutting you off and giving out shots of water," she warns. "We're not looking to kill anyone."

"I'd like to start the game," my mother announces. "I have a good one."

"Go ahead," Joe says, nodding to an already very tipsy DeeDee.

"Never have I ever…had a threesome!" she covers her mouth as soon as she says it, giggling so hard I think she might pee her pants. How was this woman married to my father?

The entire band, Raven, and Brock toss back shots.

"I'm totally judging you right now," I tell my fiancé. "Groupies?" I sneer, shaking my head with disappointment.

He shrugs, with an "oh shit," look on his face.

Cal is seated to my mother's right and up next. "Never have I ever sucked a penis," he says, cracking up as he watches all of the girls but Anika and Kline slurp down a shot of Fireball.

Then all of our heads whip over to Aiden when his hand rises into the air. "What?" he says, giving his hair the Justin Bieber flip. "Went through an experimental phase…don't judge me, fuckers." He downs his shot then gives the rest of us a look that dares us to say another word.

I glance over to Rhett to revel in his stunned reaction and crack up. "Jesus, all the skeletons are coming out tonight."

"My turn," Raven squeals, giddy over whatever she's got cooking up over there. "Never have I ever fucked in a toolshed during a game of paintball!"

"Well, that's rather specific," Judy says, her mouth dropping when Rhett and I raise our hands for a drink.

"Such a bitch," I mutter, eying my best friend.

"So, that's where you two ran off to." Essie shakes her head as she pours the liquid down each of our throats.

"Never have I ever..." Nick trails off for a moment, searching the crowd for his victim. "Kissed someone of the same sex," he says, smirking at Anika, who is seriously about to murder his drunk ass.

I can't believe he just did that to her.

Kline's hand shoots up, followed by Lisa's, and finally Anika lifts one finger into the air. "What happens at Pour Judgment—" she starts.

"Stays at Pour Judgment," the rest of us chant in unison.

"Never have I ever flashed my tits for beads on Bourbon Street," Ryan announces, staring at Judy with a knowing smile.

"Ew, gross. Not my sister," Rhett moans, covering his face in mock horror when her hand is the only one to go up.

"Don't feel bad, Judy. It's only because the rest of us have never been to New Orleans. I'd totally let a nip slip for some beads!" She does a little shimmy, poking her boobs out. "Do you booboo."

Judy gives her husband the evil eye, wracking her brain for what she can divulge to the group to embarrass him. "Never have I ever busted a nut. And let me be clear that by busted, I mean fallen on the bar to my mountain bike so hard that the ball did not survive."

Ryan's face turns so red it's damn near purple.

At once, the guys all hiss in pain.

"So, you only have one testicle?" Essie asks curiously, her right brow shooting up.

"Just give me the damn shot," he grumbles, his head hung in shame.

Abby Jane is next, and I swear the girl is just bursting at the seams to humiliate someone. Being she only knows Brock and myself, I certainly hope she's chosen her husband as her victim. "Never have I ever jacked off in my tutor's shower using her Victoria's Secret Love Spell as lube."

"Payback's a motherfucker, Abby Jane," he threatens, lifting his hand into the air for his shot.

And so the game continues, until we've all far surpassed our three shots of Fireball and learned more about each other than we should. I'm fairly certain by the time we call it quits, half of the couples are no longer on speaking terms, and none of us will be able to look each other in the face in the morning

As Rhett scoops me off the log, cradling my head to his chest, I get a fleeting feeling of deja vu. At least this time, I'm not the only one who has to be carried to bed.

Chapter 49

RHETT

"Well don't you lot look like something from an episode of *The Walking Dead*," Essie teases as the guys and I make our way to the field for today's color wars.

It's a scorcher. My skin burns where the sun's beating down on the back of my neck. The smell of alcohol seeping from my pores adds to the bout of nausea I'm fighting. "Mornin', Essie," I say, nodding her direction. "Joe." I angle my head his way, swallowing down the bile climbing in my throat.

"Ah, there you are ladies," she chimes into the megaphone. "There ya go, Kline…yup. Right there, sweetie. Just let it all out—" Her hand lifts to cover her mouth and she gags. "Ew. I smell it." She looks over to Joe. "Babe, go hose that, will ya?"

Korie looks positively miserable, I almost want to call the competition off, but then I remember what's at stake, and that I'm currently losing. I reassess the situation. Pale, a little green, hair knotted in a rat's nest atop her head. Moving like a slug. She's definitely seen better days. On second thought…

her discomfort is a small price to pay in the grand scheme of things, right? She can always nap after we whoop that ass.

When her tired eyes finally connect with mine, I send her a kiss. "Mornin', beautiful!"

She snorts, plopping down in the grass and lying back on her elbows. "Prepare to get your ass handed to ya, Hollywood," she snaps back. "Don't let this sexiness fool you." Her hand glides up and down her body.

Stick's competitive nature is one of the things I love most about her. But it'll take some divine intervention for those girls to beat us at anything today with half their team puking their guts up on the sidelines.

"Joe and I watered down the competition after seeing how trashed you all were last night. We've got a few games and relays planned, then you can all go rest up for rehearsal supper tonight, how's that sound?"

"Here, here!" Aiden shouts, before slamming his hand on his chest and letting out a huge belch.

Essie shakes her head, laughing. "There will be a total of four games today. The girls are already ahead by two. If they get two wins today, they are our champions. So, guys, step it up!" She points a finger our way. "Okay, so our first competition is a little game we like to call Bump and Grind."

Joe puts his hands behind his head and starts gyrating in the middle of the lawn. It's fucking hilarious.

"Yeah, so…each of you will have a balloon tied to your front, over your crotch, and another on your butt. The girls will line up behind that pink chair. Guys, you'll line up behind the blue one. The first person will run up to the chair, holding onto the back for balance. The second in line will then have to pop the balloon on their front and your back without using anything more than the force of their hips."

"What in the gay fuckery is this?" Lyle shouts.

The counselor shakes her head and continues. "Once both balloons have burst, the first person goes to the back of the line and player two grabs the chair while the third person becomes the thruster. The game ends when the first person busts their front balloon on the caboose's well...caboose." She smiles at her cleverness.

Sounds simple enough. We've totally got this. I mean, we have way more experience with thrusting hips than the girls do.

After we've all been strapped down with balloons, the whistle blows. Once again, Korie and I are first. And just my luck, Lyle's homophobic ass is my thruster.

The whole time he's ramming into me, he's cursing up a storm.

"Come on, Lyle," I shout when the girl's line keeps moving and he's still fucking around behind me. "Harder," I moan, to mess with his head.

All of a sudden, he shoves into me, and I'm sent flying over the fucking chair, landing hard on my ass. But wouldn't you know, the damn balloon is still intact. Before I've even gotten myself back into position, the whistle is blown, and there's another tally in the girls' column.

"And here I was thinking of making you godfather," I mutter, shoving hard past him to rejoin the group.

The guys and I finally get on a winning streak and take the next three events easily: three-legged race, wheelbarrow race, and a sack race.

"All right," Joe announces. "Looks like we'll have to go to the tiebreaker. The winner of this game takes all! We like to call this one Impale the Paper, and it's as naughty as it sounds." His old man laugh has us all cracking up. "The game is played with a plunger and a roll of toilet paper. The first person in line will go out to stand behind the tape with a roll of toilet paper gripped between his or her thighs. The second will then waddle over with a plunger tucked between their legs, the rubber to the back, pole sticking out the front like so." He motions to Essie who's giving a demonstration. "Your job is to get the stick through the hole. Once you've successfully transferred the roll from between your partners legs to your plunger, you swap positions. The plunger becomes the toilet paper holder and the person who was holding the paper runs the plunger to the next in line. The game ends when the original paper holder has had a chance to plunge successfully."

"I'm going last this time," Lyle growls.

For a bunch of dudes who actually have experience working with sticks between our legs, you'd think we'd be a little more coordinated. Three girls have already impaled their paper before Nicholas finally steals the roll. We swap places and I pass the plunger to my father, who surprisingly gets it in his first try. Next up is Lone Star…uh, I mean Ryan. I don't know how this fucker ever managed to get my sister pregnant. The plunger keeps slipping out from between his legs, and the whistle is blown, signaling the girls' win, before he ever gets it anywhere close to the hole.

"Aren't you going to congratulate me?" Stick asks, sauntering over with a triumphant sparkle in her eye.

"No." I pout, hanging my lip. "I hope your birth control fails and we get pregnant with twins."

She shakes her head, trying not to laugh. "I have something special for you tonight," she teases, running her tongue over the seam of my mouth, getting Ollie real excited.

"Do you now?" Suddenly, I've perked up.

"Not that," she says, slapping her palm to my chest. "We agreed not till the wedding night."

"Well, I think that was a really stupid decision, and I wanna take it back."

She rests her hands on her hips. "It's one more day. You can do it. Plus, I really need to rest up for tonight. I feel disgusting."

I reach into my pocket retrieving the Zofran I brought from home, just in case.

"What's this?" she asks when I hand her the bottle.

"Zofran…it's for nausea."

Her eyes turn lethal. "Why the hell didn't you give this to me when you saw how miserable I was this morning? Poor Kline was puking her guts out."

I shrug and wink, taking a few steps back before answering, "I wanted to win."

Chapter 50

KORIE

FEELING INFINITELY BETTER THAN I DID WHEN I AWOKE THIS morning, I unzip the garment bag containing the outfit Anika chose for me for tonight. Yes, I let her dress me. If it were up to me, I'd be in jeans and a tee, but I'm smart enough to realize that I'll someday regret that choice, and also, while we've managed to keep the ceremony completely on the downlow, pictures of our union will have to be made public, due to the nature of Rhett's career, and I'm making it my duty not to embarrass my new husband, at least not on the first day.

Plus, if I'm being honest, Anika has impeccable taste. "This is really cute," I say, taking the white chiffon romper off the hanger. It's spaghetti-strapped, with a faux wrap neckline, lightly lined with a ruffle. The waist is cinched with a side tie ribbon. Simple. Elegant. Perfect.

I slip into the outfit then let Raven and Anika work their magic on my hair and makeup. But when that prissy brunette comes out with a pair of four-inch strappy silver heels, I sort of want to punch her in the tit.

"Seriously, Annie?"

"No one with any class attends their own rehearsal dinner in anything but a sexy pair of heels," she returns, crouching to strap them around my ankles with a triumphant smirk on her too pretty face.

I hardly recognize the cafeteria when I walk through the double doors. It's been transformed into something I can only describe as magical. Right near the entrance is a white painted wood sign with "How sweet it is to be loved by you," in black script. Behind it is a table filled with tiered glass trays of donuts, cookies, and cakes.

The ceiling's been draped with white fabric and twinkle lights. The picnic-style tables were replaced with one long wood table big enough to seat our entire party and more. It's lined with a white cloth and topped with greenery, blush and white roses, and tealight candles.

"Damn," Rhett hisses, suddenly appearing in front of me, and I certainly concur. He looks fucking edible in a pair of khaki slacks with a white button down and slightly darker tan blazer. His suspenders, belt, and shoes are all a deep chocolate brown, and a baby blue bow tie adds the perfect pop of color.

"I've changed my mind," I rasp, undressing him with my eyes. "Meet me at the toolshed at midnight."

His hearty laughter makes my heart soar. "Yeah...I think I'll make you wait." He bites his lower lip, and my thighs clench with need.

With a shake of my head, I link my arm through his. "Such

a tease," I mutter as he leads me to my seat.

All of our guests are already settled around the table and looking so fancy in their formal attire.

"I'd like to start the evening with a toast," Nicholas says, rising to his feet and tapping a butter knife to the side of his glass. "I wanted the chance to say a few words tonight, before these two run off on their honeymoon tomorrow."

We all turn to give him our attention, and I feel Rhett's hand squeeze my knee.

"As most of you know, Rhett has been my best friend for damn near all my life. I think it's safe to say that just about no one knows him better than I do. There were a few years there where we got caught up in the rock and roll lifestyle. We were wild and reckless, and lost sight of who we really are at our core. That's the reason when Rhett set his sights on my baby cousin, Korie…well, to say I had my reservations would be putting it mildly." A soft chuckle erupts from our guests. "I was wrong," he says, his eyes connecting with Rhett's. "You are more than good enough. You are everything I hope to someday be, and tomorrow, when I give you my cousin's hand in marriage, it will be without reservation. You two are what dreams are made of, and I'm honored to be able to witness your fairy tale brought to life." He lifts his glass into the air. "To Rhett and Korie."

Eighteen champagne flutes take turns clinking with a resounding, "Cheers."

The night's only just begun, and I'm already dabbing at tears, trying to save this cursed mascara.

Nicholas waves toward the kitchen as he lowers back down to his seat and a line of servers file out with trays of food. I lift the domed lid from my plate, finding a lobster pasta with French bread and butter and a side salad. My stomach growls when I get a whiff of delicious aromas.

322 HEATHER M. ORGERON

Once everyone has received their dinner, Judy offers to bless our meal.

"Heavenly father, we ask you to bless this food which we are about to receive and to bless Rhett and Korie as they take this huge leap of faith into married life. We thank you for bringing our families together and for blessing us with such wonderful friends to share in our joy of this glorious union. In your name we pray."

"Amen."

"Make sure you leave room for dessert," Rhett warns when he sees me shoveling pasta into my mouth.

I chew and swallow, then dab at my lips with a napkin. "I saw the cakes at the entrance. So cute."

"I have another little surprise coming," he says with a wink.

When we finish our meal, Nick calls the servers back to retrieve our dishes with another wave. Are they seriously just standing back there watching for his signal?

"Be right back," Rhett says, as he and the rest of his bandmates get up from the table. He bends to place a kiss to my forehead.

"Wai—where are you going?"

"You'll see," he says, rushing off.

"What's going on?" AJ asks from across the table.

I shrug. "Not a clue."

A side door off the kitchen swings open, and a huge wood sign on wheels is rolled out. In black cursive letters it says, "I'll stop the world and melt with you." Beneath that are painted waffle cones with rose colored ice cream to match the decor. Then an ice cream cart follows, with a variety of flavors and glass bowls filled with every topping you could imagine.

I still have no idea why the guys have run off, until I hear the sound of his guitar. Rhett, Nicholas, Aiden, and Lyle come out looking every bit the boy band, with their suits and carefully styled hair.

"I was going to come up with a toast of my own," Rhett says. "Then I thought...well, all we really need is love, right? And maybe a little ice cream?"

Nick bangs his drum sticks together three times, even though the drums are nowhere in sight. They perform a mash up of songs starting with a twangy, more country rendition of "I Melt With You," by Modern English. After the chorus they seamlessly blend it in with their own take on "All You Need Is Love," by the Beatles. And finally, they conclude with "My Best Friend," by Tim McGraw.

I'm nothing but a blubbering mess of emotion when he passes the mic to Lyle and saunters across the room, scooping me up into his arms. "I can't wait to be your husband, Korie Potter."

As if the ice cream bar and live performance aren't enough, he pulls a velvet box from his back pocket and lifts the top. Inside is a platinum necklace with an ice cream pendant, engraved with the words "I melt with you."

With trembling hands, I remove it, examining the delicate piece from every angle before handing it to him and turning so he can fasten it around my neck. "Thank you," I say, pressing my tear-soaked lips to his. "I umm...I had a surprise for you too, but now I'm a little embarrassed."

While we're still standing, wrapped in each other's arms in the center of the room, the lights dim and music filters from the overhead speakers. Slowly, we begin to sway along to the beat, my body a livewire, tingling every place we touch.

"Don't be embarrassed." He grips my chin, turning my face up to his. "Show me."

Thankfully, everyone else has taken to the dance floor—

324 HEATHER M. ORGERON

their attention no longer fixed on us.

"I changed my mind," I say, unclasping the fastener on the top of my clutch.

"About?"

I retrieve the disk of birth control pills and place it in his hand.

"It's empty," he says, examining the open slots. "Does this mean?"

"Flushed them down the toilet this morning. I want to have your baby almost as much as I want to be your wife, Rhett Taylor."

Chapter 51

RHETT

IT'S A GREAT DAY TO BE MARRIED, I THINK TO MYSELF AS I MAKE my way to the pavilion. The sun is high, shining bright, and there's not a cloud in the sky. A cool breeze blows through the glass chimes, and the sound reminds me of wedding bells.

"Lookin' good, man," Nicholas says, dressed in the same camel-colored linen suit as mine. "You ready for this?"

I adjust the dusty rose bow tie at my neck. "Yeah," I answer with complete confidence. "I am."

I look out at the glowing faces of our closest friends and family, so happy with our decision to keep the ceremony small and intimate. So much of our life is shared with the world. I wanted this to be something sacred. A moment we could claim as our own.

The wedding planner did an excellent job decorating the place. The wood pillars are draped with thick white fabric, tied back with dusty pink ribbon. A huge chandelier was brought in for the occasion, hung from a wood beam above the center of the cake table. The cake Korie chose is simple, yet elegant. Two tiers of almond-flavored cake coated in antique white buttercream icing. The edges are piped with gold foil and a small cluster of roses sits on top and another a little bigger on the bottom tier. The flowers are varying shades of dusty pinks and creams to match her bouquet and the centerpieces on the white linen-covered tables.

At the edge of the pavilion sits a wood-beamed arch that was brought in for the occasion. It's draped in blush tulle and dripping in baby's breath. Directly through the arch is the rippling water, making a perfectly serene backdrop for our nuptials.

"It's time," Essie says, giving my shoulder a gentle squeeze as she walks past to make sure everyone is in their proper places.

Lyle takes his seat behind the keyboard, and as the curtains part, I recognize the beginning notes to "Somewhere Over The Rainbow," at the exact moment I see my bride. I'm hit with a barrage of emotion as I try to digest it all.

Her long blonde hair is curled, with a floral crown threaded through the strands. The dress is ivory—long and fitted, flaring out where it reaches the floor. Comprised of nude lace, it fits her body like a glove. She looks elegant and dainty.

I keep thinking there's no way I could possibly love her more, but every day she proves me wrong. That she found a way to include my mother in this momentous occasion has my heart feeling like it might burst, unable to contain the ever-growing love I have for this woman.

With her arm threaded through Nick's, she makes the slow march down the aisle. She raises her head, and her emerald eyes latch onto mine. For a moment I'm struck with a feeling of sheer disbelief—that this is happening—that she's truly mine.

The way all of this came to be seems too good to be true.

But here we are, coming full circle in the place where we began.

Who knew Pour Judgment would lead to the best decision of my life?

Epilogue

KORIE

"Up next in our Chicks with Tricks junior division, we have the daughter of X Games gold medalist, Korie Potter, and country superstar, Rhett Taylor. Please welcome six-year-old Hadley!"

"I'm gonna be sick," Rhett says, scrubbing a hand over his face before hanging his head. "Tell me when it's over."

I stab an elbow into his side. "That kid will have your ass if she finds out you didn't watch her skate."

"Fine," he says, taking my hand in his and squeezing it tight as our little girl drops in for her very first run of her first competition ever.

"She looks so tiny," I whisper as she climbs the high wall and lands a gnarly kick flip. "Yes," I hiss, clapping my hands together. "Good job, baby," I scream.

"Damn board's bigger than her," he grumps beside me, swatting a fly away from his face.

She pumps her little legs, her long blonde hair flowing

behind her from beneath her pink helmet as she picks up speed then lands her little rainbow board on top of the grind rail, sliding all the way down, just like I taught her.

"Jesus Christ!" Rhett shouts, lunging forward when she tries for an invert and her hand misses the ledge. She lands on her helmet then tumbles down the ramp.

"She's fine," I say, pulling him by the back of his shirt so he doesn't jump into the bowl after her. "See?" I wave at our daughter as she climbs out with the biggest smile on her face.

"Gimme your hand," I say, placing it on my growing stomach. "You feel that?"

A smile splits his gorgeous face. "He's active."

"Ryder already wants to take off after his big sister."

Rhett's eyes grow wide. "Nuh-uhn. Not this one too. This one's my little crooner."

"Good luck keeping him off the ramp in our yard," I say, rolling my eyes.

"Dammit, Stick. You gonna turn all twelve of our kids into daredevils?"

I smile, planting a kiss on his heart-shaped lips. "Damn sure gonna try."

THE END

If you'd like to read AJ and Brock's story, download *Rebel Heart by LK Farlow* on Amazon and read free in Kindle Unlimited.

Acknowledgments

First off, I'd like to give a collective thank you to you, my readers, for sticking with me. It's been almost a year since I've published—my longest break yet. It's a scary thing to be a writer who's not writing. But, I'm not a person who can force it, and it means everything that you stuck by me while I waited for my voice to return. Waited is probably not the right word—begged...pleaded...cursed the literary gods. But you get the picture. Korie and Rhett brought me back, and I hope you enjoyed reading about them as much as I did writing them!

To my family. My husband, Adam. My children Xavier, Kari, Bari, Parker, Amelia, and Kellan. Thank you for being ridiculously cute and funny and sarcastic, and giving me endless inspiration for my novels. Thank you for sacrificing time and cooked meals when inspiration struck so I could pen this story.

Mom...thank you isn't enough, but it's all I've got. Thank you for always showing up when I need you. For everything from babysitting the kids to cooking meals to cleaning my house. You're always here for me with a smile on your face and an encouraging word. We appreciate you more than you know.

Kate Farlow...there aren't words for what you mean to me. You are the definition of a true friend. Thank you for always being here day or night to assist with anything...and I do mean anything from advice, to teasers, to newsletters, to listening to me vent about my kids or cry about my hurt feelings. I love you more than Pepsi and Tootsie Rolls and that is SO MUCH!

Lo, you beautiful, sexy thang. Thank you for being such a light in my life, and a shoulder I know I can always lean on. I love you so freaking much, and I'm so lucky to call you MINE! #wifey

My P.A., Renee McCleary. I feel like you dropped down from heaven at a time I didn't even know I needed you. I'm so thankful we met in Boston, and I suckered you in to taking me on. You're stuck with me now. Thank you for forcing me to set a date and nagging me daily for my word count. For reading every scene fifteen times as I wrote it. You are a gem, and I'm so lucky to have you on my team.

To my beeches, Harloe Rae and K.K. Allen. I don't know that I could have pushed through without your love and encouragement. Thank you for being the beautiful souls that you are. Honest, selfless, kind, and genuine friends are so hard to come by, and I know how lucky I am to have found that in each of you. Plus, I marked you…you're mine. #sploogesisters #baptisedintheocean

Nicole and Dani. What can I say that hasn't already been said in the last five books? Everyone should have a team of betas as loyal and giving and dedicated as the two of you. But they need to get their own because I'm never giving you up. From the bottom of my heart and soul, I love you two to freaking pieces. Thank you for EVERYTHING!

Katherine and Keri, how did I get lucky enough to land the two of you? Not only are you the best and some of the most supportive readers around, but truly incredible humans and friends. I don't think you have any clue how much I admire you both. Thank you for reading and for your feedback, and most of all for being you. I love you.

Nikki. Girrrrrl. Thank you for always checking in on me. For asking how my words are going. For kicking my ass off of Facebook and calling me on my shit. You are real and honest and such a great friend. Love you, forever!

To my editor, Kiezha, THANK YOU for being flexible and working around my chaotic life and writer brain. You are the absolute best, and I love you to bits!

Jules, lawd hammercy. You've been with me from the start, and I can't imagine doing this without you. Thank you for always doing your best to accommodate me. You give my work a face, and you always do such a brilliant job. I love you, woman!

Thank you to my proofreaders: Sammi, Sara, Misty, and Aundrea. I appreciate you so freaking much!

HUNNIES!!! Dear Lord. I don't even know what to say. All of my friends gush about what an active and supportive group you are, and every bit of it is true. I feel like the fan girl when you come to my table to meet me at signings. Thank you for not only getting my brand of crazy, but embracing it. Love y'all!

To the girls at Give Me Books, thank you. Thank you for your loyalty and support and, most of all, your friendships. You are a shining star in this industry and make my job infinitely easier.

To every single reader and blogger who has picked up my work, whether you've loved it or hated it, thank you for giving me a shot. There are so many books out there, and that you gave me a chance means the world.

About The Author

Heather M. Orgeron is a Cajun girl with a big heart and a passion for romance. She married her high school sweetheart two months after graduation and her life has been a fairytale ever since. She's the queen of her castle, reigning over five sons and one bossy little princess who has made it her mission in life to steal her Momma's throne. When she's not writing, you will find her hidden beneath mounds of laundry and piles of dirty dishes or locked in her tower (aka the bathroom) soaking in the tub with a good book. She's always been an avid reader and has recently discovered a love for cultivating romantic stories of her own.

For more information at Heather
www.heathermorgeron.com

CPSIA information can be obtained
at www.ICGtesting.com
Printed in the USA
LVHW081542271019
635482LV00005B/26/P

9 781698 876139